HACKER

THE OUTLAW CHRONICLES

TED DEKKER

WORTHY
PUBLISHING

Copyright © 2014 by Ted Dekker
Published by Worthy Publishing, a division of Worthy Media, Inc., 134 Franklin Road, Suite 200,
Brentwood, Tennessee 37027.

WORTHY is a registered trademark of Worthy Media, Inc.
HELPING PEOPLE EXPERIENCE THE HEART OF GOD

Library of Congress Control Number: 2014934708

ISBN: 978-1-61795-275-3 (trade paper)

Published in association with Creative Trust, 5141 Virginia Way, Brentwood, TN 37027.
www.creativetrust.com.

For foreign and subsidiary rights, contact rights@worthypublishing.com

Cover Art and Photography: Pixel Peach Studio
Interior Design and Typesetting: Kimberly Sagmiller, Fudge Creative

Printed in The United States of America
14 15 16 17 18 VPI 8 7 6 5 4 3 2 1

HACKER

THE OUTLAW CHRONICLES

EPISODE ONE

1.0

ONE FRAGILE moment—that's all it takes for a life to be un-made, to shatter into a million pieces that will never fit together the same way. Hard as you try to change it, you'll find—just as I did—that some things, once broken, can't be fixed.

Some things have to be re-created completely.

Some people too.

The ancient book says that it took God seven days to create the world. It took him only three to shatter my little life and remake it in a way that I would've never chosen for myself. It's always like that—one story ends; another one begins.

This is my story, and I couldn't have possibly known how hard it was going to be.

None of us could've known.

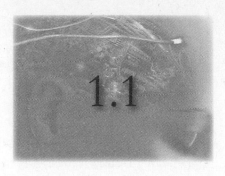

Day One
12:12 PM
Silicon Valley, California

EVERYTHING CAN be hacked. Everything—the cell phone in your pocket, the onboard computer of the 737 you're flying on, the security system guarding your house while you sleep. Nothing is safe.

Anyone who says otherwise is selling something.

Most people don't believe it, and that's fine. I totally get it. Whoever said ignorance is bliss wasn't so ignorant. Still, despite our unwillingness to accept it, deep down we all know the truth: safety is an illusion and nowadays the castles we all think will protect us are nothing more than little ones and zeroes, tiny bits of code no more substantial than the air we breathe. They're castles built on clouds, nothing more.

I should know; it's my job to demolish those castles. Some would call me a hacker, but I see myself as something more—a reality check for hire. I crack corporate servers to prove I can; then panicked companies pay me to fix their problems. I open their eyes to the cracks they fail to see.

I'm good at it. One of the best, actually.

Nyah Parks is my name and I'm seventeen. I suppose I'm not typical, whatever "typical" means. I aced high school by age twelve. Could've done it by eight, but my parents thought I should mature a bit before walking into the ivory halls of higher education. Maybe they were right, but it's not like age would make me more normal. I was a freak at eight and time didn't change that.

While other teen girls were fussing over boys and things like hair and makeup and how many Facebook friends they had, I was learning computer code—PHP, C, C#, AJAX, Java, JavaScript, Perl, and Python just for starters. Programming, I came to realize, is my native tongue. And I rock at it. Wrote my first stochastic stock-trading algorithm at thirteen and sold it to a Wall Street hedge fund for enough bank to pay for college. Stanford, in case you were wondering.

I never fit in at high school, and it was even worse at college. I got in and out as quickly as I could, graduating at fifteen with a double major in computer science and mathematics. No one was lining up to hire me, though. One recruiter told me I needed better social skills. I told him where he could put his opinion, which I guess proved his point. Like I said, a freak.

My childhood shrink diagnosed me with arithmomania, an obsessive compulsion to count, which I do constantly: the number of Cheerios floating in my cereal bowl, the percentage of drivers yapping on cell phones, the statistical probability of being run over by them as they change lanes, how often the letter Q appears in every magazine article and book I read. I don't know why Q specifically, but there you have it. It's a thing.

None of this has won me any friends. Despite what everyone says, being different is a curse. People don't want different, not really. They want to be around people like themselves: safe, predictable . . . boring.

People don't like surprises. Not the big kind, anyway. Not the kind that leave scars.

Lettie, my dad's mom, says that the traumas that leave scars happen for a reason, and those things are among the most beautiful things on earth, like diamonds and sunsets.

I told her that was total garbage, that all she was doing was trying to make sense of the chaos all around us. She just smiled and said nothing.

If the universe made sense, then Harlan Schmitt, age twenty-three, would've never run a red light at 64th and Pine seven hundred sixteen days ago. He would have never broadsided a minivan—*my* family's minivan—doing eighty-three miles per hour, according to the police investigation. He would have never killed my dad and little brother. And my mom wouldn't be stuck in the nightmare that she is, alive but not living because of the brain damage.

If the universe made sense, and there was a God who knew what he was doing, none of that would've happened. I would be telling you a different story. Not this one, not one in which my life shattered for the second time, two weeks before my eighteenth birthday.

The first time started when a certain dimwit climbed into his crappy ten-year-old Corolla after too many beers at O'Shanahan's Pub—celebrating, it turned out, a fifty-cent raise that brought his hourly wage to a whopping $10.74.

The second time began when I pulled into the parking lot of Blak-Box Technologies on a bright Tuesday afternoon. It was July and the asphalt rippled with heat, so I found a shady spot near the front door and sat in Mom's old blue Honda Civic, staring at the shiny building.

Being there was unreasonable and dangerous, especially if things went sideways on me, but I had no choice. I wasn't there because I wanted to be. Not really. I was there to get my mom what she needed, and what she needed was $250,000. That was the price of her salvation if I could find a way to afford it.

The accident had left her with severe brain trauma. During the first days, doctors saw hopeful signs and thought she might make a full recovery. She could remember her name, who I was, and even some details about the accident. Encouraged with her progress, they moved her out of the hospital and into an assisted-care facility.

Two months ago, everything that made Mom who she was—her

laugh, her smile, the memories we shared—began to disintegrate right in front of me. Her brain began to die. *She* began to die. Doctors said she had three months to live, best-case scenario.

Three months. That was the measure of her life, her expiration date.

My entire life became focused on helping her get better. Doctors said nothing could be done, but I couldn't accept that. I was going to find a way. Every waking moment, every job I took, every dollar I made went to finding a cure. All the while, she spiraled down into a waking nightmare.

My persistence paid off when I came across a post on an obscure neurology online forum, an old-style message board still used by scientists. The conversation thread was about a privately funded, experimental—and apparently successful—program to help soldiers recover from brain injuries. PREMIND, as they called it, was being run out of the Helen Wills Neuroscience Institute at UC Berkeley, not a half-hour drive from me.

That night I hunted down the program director and was waiting on her front doorstep the next morning. It took days of pleading and borderline stalking, but I convinced her to accept Mom into the program, as long as I covered the $250,000 required for the medical procedures, and paid it in full before the clinical trials began.

I had $101,243.12 scraped together from consulting jobs I'd done over the past year. If I couldn't save Mom myself then I would use my skills to hire the people who could. Problem was, I needed a big job, one bigger than any I'd ever done before. I'd never made a hundred grand from a single job. If I had any chance, I would need to go big, and that's where BlakBox came in.

I picked up my cell phone and tapped the screen to dial a number. It rang once and Pixel picked up.

"Hang on. Almost ready," he said. His voice was tense. Jason Piksky had been my brother's best friend. At fourteen, he was a better hacker than most people three times his age, and he was the only one I trusted to be my second set of hands on this job. It was too important, too complex to do on my own. I pictured him on his bicycle, a Mac Power-Book strapped between the handlebars.

"Are you in the right place?" I asked him. "The Wi-Fi signal is strongest—"

"On the west side of the parking lot, behind the shrubs. I know. We've gone over this a million times."

"This has to be spot on. No mistakes."

I could hack nearly any company from my living-room couch while watching *Doctor Who* reruns in my pajamas. But sometimes *how* you get someone's attention is everything. Landing the biggest job of my life required going radical. Some people won't look you in the eye unless you first grab them by the throat. Easier said than done when it's Goliath you're gunning for, and that's exactly what I was doing.

A long silence on the other end. "You sure about this?" Pixel said.

"No," I said, staring through the dusty windshield.

"We're going to ace this."

I drew a long breath and let it out slowly. "Right."

I climbed out of the car and angled toward the front door, wiping a sweaty palm on my pants.

"I'm going in," I said into the phone. "Watch for my commands. Just like we practiced."

"Got it."

I ended the call and pocketed the phone. One way or another the outcome would be epic.

I climbed the marble steps to the front entrance. As corporate offices went in Silicon Valley, BlakBox was unremarkable: a steel-and-glass building the size of a football field, with windows tinted the sheen of volcanic glass. No sign or logo announced the company's name; nothing indicated what went on behind its black walls. It was tucked in the back corner of a business park surrounded by distribution centers. It could have been just another warehouse shipping out tennis shoes, yoga mats, and baby food to online customers.

I knew better.

BlakBox dealt in information. It ran data centers all over the world, vast server farms that companies depended on to keep their files backed up and secure. Some of the largest dot-coms on the planet used its services. If the BlakBox network was a global wheel, this obscure building was the hub. It controlled everything.

The double doors parted with a hiss, and a rush of chilled air caught my hair as I stepped in. The mahogany-floored lobby was morgue quiet as I made my way toward the reception desk, a massive, arching counter between the entrance and an alcove beyond it. Other than the emergency stairwells, a bank of four elevators was the only access point to the four floors above and the eight floors below: office space overhead; server rooms and the control center deep below my feet.

A pair of security guards sat behind the desk. A man, bald and NFL thick, stood as I approached, tablet computer in hand. The other guard was glaring at a big monitor.

"Good afternoon," NFL said. A black name tag pinned to his lapel read M. Small. His first name was Marion. Age thirty-four. Divorced with one child. It's amazing what you can find online without much effort.

"Hi. I'm meeting someone for lunch," I said. "He said I should wait for him in the lobby."

The man's eyes lingered on me. They were deep set and grey, like the ocean after a storm. "Your name, ma'am?" he said.

"Williams. Heather Williams."

He swiped his finger down the tablet, stopped, then nodded. "I see you're here for—"

"Brant Thompson," I said, my voice cracking. "Yes, sir."

"You okay?"

I shrugged and coughed into my hand. "Sorry. I'm just a little nervous. He's interviewing me for an internship. You know, he and my dad are kind of friends and it's a favor. I'm trying really hard not to screw this up."

He chuckled and lifted a phone. "I'll let Mr. Thompson know you're here."

"No!"

He glanced up, one eyebrow raised.

"That's not necessary," I said. "Really. He said not to bother him when I arrived because he'd be in a meeting. I'm supposed to just to wait down here." I shifted on my feet.

The man stood silent.

"Okay if I wait over there?" I pointed to a sitting area—an L-shaped, white leather sofa and two white chairs surrounding a glass-and-metal coffee table.

"That'd be fine," he said and set the phone down.

I glanced around. Midday light illuminated the glass sculpture that hung from the ceiling by wires. It was a beautiful abstract meant to look like links in a chain. "Wow, this place is *sweet*. Seriously. Way nicer than Bayside."

NFL's hard face softened. "You attend Bayside High School?"

"Yep. Senior year."

"Mr. Palmer still principal?"

"Him and his bad toupee."

He laughed quietly and shook his head. "Like a ferret perched up there."

"That's it."

"I went there ages ago."

Sixteen years, to be exact, Marion.

"No kidding," I said. "Wow. Small world. You must've played football."

He waved off my comment. "Too violent. Flag corps captain. Two-time state champ." He was grinning now. "Good luck with your interview. Hope you make a big impression."

I gave him a smile. "That's the plan." I walked to the seating area and sank into an oversized leather chair. I had a sweeping, unimpeded view of the lobby from entrance to elevators.

This is insane, Nyah. Absolutely certifiable.

I smeared my hands across my jeans and scanned the room, trying to ease the relentless itch that gnawed at the edge of my mind.

Eight magazines stacked on the coffee table. Two vases. Thirteen flowers in one, eleven in the other.

I diverted my attention down, tapped my foot twice—a ritual my counselor taught me to bring me back to the present.

Breathe . . . breathe . . .

I slipped my iPhone from my pocket and thumbed it awake. Swiped my finger across the screen and a digital dashboard appeared. Three days of sitting in the parking lot, just within range of the building's Wi-Fi signal, had given me enough time to crack the building's utilities network. That was the only chink in BlakBox's armor; I hoped it would be enough.

I drew a deep breath and, after a last glance at the security guards, called up my texting app.

Time to give Goliath a sharp poke in the eye.

1.2

Day One
12:27 PM

MY THUMBS skimmed over the virtual keys, typing a single word:
READY?

The response came six seconds later from Pixel's Mac—*rock n roll.*
The plan was simple: all he had to do was execute the programs on my
command. Normally, I hacked alone and never from inside the building
I was targeting. To pull this one off, though, I needed on-site access and
a wingman.

I inhaled then texted the first cue.

INFERNO.

After a delay of 876 milliseconds—the time it took for him to click
the track pad—the lobby's airspace was ripped in two by a screaming
fire alarm. White strobe lights flashed at both ends of the lobby and
near the exits.

Startled, the second guard grabbed his computer monitor and
leaned in close.

"What floor?" NFL asked.

"Looking." The man shook his head. "Can't tell."

"C'mon, Jack!"

By now, the information panel must have been lit up like a psyche-
delic Christmas tree.

"It's going crazy," Jack said. "L-4! Lower-level four! No, wait. The system says it's on L-3 now."

Hacking into the corporate security network had proven impossible, but I'd found a thin crack to slip through using the building's alarm system.

"Well, which is it? Three or four?" NFL's voice had taken on the qualities of a whiny little girl.

"I don't know! The whole thing's glitching out. Now it's saying the alarm's coming from *all* floors." Then the color drained from his face as he bolted upright, sending his chair skidding back behind him. "Sprinklers! They're deploying in the executive wing."

"What? Get up there now!" NFL ordered and snatched up a walkie-talkie. "Start evacuation procedures. Go!"

Both men scrambled around the security desk and sprinted in opposite directions—one to the east stairwell and the other to the west.

As NFL ran past me, he waved and yelled, "You need to move! Get outside!" He slammed through the stairwell door on the far end of the lobby, raising the walkie-talkie to his mouth as he did.

"Well, since you asked so nicely," I said, heading nervously toward the elevators. "Just need to make one stop first."

My heart was hammering and my entire body buzzed with adrenaline. All four elevator doors yawned open by the time I'd reached them. The cars had returned to the lobby level and shut down—an automatic protocol triggered by the fire alarm.

I stepped into a car. This was the point of no return. The control-panel buttons flashed on and off. I pressed L4 and was rewarded with an irritating buzzer sound. Having researched Walter Bell, BlakBox's founder and CEO, it would not have surprised me if the button had also jolted me with a high-voltage shock. He was known as a ruthless dictator who accepted nothing less than perfection from his employees. Performance earned you staggering bonuses; failure brought ridicule and, often, a boot out the door.

My phone trembled in my hand. Text: *DOWN*.

I glanced up at the buttons. "C'mon, Pixel. C'mon . . ."

After five seconds, the buttons dimmed off, the L4 button came on and the doors shut.

L-4: the company's mission control center. The pulsing, beating heart of BlakBox's corporate infrastructure.

The building was one of three informational "meta-hubs" scattered around the globe—because naturally a monster the size of Blak-Box needed three hearts, and they all needed to be in different places in case one stopped. From here, technicians constantly monitored forty-two data centers, housing a total of 80,411 servers, running nonstop diagnostics on the servers' temperature, energy usage, streaming speeds, data storage—every possible measure to ensure peak performance and predict problems.

They likely never predicted a teenage girl hacking them from right inside their own building.

The elevator hummed as it descended, five hundred feet per minute according to the manufacturer's specifications. It would take a mere nine seconds to reach sublevel four. An additional twenty seconds of fast walking would bring me to the data center, and sixty-two more to finish my task. Hopefully.

The plan was risky, but simple: get into the mainframe room, transfer a couple data packets to Pixel's computer in the parking lot, and then turn myself in. If this job played out like the others I'd done in the past, BlakBox would be sufficiently impressed with my capabilities and hire me on the spot as a security consultant.

And I'd get the money I needed for Mom.

I stared at my reflection in the polished steel doors. The girl gazing back looked terrified. This was insane . . . and insanely illegal, too. Blak-Box *better* be majorly impressed.

The doors opened and I stepped into a sterile hallway. Strobe lights flashed on the walls, making the corridor itself appear to vibrate. Half a dozen people brushed past me, rushing for the stairwell without a second glance at me. Pushing against the flow of traffic, I made my way toward the far end of the corridor and a black steel door that marked my destination.

As I approached, my gaze flicked to a keypad beside the door. A light shined green: Unlocked. Pixel was ahead of schedule and had already tripped the lock for me.

I reached for the door handle, but it swung open and a man stepped into my path, nearly knocking me over.

"Who are you?" he asked, scrunching his eyebrows.

"IT intern from L-6," I yelled over the din. "Binkman told me to check the floor, make sure everyone's out."

His face softened into an expression of bafflement. "It's not a drill?"

"No."

"No need to check." He jerked his head, indicating the dark room behind him. "I'm the last one out. Everyone else is gone already."

"Gotta check anyway. Binkman's orders. If he finds out I didn't do what he said—"

"There's no need—"

"What's your name?" I said. "He's gonna ask me why I didn't check and when he does, I want to be sure I pronounce your name right."

He thought about it, eyes flicking around, unsure if he should let me into the unguarded room. But Joseph Binkman was the head of data management—this man's boss.

"Fine," he said, "But hurry. And don't touch anything." Then he ran—I mean a full-on sprint—toward the stairs.

I shoved through the door and stepped into the cool darkness of the room. The heavy door slammed closed behind me. I punched a code into another keypad on the wall. Simultaneously, a green light turned red and the door's locks *thunked* into place. I turned to face the control center.

The room was large, with rows of tall computer banks arcing from one side of the room to the other. Like congregants at a church of robotic giants, they all faced a floor-to-ceiling wall of seamless plasma screens streaming real-time data from around the globe. A world map indicated the location of each data center. Multicolored lights and numbers flashed, seemingly at random, all over the glowing wall. Workstations filled a large space between the wall and the computer banks. It looked like something NASA had designed.

I wove my way through the workstations until I came to the one that was still logged in, its screen glowing with the image of a star field. There, I plopped down in the chair and wiggled back into it. I lifted my phone, and sent another text: *BREAKDOWN*.

"Who are you?" a gravelly voice boomed over the alarms and my thumping heart.

I jumped and snapped my eyes up. A chill shot through me.

A video feed of a balding man with a mustache filled the screen. He scowled. "What are you doing? Who are you?"

Frantically, I palmed the mouse, moving the cursor to an icon of a video camera and closed the webcam application. Whoever had been sitting here before had left the chat window open. The man's face disappeared.

Pounding erupted from the metal door off to my right. Angry shouts penetrated from the other side. Pixel had disabled the keypad and lock system so they'd have to knock the door down if they wanted me. It sounded as though they did.

Keep calm.

I had to move fast on phase two, snagging a few packets of data then streaming them to Pixel outside. I navigated to a file manager and a window expanded on the screen.

I grabbed my phone and texted Pixel. *Sending now. Be ready.*

Getting into the building was one thing, but tapping into BlakBox's servers—right into their encrypted data—was altogether more serious. A chill of excitement mixed with unchecked terror shot through me. When they realized I could snatch their data like coins from a fountain, I was a shoo-in for a job. I just needed a few files to prove I could do it.

I established a connection between the workstation and Pixel's Mac and navigated through a directory of folders labeled only with numbers. With the transfer protocol initiated, I typed furiously as the banging at the door grew louder. The data streamed through the link to Pixel's laptop.

Text from Pixel: *i see it.*

A louder slam against the door startled me. The steel entry bulged inward. They were almost inside.

I watched the screen as a bar graph showed file after file being exported. It was the digital equivalent of walking out the front door with the folders under my arm.

As the data streamed, preview images of each document rapidly flickered across the screen. I clicked on one as it crossed the screen and it expanded—bank statements with transactions in the tens of millions of dollars, all transfers from other international banks to this one account.

"What is this?" I said and clicked through the document's pages. My eyes skimmed the data on the screen: Tripoli, Damascus, Tehran, Shanghai . . .

I clicked on the next file. I sucked in my breath and leaned closer, not believing my eyes. Close-up photographs of dead bodies and charred buildings and smoldering cars cycled on and off the screen, interspersed with multipage documents. Then: a photograph of a man stepping out of a car. I recognized him from the news: a congressman who had died in an embassy bombing.

My stomach twisted in knots.

I clicked on another file and it filled the screen. More images then a list of names and addresses, and beside the names were acronyms: MOS, MI6, CIA, ASIS, MAD. Some had black X's beside the name. Page after page of documents, all stamped TOP SECRET UMBRA and all marked with the header *United States Department of Homeland Security.*

Why did BlakBox have top-secret files? I didn't know what I was looking at exactly, only that I'd stumbled onto something I shouldn't have. This was way over my head. Panic gripped me and I felt the room constrict around me.

Frantically, I cut off the file transfer and closed down the windows. My phone chimed. Text: *it stopped.*

I dialed and pressed the phone to my ear.

"Hey," Pixel said, "the connection dropped—"

"Get out of here."

"What? What's wrong?"

"Now. I'm serious. Something's wrong. Go! Go now!"

The pounding at the door had gotten thunderous. I glanced at it as another bulge popped out from the door's surface and one of the hinges pulled free.

"You're scaring me," he said. "What's wrong?"

"I don't know. Just . . . go! Now! Get rid of that data."

I hung up and flipped through my contacts. *C'mon, c'mon, where is it?*

I pushed the dial button and I looked up at the screen as a man appeared. He'd remotely launched the webcam. He was thin and twitchy, and glared at me from the screen. He wore John Lennon glasses and twin images of his computer monitor—with me on it—reflected back at me. My stomach tightened.

He watched me without a word.

Through the iPhone's tiny speaker, I heard ringing.

"Pick up, pick up, pick up," I said.

"You've reached Jill Corbis . . ." Voicemail. *No.*

The man on-screen sneered, seemed ready to say something. I yanked the camera cord, killing his image.

"Leave a message," Jill's voice said in my ear. *Beep.*

"It's Nyah. I think I'm in big trouble. I found something—"

The door crashed open and three men dressed in SWAT gear burst into the room, shouting and leveling assault weapons at my head.

"I'm at BlakBox," I said in a rush and jumped to my feet.

"Drop it!" one of the gunmen yelled. "On your knees!"

"Help me!" I said. "Please—"

"Show me your hands!"

"They're going to shoot me!" I screamed—anything to make Jill drop everything and come running. At the moment, she was the only person in the world who *could* help me.

I let the phone slip from my hand. It hit the toe of my shoe and clattered on the floor as I placed my hands on my head.

Well, guess I'd gotten what I wanted: Goliath's attention.

One of the men grabbed a fistful of my shirt and spun me around. In less time than it took to draw a breath he shoved me to the ground and drove his knee into my back, pinning me under his crushing weight.

I gasped for breath, but none came. Face pressed against the cold floor, I felt dizzy and watched a pair of black shoes approach me. They stopped inches from my face.

"Take her to the holding room," a voice said. "I'll deal with her myself."

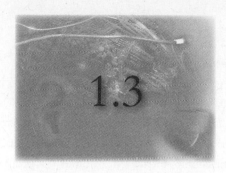

1.3

Day One
1:34 PM
BlakBox, L-8

THE GIRL was a problem and problems had to be handled.

Jon Stone studied her carefully from behind the holding room's two-way observation window. She sat alone at the room's one table. Other than her trembling hands, she hadn't moved since being apprehended an hour earlier.

Nyah Parks was her name according to her driver's license, which he'd taken along with her phone. She was terrified despite her best efforts to conceal it. One thing was certain: the girl wasn't nearly frightened enough, but that would change soon.

The child was rail thin and short—five feet two—with shoulder-length, raven-black hair highlighted with faint purple streaks. Brown doe eyes. Her complexion was smooth and deep olive brown, perhaps a child of Asian or Middle Eastern descent, and the only sign of typical teenage rebellion was a simple gold ring piercing her right nostril.

Her story was practically etched on her face: smart kid, a nearly friendless misfit who preferred computers to people and shunned the world because it had shunned her first. But she was more than just the garden-variety honors student. The quick background check he'd done had proven that. She was exceptional, dangerously so if her little stunt was any indication of her abilities.

The real question was, why was she here?

Stone watched one of the three cameras mounted high on the wall of the holding cell and he knew at least one person was watching the live video feeds. *Holding cell*—few private companies had them, but he'd insisted on its installation when Walter Bell brought him on as a security contractor, an innocuous term better suited for human resource files than for describing the reality of his responsibilities. At first, Bell hadn't seen the necessity of having the room, but with time he had come to appreciate its utility.

Near the ceiling, the camera rotated a few inches, confirming Mr. Bell's presence on the other end, twelve stories above in his executive suite.

The cell phone on Stone's belt rang. He pulled the phone out of its sheath and answered it. "Sir," he said.

"Where do we stand?" Bell's voice was taut, the words measured and sharp. Always sharp. Mr. Bell did everything with calculated efficiency, ruthlessly cutting to the bone of every situation.

"The boy outside has been contained," he said calmly. "We recovered a laptop and a cell phone. Both are being scanned as we speak."

Stone imagined Bell pacing like a lion, his upper lip curled in that perpetual sneer of his. Some underestimated the firm's sixty-three-year-old chief executive, but such people were fools. He'd witnessed first-hand Bell's unchecked ambition to grow his empire at all costs. Boundless desire always led to ethical compromises, and Bell's unscrupulous ways had been handsomely rewarded by the firm's less reputable clients. He was a master at cyber sleight of hand, and had the uncanny ability to bury secrets for those who needed them to disappear and uncover others' secrets when the price was right. His loyalty always sided with the fattest wallet.

"And our exposure?" Bell said.

"I'm still assessing the situation," Stone said. "However, it seems minimal."

"Seems? I want certainties, not guesses. How long?"

"Give me an hour."

"Don't mess this up, Stone. Find out what she knows and who sent her. I want this thing sealed tight."

"Of course." Stone's gaze lowered to the girl. She could not possibly understand the death and destruction contained in the box she'd opened. "I'll take care of it."

"I know you will." With that, Bell ended the call and Stone returned the phone to its sheath. He licked his lips.

The girl looked toward him, but he was hidden behind the glass. She was in deep, with a crushing mile of water over her head and no way to the surface. She seemed too naïve to be a hired gun. If someone had wanted to hack BlakBox, they wouldn't have done it from inside the building. Too risky. Then why was she here?

He straightened his suit jacket and entered the holding room. Without a word he drew the chair out and sat opposite the girl, who watched him with desperate eyes while the overhead fluorescents hummed. The concrete-walled room was cold; he kept it at fifty-eight degrees, the temperature of the grave—and gooseflesh covered the girl's bare arms. It was a tactic he'd learned in his time overseas. Depriving the body of comfort was the easiest way into the mind.

She tried not to break his gaze, but fear had taken over and her attention flicked between him and the door. "I was beginning to think no one was coming for me."

"Not to worry," he said. "We always follow through here at BlakBox."

Her eyes lowered to the table. There was deep-seated fear behind them.

Stone pulled the girl's driver's license from his breast pocket and glanced down at it. "Nyah Parks." He looked up at her. "Seventeen years old." Stone's attention lingered on her face. "You're an old seventeen. An old soul, I can see that."

She shifted in the chair, uneasy. "The nose ring adds a few years."

"Yes, I think you're right."

She forced a nervous smile.

"You've had quite a day," he said. "No one's ever visited our offices in quite the way you did. Care to tell me why all the theatrics?"

She hesitated. He could practically see her mind stuttering.

"No need to be shy," he said. "We're just talking. You help me; I'll help you."

"I'm here to do Mr. Bell a favor."

"I see." He nodded once. How many times had she practiced that in the mirror? "As you can imagine, my employer doesn't see it that way."

"Maybe he needs a little convincing," she said and lifted her gaze to the video camera perched high in the corner. She was scraping together bits and shreds of courage. "That's why I did all of this. To get his attention."

"Well you certainly did that." He laced his fingers together on the table. "So you caught the tiger by the tail. Now what?"

The girl fidgeted. "I'm . . . I'm here to offer Mr. Bell and BlakBox an opportunity."

"Which is . . . ?"

"Me," she said. "Actually, a chance to hire me."

Stone liked the girl's backbone, even if she was too naïve for her own good. "Why would he do that?"

"Because I have a very valuable skill set that's lacking here."

His eyebrow arched. "Lacking?"

"Your corporate security is not all it's cracked up to be."

"Is that right?"

"Yes," she said with uncertainty. "It is."

"Yet, here you are." His gaze flicked around the room—the *cell*.

Realization settled onto her face. Whatever she thought the outcome of her little stunt would be, it certainly wasn't this.

"Maybe you're not as smart as you think you are," he said.

"Or maybe I'm much smarter than you realize, which is why Blak-Box should hire me. I came here to make an impression, to prove how easy it is to get to you."

He dipped his head, conceding that she'd accomplished at least that much. "Your point?"

"If I can hack you, others—not-so-nice ones—can too. I can stop them before they do. BlakBox provides secure data archiving for millions of users. Most of them are everyday people backing up term papers and photos of their friends dancing on tables." She paused and he could read the uncertainty in her eyes. "But then you've got the important ones—intelligence agencies, the military, foreign governments . . ."

She stopped, her confidence faltering. She was obviously unsure how far to reach.

"We're nothing more than a data storehouse," Stone said with a shrug. "A parking garage for computer files. What our clients do isn't my concern. People like you are."

"Right." She swallowed, nervous. "Because I breached your secure data center and accessed your mainframe in under ten minutes. That's a problem I can fix for you."

His jaw flexed.

"I'll show you how I did it," she continued, "and how to make sure it can't happen again." She assessed him for a moment. "Look, we're on the same side. If I'd wanted to do real harm, we wouldn't be having this conversation. Instead, you'd be scrambling to stop your clients' secrets from bleeding out all over the Internet."

"And that's what you're trying to convince me of?"

"I think I already have."

It was true. The girl was a genius, no doubt about it. BlakBox had hired plenty of hackers to attempt breaking through its firewalls and other digital security, but no one had ever succeeded. Until now.

She said, "I'm here to make you a business proposition. I've shown you what I can do. I'm here because I want to work for you." She looked at the camera. "I exploited one weakness: a missing software patch in your alarm system. No one else had thought of it, not even you, and I was able to get into your control center. Think about what a sophisticated, coordinated attack would do. Everything would come to a grinding halt. What I did was just the tip of the iceberg."

"Thank you for pointing it out, but I think we're done with you now."

She shook her head. "It's not the only vulnerability BlakBox has. There are other, more serious ones. If you hire me, I'll show you how to close the gaps for good. No one will be able to do what I did. Ever."

"What's in it for you?" Stone asked.

"A job, obviously. My consulting fee includes implementation of the necessary repairs to your firewalls."

"Consulting fee . . ."

"Yes. One hundred fifty thousand dollars."

He paused, considering the girl. "That's a lot of money."

"It's a drop in the bucket compared to the revenue you'll lose if someone hacks your system for real. When that happens, you're looking at hundreds of millions in red ink. One major incident and your clients will bolt from BlakBox faster than they would from a burning house. You know I'm right. What if they found out about this?"

"That sounds like a thinly veiled threat to me."

"It's not. I'm just . . . I'm offering you a chance to fix your security gaps." She took a deep breath. "Look, someone *will* hack your servers; probably very soon." She was flustered now, grasping because she'd lost all traction.

"Oh? What makes you so sure?"

"I—"

"You know what I think?" he interrupted, leaning toward her. "I think you're planning it yourself and this little stunt was merely a test run gone wrong." He grinned "How close am I?"

"No, *no!* It's not like that."

"Tell the truth. Things will go better if you just come clean. Who sent you?"

She began to speak then fell silent as tears gathered in her eyes. After a few moments she caught her breath. "No one. It's just me. I'm not working for anyone."

"We both know that's a lie, don't we?"

"It's not."

"You've hacked your way into BlakBox. Granted. You caught our security team off guard. I'll also grant that you're exceptionally intelligent and resourceful, but look at me when I tell you this." He paused, narrowing his gaze at her. "You're dealing with an organization with tens of billions of dollars and a global reputation at stake. It's my job to ensure that nothing jeopardizes either of those things. *Nothing.*"

The words hung in the air, thick and heavy. The girl sat there, stunned. Any attempt to hold together her threadbare courage had failed. There was nowhere to run, no one to call for help, and she knew it.

He continued, his voice forceful, but calm. "You need to understand that we possess a depth of resources that your tender young mind can't possibly fathom. More than that, we possess the will to use them to protect our interests. You've made a grave error in coming here. Do you hear what I'm saying?"

She nodded weakly.

"Good. Now, I don't know what your true intentions are, but I promise you this: I will find out no matter how long it takes. And whatever data you transferred to your friend in the parking lot is already back in our hands." It wasn't true, but she didn't know that.

Her eyes went wide. "Where's Pixel? What'd you do to him?"

"There's only one unanswered question here, and that is what to do with *you*."

"Listen," she said, fear practically strangling her now, putting tiny beads of sweat on her forehead and upper lip. She was looking for a sliver of hope to dig her nails into. "I'm really sorry . . . I didn't mean for any of this to . . . I just thought . . ."

"You didn't think. That's where you went wrong."

"Please, we can work something out."

"There's nothing to work out. This isn't a negotiation, and there will be no leaving, no attorneys, no phone calls until I say so. Now, you're going to tell me everything—why you're really here, who sent you—"

"Nobody sent me," she said, staring absently at the wall.

"Tell me what you accessed on our servers and why."

"I didn't see anything," she said. "I swear. I was just—"

"Start at the beginning. Tell me everything."

She lowered her face into her hands, beginning to cry now.

"Don't disappoint me, Nyah. I'll know if you're lying. And, trust me, I'm not the kind of man you want to lie to."

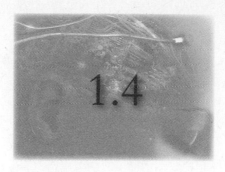

1.4

I WANTED to scream, but I knew no one would hear me. Not in this concrete bunker deep underground.

The man across the table studied me. His eyes seemed like black pearls, impenetrable and cold. I knew I wouldn't be leaving that room anytime soon, maybe never. Whatever I'd stumbled onto, it was dangerous enough for Bell to sic this lunatic on me. What were in those files I'd transferred to Pixel? Something big, obviously, and very dangerous.

I looked up at a video camera, and the man settled back in his chair. "They've been turned off," he said. "We're quite alone and these walls are very thick. I assure you."

I swallowed, said nothing. I believed him. I also believed he was capable of much more than I was imagining, which was pretty awful. I sat up as straight as I could and tried to speak without coming completely undone. "There are people looking for me. I've been gone a long time."

He glanced at his watch. "Really? Who would be looking for you? Your friend on the bike?" He shook his head and stretched his lips into a tight smile. "Not anymore."

I felt like puking right then and there. "Where is he?" I asked again. "Please tell me you didn't hurt him."

"Pixel," the man said slowly, as if he were chewing on the word. He shook his head.

"*What did you do?*" I felt the last seams of my resolve pulling apart. I had to get out of that room, out of that building, but there was no way I could overpower him. And I was deep underground. I could never

27

escape before they reeled me back in. That's exactly how it felt: like I was a fish on a hook.

"Your friend's in very serious trouble, just like you. Apparently, he understands what's at stake, and he is cooperating fully with authorities as we speak."

"He's with the police?"

"He's told us everything. Like I said, if you lie to me we'll know. Now, start at the beginning. I won't ask again."

The man's face was hard as a statue's, but I knew he was lying about the authorities being involved. If Pixel was in custody then why wasn't I? Why was I being held in a concrete room? It made no sense. Chances were that Pixel sat in another room just like this one, maybe next door, and the only path out for both of us was to tell them everything. I had nothing to hide, after all. I only hoped he'd believe me.

"All of this is very simple," I said. "The reason I came here was to help my—"

Before I could say *mother*, the man's mobile phone rang, cutting me off.

"Yes?" he answered, irritation making the word sharp as a rock dropped on the table. His gaze flicked toward me and his mouth twisted into a frown. "How long ago?" He squeezed his eyes closed. "I see. No, no, keep them there. I'll bring the girl up."

Hope kindled inside of me as he holstered his phone. *Bring the girl up.* Was I leaving? Or was he just taking me somewhere else to question me? He seemed uncertain for the first time, and caught off guard.

He crinkled his nose at me. "Smart girl," he said. "Apparently that call you made worked out, though I had my doubts it would. The FBI doesn't come running for just anyone. Jill Corbis, was it? She's waiting in the main lobby to take you into custody."

Jill. She'd gotten my call. She came to my rescue. "What—?" I started.

He held up a massive hand, stopping me. "The question is, why? Why would the FBI come for a teenage hacker like you? I suppose I'll find out soon enough." The man leaned close. "Though let me give you some advice. If I were you, I would consider carefully what I told the authorities. Your actions just might have far-reaching consequences."

I knew he meant Pixel and my family. I had no doubt this man was capable of anything.

He pushed back from the table, stood, and turned toward the door. "Follow me," he said.

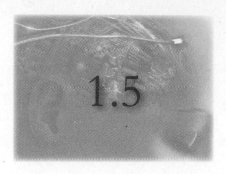

1.5

Day One
3:46 PM
FBI Field Office
San Francisco, CA

"NYAH, WHAT were you thinking?"

Jill Corbis glared at me from the end of the conference room where she stood with hands gripping the table's edge. Thankfully, she'd gotten my message and taken it seriously enough to bring a pair of agents with her. She had made a spectacle of arresting me in BlakBox's lobby. It was a show mostly for Bell's sake, she'd said. They could have carried me out in a bag of trash for all I cared, as long as they got me out of that place.

"Look, I'm sorry," I said. "I just . . . I wasn't thinking."

"Well, that's obvious. What you did was not only dangerous, but highly illegal."

"I said I'm sorry," I repeated.

"Not good enough this time. I just defended you to the deputy director, who, by the way, has already gotten a call from BlakBox's legal counsel. I want to help you, but you need to give me more than just *I'm sorry*. Let's go through this again, and this time I want you to tell me everything."

"I did tell you everything."

Jill narrowed her focus. "My gut tells me you're not."

31

I pushed my chair back from the table. "I already told you, I was just trying to land a consulting job. I need the money," I said. "That's it."

"Everybody needs money."

"Not *this* badly, they don't, and not this much. I'm trying to get Mom into a clinical study, which is crazy expensive. Her doctor thinks she doesn't have long to live. This research program could help. It's the miracle I've been looking for and the money from BlakBox was going to pay for it. But now . . ."

I let my words trail off. It was all too much—getting caught, watching the money slip through my fingers, along with it my last chance to help Mom. Worse still, Pixel was missing, and it was my fault.

Jill's face softened. "So you take a risk, swing for the fences with BlakBox, hoping they'll hire you and pay the money you need."

"Yes," I said, not hiding the frustration in my voice. "We've already gone through this."

"And we'll go through it again, if need be. It's important that I know everything." She sighed. "You know, kid, every grey hair on my head is from you."

That was probably true. We'd met a year earlier when her team scooped me up as part of a hacking sting. I'd been cleared of any crime, mostly because, while my snooping had crossed paths with malicious hackers, I had no affiliations with them and hadn't vandalized anything. I'd simply been in the wrong digital place at the wrong digital time.

Where others in the Bureau saw a threat, Jill had seen a young girl trying to get her bearings after a tragedy had shattered her world. Incredibly, we'd become friends, and I'd started tipping her off when I caught whiff of something fishy on the cyber wind. She owed her last promotion to me after I uncovered a hacker's plan to breach a global payment system and snatch a hundred million credit card numbers.

"Do you realize how connected and influential Walter Bell is?" Jill continued. "If BlakBox decides to come after you—"

"Let them! I don't care!"

"Well, you need to start caring, because right now there's no scenario that ends well for you."

"It doesn't matter," I said. "All that matters right now is finding Pixel." I softened my voice and sat back in the chair and hugged myself. "I have a really bad feeling."

"We'll find him," Jill said. "He probably got scared, ran away, and now he's laying low until things cool off."

"Then why isn't he answering his phone? He always answers. That creep at BlakBox said the authorities had him, but that's a lie. What if they grabbed him? What if they've done something to him?"

Jill was silent, her mind grinding away. I knew in my heart the man in the black suit had Pixel. That's why he'd mentioned him, to scare me. To pressure me and let me know that he held all the cards.

"What if they hurt him?" I said.

"At this moment we have no reason to believe anyone at BlakBox would harm either you or your friend. They're a corporation, not the mafia. Walter Bell is a lot of things, but stupid isn't one of them. Holding a kid is too risky."

"Risky?" I threw up my hands. "They locked me in a concrete room in their basement and sent a man to interrogate me. Do you really think they were just going to call the police? If you hadn't come for me there's no telling what they would've done. They were just going to deal with it themselves and make me disappear quietly. And Pixel too."

"That's an assumption. We don't know that."

"Then where is he?" The words came out sharper than I'd meant, and more desperate.

"I don't know." She stopped. "But we'll find him, I promise."

"Not sitting here we won't."

My words hung in the air as Jill settled into the seat next to me and leaned close. "I know you're upset. I would be too. I want to help you, but you're not giving me much to go on."

"These people are dangerous," I said. "I'm scared."

"You should be. Remember, you're the one who crossed the line here, not Bell. I should be investigating you."

"But the pictures, the things I saw on their server . . . I don't know, it was like something straight out of a spy movie. Something isn't right there. I mean, how many companies have an interrogation room?"

"More than you realize," Jill said.

A thick, dark cloud descended on my mind. Every moment that passed without word from Pixel lowered the odds of finding him safe. Everyone knew that. Plus, time gave BlakBox the advantage of covering their tracks—masking whatever it was I'd seen on their servers and whatever they'd done with Pixel.

"You have to raid that place before they move everything off their servers," I said. "It's all right there; you just have to go get it."

Jill shook her head. "I can't do that, not on the word of a teenage girl."

"Don't you believe me?"

"I don't know." She was quiet for a moment. "I don't know."

Her words stung. "Jill . . ."

"I trust you far more than I do Walter Bell, but that's not enough. I need evidence."

"Then find Pixel. Find his laptop. I transferred the files from Blak-Box's server to it."

"Could he have sent the data somewhere?" she asked. "As a . . . I don't know . . . a precaution? An e-mail account, a cloud backup service, anything?"

"Yeah, if he had time. The plan was for him to upload the files to an encrypted site on the Internet, which I'd then give BlakBox access to after they hired me."

"And?"

"It's not there. I checked the account using my phone. I was the last person to log into it, and that was last night."

"What about e-mail? Could he have sent it to you?"

"I checked that too. I've gotten nothing from him." I shook my head. "They have him, I know it. And the data too. If that's the case it's their word against mine."

Jill reached out and put her hand on top of mine. "We'll find Pixel and we'll figure this out."

I felt the tears welling, but I shoved them down. I didn't say anything.

"I had your car towed to impound. It's waiting for you downstairs. Now I want you to go home," Jill said. "Get some rest. We'll look at this with fresh eyes tomorrow. My people will keep looking for Pixel, all right?"

"You're letting me go?"

"It took some work on my part, but yes, for now. You have to promise me you'll keep your head down. And if the thought crosses your mind to go anywhere near BlakBox, don't. Understand?"

I nodded. "Thanks."

"It's going to be all right," she said and squeezed my hand. "I promise."

It wasn't a promise she could make, though. We both knew that.

I left the conference room and headed out, feeling small in the FBI building's wide, tiled halls. I tried Pixel's number and wanted to scream when my call went directly to voicemail again.

Where are you, Pixel? Please be all right.

I don't remember the ride to Mom's apartment. My body was running on autopilot, which was good, since my mind felt like a fried circuit board. I pulled into Cedar Ridge, the assisted-care facility where she and my grandma lived, and sat in the stuffy car, watching the sun drop lower in the sky.

After a while, my nerves felt a little calmer. I climbed out of the car and headed for the front entrance. It was a campus of five buildings that housed over five hundred people. Most of them were retirees living out their twilight years in style. Others, like Mom, were there because the hospice care was the best in northern California.

When I entered Mom's apartment my grandmother Lettie was standing at the kitchenette, sorting mail. It was a small, two-bedroom unit on the ground floor that reminded me of my own apartment—kitchenette on the right as you walked in, cramped living room ahead, and a narrow hall beyond the kitchen counter, leading to the bedrooms.

Lettie dropped the stack and attacked me with a hug. "There you are! Don't you answer your phone anymore?" She said, squeezing me tight. "You had me worried."

"Sorry. I got held up." I tightened my arms around her. She felt so frail, like holding a bird.

"I saved you a plate," she said, turning and heading for the refrigerator. "I'll heat it up."

"Maybe later. I grabbed a bite on my way home," I lied. You have to understand, food was her love language. Lettie saw feeding me as a way of putting into action what she felt in her heart. She was taking care of me, and rejecting her food offerings was like turning away from a hug. You just didn't do it without good reason. Truth was, my stomach felt as though it'd been used as a punching bag.

She turned to face me, her hands fluttering in front of her, now that they had nothing to do. "Oh," she said, disappointed.

Lettie was my dad's mom. She was short and stocky with hair the color of cobwebs. Grandpa Rick had died three years earlier, one week after he sold his service garage and retired. They'd planned a trip around the world, but never made it. She'd gone back to work because sitting around the house was driving her "batty as a banana," an image I didn't quite get, but I understood. After the accident she'd dropped everything to take care of Mom, and had recently moved into Cedar Ridge to be with her around the clock.

"How was the job interview?" she asked. "I'll bet they just loved you."

"I didn't get it. I wasn't a 'good fit for their corporate culture.'" I made quote marks in the air.

"They said that? To your face?"

"I think it *was* my face they were referring to." I touched my nose ring.

"Psh!" she said, waving her hand. "People are too hung up on what they can see, when all that matters is what they can't." She tapped a finger against her chest, over her heart. "Well, their loss." She shrugged and smiled. "Someday they'll regret their decision."

"I seriously doubt that."

Lettie knew I was a computer consultant and that I was extremely good at it. Large companies hired me to fix problems and gave me monster paychecks to do it. But I couldn't tell her how I acquired clients. She would never understand or approve.

"Wait and see." She ran a finger along my temple, catching a stray strand of hair and tucking it behind my ear. "You're brilliant and beautiful. Things are going to get better, you'll see. If there's anything I know in these old bones it's that everything happens for a reason."

"I was hoping this project would work out. The money would've taken care of us for a while and paid for that experimental trial."

"It wasn't meant to be."

It was unfair is what it was. The trial was a miracle in waiting. PRE-MIND was short for *Post-traumatic Restorative Encoding Med-Integration Neural Device*. It was a neural implant that held the promise of reversing some of Mom's brain damage and nudging her a bit toward *normal* again. But it didn't matter now: BlakBox hadn't taken the bait so there was no money to get Mom into the program.

Anger grew deep inside me, like the fitful heating of charcoal in a grill. Anger at the situation, at our life, at God. It felt as though we'd become a punch line to a cosmic joke, and that God took perverse pleasure in dangling hope in front of us only to snap it away when we reached for it.

"I have to find a way. I don't know how yet, but I'll get the money."

"Honey, that's impossible. Let it go."

My mind was churning. Lettie looked at me with concern. There was something else in her eyes as well, something small but powerful. It was hope, and I knew it would turn into either disappointment or joy.

"How's Mom?"

"It's been a tough day," she said with a fading smile. "She's . . . I should check on her."

I took Lettie's hand. "It's okay. I will. You sit down."

She pecked me on the cheek. "She knows who you are, you know. She remembers, even if only deep inside."

I smiled and nodded. "I know."

Without another word I veered down the short hallway to her bedroom. Lettie had created a gallery of family photos—"The Hall of Memories," she'd called it.

I walked slowly, my fingertips skimmed over the photographic bodies and faces, remembering each event: Mom nailing Dad with a Super Soaker as he came out of the sliding-glass door onto the back patio, her mouth open in a laughing grin, her eyes made into joyful crescents; Mom and my little brother Tommy, wearing big mustaches and hats, each with both hands on a cane and kicking up one leg during a home-brewed vaudeville act they'd put on three years ago in the living room; me, holding Mom in my arms in the surf on a beach in Pensacola, Florida, mom acting afraid of the water. Right after the picture had been taken, I tossed her into a big, breaking wave and she proceeded to drag me into the water, both of us stuffing sand down the other's bathing suit and smearing it into each other's hair. I'd never laughed so hard.

No one ever tells you that being a survivor is a kind of curse. Not the doctors who remind you that you're lucky to be alive. Not the counselors who mean well, but have no more answers than you do. Not your friends who are afraid of saying something wrong so they say nothing at all.

What's worse is the knowledge that it didn't have to be this way, that life would be the same if only one little thing had unfolded differently.

If only we'd left the house ten seconds earlier.

If only Dad had taken a right on Chestnut instead of Palmer, which he rarely took because of the traffic.

If only I'd sat on the driver's side instead of Tommy.

If only . . .

Doctors were shocked that I'd survived the impact. When I told them that I never lost consciousness they thought I was lying. I wish I were.

I remember everything: how time slowed just before the other driver slammed into us; the screeching, grinding metal sound our car made when it flipped and slid to a stop in the grassy median forty yards away.

I remember it all.

When the first responders arrived, they found the van on its right side leaking gas onto the ground. Dad had been killed instantly and Mom was bleeding out. Tommy was dead too. That was the worst part, seeing him.

His body hung above me by his seatbelt. His eyes were still open and his arm hung limp. Blood streamed down his arm and onto my face. He just stared at me, his eyes still frozen with the fear he must've felt as he died. I heard his last breath.

When the firefighters cut me from the car I was hysterical, they'd said. That's the only part I don't remember.

I went into the bedroom at the end of the hall. Mom lay motionless in her bed, propped up by a couple pillows. The brain trauma she'd suffered in the accident had paralyzed her from the waist down, and in recent months she'd begun deteriorating at a frightening pace. She could still speak, but she had no memories of her past and couldn't form new ones. Every day was like starting over—remembering and forgetting who she was, who I was, who Lettie was. And there was the *pain*, which came in agonizing waves that sent her into near delirium. It wouldn't be long, doctors said, before she would be gone.

I sat in a chair beside her.

"Hey, Mom," I said quietly.

Her eyes were glassy and fixed on the ceiling. They were a deep brown. Dad used to call her Angel Eyes.

"Are you the nurse?" she whispered.

"I'm your daughter, Nyah."

"Nyah." A lost look came over her face. Her eyes drifted left and right like someone trapped between waking and sleep. "A pretty name."

"You came up with that." I noticed her nails were freshly painted, a sparkly blue, like something you'd see on an expensive sports car. Lettie did her daughter-in-law's nails every week before her neurology appointment so she'd look her finest. "I like that color on you."

She winced. "My head hurts so much. Make it stop." Her voice was barely a whisper.

"I wish I could," I said.

"Please . . . ," she begged.

I checked the IV used to deliver the steady doses of pain meds that Dr. Benton had prescribed to keep her comfortable. It was already maxed out and there was nothing more I could give her.

"I'm sorry," I said, hating myself for feeling so helpless. "I'm sorry . . ."

She moaned quietly and closed her eyes.

I took a deep breath and let it out slowly. I sat there for a long time, listening to the gentle sound of her breathing.

"Why is life so unfair, Mom?" I said and shook my head "This shouldn't have happened to you. You and Dad and Tommy were good people, the best kind of people. You were this family's laughter. You laughed so often and got everyone else doing it too." I laughed then, thinking about it, but the sound was choked and came with tears. "And Dad, boy he just wanted to try anything and everything, didn't he? Remember when he bought all of us Rollerblades?" Another short laugh, more tears. "We must have looked like the Four Stooges, arms and legs flailing, going down the street. Tommy fell and broke his arm! But you had him laughing all the way to the hospital."

She opened her eyes and looked at me, a look of puzzlement on her face. "Don't cry."

"I messed up," I whispered. "Nothing's gone the way I'd planned and now everything's wrecked. And it just keeps getting worse."

"Please don't cry," she said again.

"I'll try not to." I leaned forward and kissed her lightly on the forehead. "I'll take care of you, Mom, I promise. I'll fix this. I'll find a way to get the money we need. And I'll find Pixel and everything will go back to the way it was."

I wasn't sure I could fix this, though. Not all of it. I'm not sure anyone could, but I had to try. Hot tears dripped off my cheeks.

"I love you to the moon and back," I said and stood. She'd already drifted to sleep, but her face was still twisted as if she were trapped in some terrible, inescapable nightmare.

Before I left her room, I looked back and vowed that tomorrow would be a better day. BlakBox may have fallen through, but that didn't mean I would give up. I couldn't. Pixel was still out there and the clock was ticking to get Mom into the clinical trial. There was still a chance, however slim and unlikely, that I could get the money. But to get it meant I had to find someone who'd dropped out of my life and off the grid.

I had to find Austin.

As I slipped through the door and closed it gently behind me, I said it out loud: "Tomorrow *will be* a better day."

But in my heart, I wasn't so sure.

1.6

Day Two
2:34 AM
BlakBox Corporate Office

STONE SAT in the dimly lit fourth-floor office suite, eyes fixed on the only other man in the room. Walter Bell stood beside the floor-to-ceiling window, hands clasped loosely behind him as he gazed beyond the glass. The outside world was still and soot dark except for the glow of distant streetlights.

"You're certain?" Bell finally spoke without turning.

"Yes, sir. I confirmed it myself. The files were fully compromised, just as we suspected."

"I see." A long pause. "And the location of the files now?"

"Undetermined. A search of the boy's phone and laptop turned up nothing. He either destroyed the files or transferred them elsewhere before we caught up to him."

"That's a problem, wouldn't you say?" Bell said as he turned toward him. "Until the files are recovered, we must assume that the girl has them and intends to provide them to authorities."

Stone dipped his head once, agreeing.

"That's a situation I can't allow, you understand," Bell continued. "Find her and recover the data. Silence the threat and make sure it never surfaces again."

"Understood," Stone said. "And the boy?"

"He's outlived his usefulness. Deal with it quietly. Tonight."

"Of course." He stood and straightened his suit coat.

"And Stone," Bell said, eyes narrowing to slits. "Take care of the girl. I can't afford any loose ends on this."

"Of course."

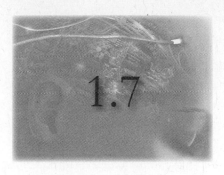

Day Two
11:14 AM

WE DON'T get to choose our lives, when or where we're born. Usually, even our names are chosen before we come kicking and screaming into the world.

Nyah means *life purpose*. My mom got pregnant with me while she and Dad were doing Peace Corps work in Calcutta, which is where she was born and lived for eight years before an American family adopted her. Doctors said she'd never have kids, but she believed her life's purpose was to be a mom. It must've been true because she became one twice.

People used to believe that naming a thing or a person defined its existence and gave it meaning. Adam named the animals. Explorers claimed faraway lands in the name of kings. Aboriginal boys survived rites of passage into manhood and were given new names. New identities.

We still believe in the power of names, hackers especially.

Every hacker has a handle, an alias that we've chosen to define how we want to be known. Maybe it's our way of redefining ourselves not for who we *are*, but for what we *could* be.

I could count on one hand how many people knew both my real name and my handle.

Austin Hartt was one of these people.

We first met at Dr. Benton's office six months after the accident. Back then, I never wanted to go to Mom's neurology appointments, and I hated myself for that. What kind of daughter wouldn't want to be there for her mom? But I couldn't bear watching her get poked and prodded while she just sat there, a numb, unknowing look on her face.

On the days I couldn't handle it, I'd sit in the waiting room while the doctor ran his tests. I hated that office and everything about it: the pine-scented antiseptic in the air, the strange patients, the hum of the air conditioner running nonstop even in winter. Most people die twice: first when they give up on life, and finally when Death comes to take what's his. The waiting room felt like a stopover somewhere in between.

Austin was the most normal person there, though he never smiled. He would sit in the same chair, always with his laptop in front of him. He had a compulsive habit of tapping each of his fingertips seven times with his thumb. I counted.

I don't think he noticed me until the day I brought my own laptop, the one with the black-and-white Anonymous decal: an image of a Guy Fawkes mask and the phrase *Keep Calm and Expect Us*.

I glanced up from my screen and caught him staring at me. He didn't look away when I made eye contact. Most boys would've looked away, but not Austin.

"That's clever," he said.

"Excuse me?"

He pointed. "That sticker. I like it."

I shrugged.

"Knowledge is free," Austin said. "We are Anonymous. We are Legion."

He paused, raised an eyebrow and nodded once as if to say, *Go on, your turn.*

"We do not forgive," I continued. "We do not forget."

"Expect us," we said together.

It was the motto of Anonymous, a global collective of "hacktivists" who'd banded together to remind big governments and corporations that they served the people and not the other way around. Anonymous was controlled chaos at its finest, a crowd-sourced cyber lynch mob of sorts that made its home in the digital world.

"Are you an Anon?" he asked.

"Isn't everyone?"

"No." There was an awkward moment filled only with the air conditioner's hum. "Do you have a mask?"

A mask. A handle.

I tilted my head: *maybe.*

"I hope it's a good one. So many of them are ridiculously unoriginal." A beat. "So what is it?"

I just smiled.

He dipped his head and went back to work on his computer. I was still watching him—wondering how old he was, why he was seeing Dr. Benton—when movement on my laptop screen caught my eye: the cursor was moving on its own. Someone was hacking me! My fingers flashed over the keyboard, telling the system to terminate all external connections and locate the source of the intrusion. Then the answer dawned on me.

I looked up and there was Austin, smiling at me over his laptop monitor. He glanced at his screen, back at me. "Trinity," he said, naming my handle. "Really?"

Ten seconds. This guy was good. He'd gotten through my firewall like a Mr. Fatty at a buffet and found my handle in no-time flat. Granted, my guard was down and I'd disabled my best firewall to tap into the local Wi-Fi, but still . . .

"Impressive," I said.

"I like it," he said.

"What?"

"Trinity. Three in one, one in three. There's a story behind that, I'm sure. Either that or you're a fan of *The Matrix* and couldn't come up with a better idea."

"Maybe I just like the sound of it."

"Or maybe you have multiple personalities."

"Possible. I am sitting in a brain doctor's office, after all. For all you know, I'm crazy."

"Isn't everyone?"

"No," I said with a wry smile.

"Well, my advice, Trinity, is this: don't wear your mask too long or you might start to forget who's beneath it. Masks are funny that way."

"Too late."

"I'll bet not."

We became friends that day. For the next few months, we'd see each other in Dr. Benton's waiting room and talk like ladies at the beauty parlor until he had to go into the office or I had to leave. Our first date—my word; I don't think he ever thought of us as dating—was to a gallery exhibit of computer art by the surrealist Christos Magganas, whom we both admired. After that, we went to movies, had picnics in Golden Gate Park, strolled through Chinatown and Fisherman's Wharf. But mostly, we chatted online—never on the phone because he didn't own one. He said the electromagnetic waves irradiate brain tissue, which was a problem considering he had a tumor.

He had moved from Boston to California to be treated by Dr. Benton about the time my family had been smashed into early graves. Austin rarely talked about his medical condition, and when he did it was only in passing. His tumor was rare, I knew that much. He said that over time it had become inoperable and when he lived in Boston he'd had a stroke, which produced some kind of delusional episode that prompted his search for better treatment.

He was two years older than I was—twenty-three months, actually—but intellectually he was on a higher plane altogether. He was a genius in every sense of the word. Something had happened to him when he was younger that made him that way, but he couldn't remember what. In fact, he couldn't remember anything before age thirteen.

I just think he was a freak of nature in the right sense.

Sometimes he'd tell me about his latest projects. If you haven't already guessed it, he was a hacker too, but if I was Pikes Peak, he was Everest. While I was cracking server firewalls, he was developing data-mining algorithms for the NSA and CIA. Those were his weekend projects, side money so he could work on other, more important, things. Passion projects, he called them.

One of those was an application he'd worked on for years. He called it MetacogNet, an artificial intelligence program that attempted to replicate the complex "left" and "right" brain capabilities of the human mind. It had the potential to revolutionize the way data becomes usable information.

Austin's findings drew the attention of a Silicon Valley venture capitalist who bankrolled the program's development. But immediately after launching the company, Austin cashed out. A larger tech company had given him ten million reasons to walk away, so he had. He'd never wanted to run a company; he had other things in mind.

That was almost a year ago. Soon after that he'd disappeared from my life: there one day, gone the next. The jerk. He'd stopped answering my e-mails, stopped logging into the online chat services we used, stopped showing up at the doctor's office. I'd gone by his apartment once to find out what I'd done wrong, but he'd never come to the door. I'd spent most of my life being ignored and had gotten used to it, but this . . . this hurt.

Soon I stopped trying. If he didn't want to see me anymore, that was his loss. I hadn't realized how much I thought of him until he wasn't there. If that sounds lame and pathetic, you've never been in love, or even in a close friendship.

Just wait, it'll happen.

The morning after BlakBox, I rode my motorcycle, a beat-up Yamaha I'd bought online, over to Austin's apartment. It was in a warehouse by the Bay that a real estate developer had converted to an upscale apartment complex. I was the only person who knew where he lived. He'd always wanted to stay anonymous to the rest of the world, which I understood.

Looking at the building from where I parked on the street out front brought back painful memories of the last time I'd spoken to him, how he'd said he had important things to do—things I wouldn't understand. He was throwing away our relationship.

That was the only time I'd ever yelled at him. It was the only way I could handle the pain and betrayal I'd felt. Anger is so much more manageable than grief. I hadn't known it would be the last time I'd see him.

But now I was there for Mom. I needed money, and Austin was the only person I knew who could help. A hundred fifty grand was pocket change to him.

I followed a cobblestone walkway to a set of black double doors. A steel callbox with the word *Sentex* etched into it was bolted to the brick wall. It had a keypad and digital touchscreen that normally would've had a long list of the building's tenants and their unit numbers. But here, there was only one.

K. Os—Unit 500.

K-OS. Austin's handle. *Chaos.*

I dialed his unit on the keypad and waited. The call system rang a dozen times then automatically disconnected after no answer. Maybe he wasn't home. More likely, he just never answered the buzzer.

Guess I'd just let myself in. I'd brought along a decryption application I'd coded to bypass the door's security protocol. Using a pocket tool, I worked the metal box's back panel free, spliced a cable with an adaptor I'd brought, and plugged the other end into my iPhone. In less than twenty seconds, the door latch disengaged with a click, and I went in.

The building was all but abandoned. Austin was the only person who lived there because the developer's plans had been bigger than his bank account, and he'd gone bankrupt before anyone else could buy a unit. Everything was half finished and covered in drywall dust, including the elevator, an open freight lift with a gated door.

I got in, pulled the gate closed, and it lurched slowly toward to the top floor.

The elevator stopped and I stepped out. Twin steel doors, black and formidable, were set in the opposite wall. A thick metal plate with the numbers 111110100 was welded to the door. Only Austin would convert his unit number to binary code.

There was no doorbell, no knocker of any kind so I pounded on the door with my fist. It barely made a sound, like punching a gravestone.

"Austin! It's Nyah!" My voice echoed around me.

I listened: only silence beyond the doors. I'd come this far and I wasn't going to leave until I'd spoken to him. No, forget that. I wasn't leaving without the money.

I tried the silver door lever. It turned easily under my hand and the latch clicked. Unlocked. What good was a having a front door like Fort Knox if you left it wide open? But I suppose it made sense when you're the only one in the building.

I eased the door open and went in.

"Austin?"

The loft was cavernous, with pitted hardwood floors, exposed brick walls, and ceilings twenty feet overhead. Daylight spilled through huge windows rising high on the walls.

"Hello?" My voice disappeared into the large space.

There was none of the furniture you'd expect—no couches or chairs, no coffee tables or bookshelves. Instead, the space was filled with organized clusters of high-tech lab equipment, panels of large-screen monitors and computers, and row upon row of blinking, humming server racks. And above it all, large rumbling ductwork that dumped cold air into the space, no doubt to cool the equipment.

Over the thrum of the ventilation, a sound pulsed—a droning *whum whum whum* that moved through the apartment like an electrical current. It was too thick and resonant to be coming from the servers.

"Austin?" I called louder. "It's Nyah. You here?"

I walked deeper into the loft, passing equipment that belonged in a hospital, not a computer lab: light boards plastered with skull X-rays taken from various angles, large stainless-steel tables meticulously organized with chemistry equipment, microscopes, centrifuges, electroencephalogram (EEG) and electrocardiogram (ECG) machines. All of it was dwarfed by an enormous, shrink-wrapped machine strapped to large pallets. The label stamped on the side read SignaTech NeuroImaging Solutions.

Neuroimaging? What was he doing with *that?*

I rounded the last server rack, and the far side of the apartment came into view. I froze and my breath caught. There he was, standing barefoot in a grey hoodie and black jeans. He wore a black knit beanie, pulled tight over his head, and large red headphones.

He hadn't spotted me yet.

Austin was leaning over a tyrannosaurus-sized control panel that reminded me of a mixing board I'd seen once in a music studio, only bigger. He seemed lost in his own world, frenetically dialing knobs, pushing buttons, sliding controllers, all of it punctuated by quick glances up at an array of screens mounted to the panel. As he tweaked the controls, the sound reverberating through the room changed subtly.

He looked past the screens and I realized the noise was coming from a sound booth of some kind beyond the control panel—a room within the room with a glass observation window set into the wall facing the control panel.

I took a step toward him and my motion drew his attention.

He jerked upright and turned. His face was drawn and thinner than the last time I'd seen him. Paler. His eyes went wide like someone shaken from a deep dream.

Without taking his gaze off me, he pushed a button, killing the sound, and slipped the headphones off.

He stood motionless for several long breaths. I was probably the last person he'd expect to show up in his apartment.

"Hey." I smiled, gave him a little wave.

He didn't so much as blink.

"Been a while, huh?" I said.

"What are you doing here?"

"You know . . ." I raised one shoulder. "Just in the neighborhood and I thought—"

"How'd you get in?" His attention flicked past me, as if expecting a SWAT team. He was twitchy, with dark rings under his eyes. He had the appearance of someone on an obsessive mission—heck, I'd been there myself: living on candy bars, coffee, and as little sleep as humanly possible.

"Seriously? I've had lunchboxes with better security than this place." I walked toward him and stopped a few yards away. "Can we talk?"

"I'm in the middle of something right now." He glanced at the control board.

"It's nice to see you too."

He sighed, turned his attention back to the control panel, and began adjusting knobs again as if I weren't there. "I'm serious," he said. "Now's not a good time. It'll have to wait."

"No." I stepped closer. "It's important."

He continued fiddling with the controls, put the headphones on again, but this time with one pushed back off his ear. "Go ahead," he said. "I'm listening."

"You stopped going to Dr. Benton."

"There was nothing else he could do for me."

"So you gave up?"

"I didn't say that." His hands moved over the control board "This is what you wanted to talk about? Why I stopped going to Benton's?"

"No. It's not," I said. "I'm in some trouble. Things have gotten complicated."

He looked at me. His eyes were puffy. Tiny veins etched them like red roadmaps. "Things are always complicated with you."

You should talk, I wanted to say, but it wouldn't help my cause. I wasn't there for me or for Austin or for the idea of us. I was there for Mom. Period.

I reached out and touched one of his constantly moving arms. "Austin, please. I have nowhere else to go. You're the only one who can help me. When I say I'm in trouble, I'm serious. Very serious."

He turned toward me slowly, this time a look of concern crinkling his brow. "What's going on? What kind of trouble?" His voice was softer.

I swallowed. "I need to borrow some money. I'll pay you back, I promise."

"Sure, okay. How much?"

"One fifty."

"That's it?" He reached around toward a rear pocket.

"Thousand," I said. "A hundred and fifty thousand dollars."

"Okay . . ." His hand came back empty. "That's a lot of money."

"I know. It's for my mom. There's a chance to get her into an experimental trial, a neural prosthesis that can rebuild brain functionality from the inside out." My words were rushing out now. "It's her only chance, but they want us to pay for it. They've had really good success so far and—"

"You're talking about the PREMIND trials."

That stopped me. "You've heard of it?"

"Enough to know it's a long shot, though it's a step in the right direction." His face became puzzled. "That's a military program. DARPA's got their hands all over it. Why would they let your mom in? She's not military."

I pulled a wad of folded up paperwork from my pocket and held it out. "They're making a rare exception since her injuries are consistent with the case-study profiles."

He took the documents and scanned them quickly. "That you could get her into this is pretty impressive. No one makes exceptions like that. You must've been really persuasive."

"Yeah, but the problem is, we now have to front the cost. Austin, it's her only hope. I'll pay you back, I promise."

"Listen, if I had it, I'd give it to you." He glanced at me. "You know I would."

"What do you mean, *if* you had it? You're a millionaire."

His face was impossible to read as he stood there.

"Right?" I said. "Austin . . . ?"

"Was. I was a millionaire. I plowed it all into my own research, every dime and then some. I have maybe five grand in cash."

I felt punched in the stomach—again.

"Besides," he said, handing the paper back. "PREMIND's more sizzle than steak. I hate to be the one to tell you that, but I've read the data. I'm not impressed with the promises they're making. They're attempting to mimic the hippocampus's neural signal processing via nonlinear transformations of multisignal input dynamics into output signals translatable to storable code."

"In English, please."

"They're creating a prosthetic that receives sensory data then processes, encodes, and stores it as a memory. Nothing more. Despite the progress they've made, their prosthetic can't heal the biological mind."

I lowered my head. "It's the best program I've found. Maybe the only one that can help Mom."

"The best program, yes, but an ineffective one at the moment. Generally speaking, I agree with one aspect of their thesis, that the physical brain is merely biological hardware running software programmed into us through nature and nurture. The PREMIND project is focused on patching the hardware so the software can run more efficiently. Seems straightforward and, for what it's worth, logical. But that's only half of the equation. They're attempting to resolve a nonlinear problem by linear means."

I scrunched a brow at him. "I don't understand."

"Brain prosthetics hold limited promise in the near term, but there's another way that bypasses the very need for them altogether."

"What way?"

"By hacking the brain just like you would any other computer. Hacking it and modifying the operating system itself in a way that changes the hardware. They won't figure that out, though, until they're willing to take bigger risks, and I don't see that happening any time soon."

"Wait . . . what? Hack your brain? Like retraining it, the way they do with stroke victims?"

"No." A smile bent his lips. "Not retraining, *rewiring*."

"The brain? Physically? That's . . . not possible."

He reached up and peeled back the knit cap from his head. Underneath, his scalp was a dome of shiny hairlessness. He looked like a chemotherapy patient or a crash-test dummy.

"Actually, I know it's possible because I've done it."

1.8

"AUSTIN, WHAT have you done?" I raised my hand to touch his scalp, but he leaned away. It was then that I noticed the small, gleaming steel studs. They looked like tiny thumbtacks that had been pushed into his skull. "Did you drill *holes* in your head?"

"I had help, of course." He said it matter-of-factly. "It's amazing what surgical technicians will do for an extra five grand in cash."

"Why would you . . ." I stared at the studs on his scalp and covered my mouth. "Why would you *do* that?"

"It was the best way to insert fiber optics through my skull."

I leaned closer to examine the shining dots. There were four: each one was embedded almost flush with his skin and had a pinhole, nearly imperceptible, in the center. If the top of his head were a clock, they would've been at two, four, eight, and ten o'clock.

My mind was reeling. He really had gone over the edge. I watched his eyes jitter about, his gaze catching me, then flittering away.

"This is crazy," I said.

"Neurosurgeons have been using this technology for decades. I've simply modified it for my purposes," he said.

"What purpose would that be? "

"Hacking." A faint smile crossed his face.

"That's what you call it? Is that what all of this is?" I waved my hand toward the lab equipment. "You're trying to hack your own brain? That's why you stopped going to Dr. Benton?"

"I stopped going because there was nothing else he could do for me. He's limited to what he was taught in med school, to the same inside-the-box thinking to which ninety-nine-point-nine percent of the world ascribes. I don't."

"Meaning what? They're smart enough to not experiment on themselves, but you're not?"

"It's this," he said, pointing to his bald head. "Or death."

His words stopped my stuttering thoughts. So that was the truth. "You're dying?"

"We're all dying," he said.

"I'm serious," I said. "Are you? Dying, I mean?"

I could hear it in his voice and see it in his eyes, however faintly: fear. In the past he had been stoic to the core, nothing ever showed. But something had shifted in him since I'd last seen him.

He nodded once. "The tumor's spread. It's only a matter of time. A very short time."

It felt like my guts were cinching into a knot. It was the same feeling I had when I heard that my father and brother hadn't survived the crash and when I first saw my mom at the hospital with tubes and wires coming out of her. "And . . . what you're doing could save you?"

He shrugged. "I don't know. My condition's advanced, but maybe what I'm doing could buy more time. The alternative is to sit around and wait to die."

"How long do you have?"

"Based on my calculations, four weeks is the best-case scenario. Worst case: two weeks, maybe less. Aggressive tumors like mine are extremely unpredictable."

My jaw unhinged. I've ordered books that took longer to reach me.

"It started here," he said, touching a finger to the left side of his head. "And spread." He drew his finger over his brow and stopped at the center of his forehead. "It's in my frontal lobe now, my prefrontal cortex to be exact. Soon, it will destroy the part of my brain responsible for complex cognitive behavior and emotive expression. Austin Hartt, the unique personality that I know as 'me' will cease to be, and everything that makes me who I am will be gone. Eventually my autonomic system will collapse and my vital organs will shut down one at a time. My brain will forget how to keep my body alive."

"Austin . . . I'm sorry." I wanted to say more, but words seemed hollow and useless. What can you say to someone who's watching Death reach out to him? "What about surgery?"

"The tumor's like a weed with roots that have worked their way deep into my brain tissue. It's inoperable."

"Chemo?"

"Would buy me maybe an extra week, two at the most."

"But it's something. It would be worth it, right?"

"Hardly. Would you want to spend your final days pumping chemicals through your veins for hours on end, hoping to eke out one more day of sitting in a hospital room pumping chemicals through your veins?"

I said nothing, but my silence spoke for me.

"Doctors are highly risk averse," he continued. "They play it safe, recycling the same old ideas, which leads to the same old results. It's the outliers who push innovation, the people on the fringe who have nothing left to lose. Nothing important ever happened without someone becoming desperate. Right now, that someone just happens to be me."

There was urgency in his words that I'd never heard before. The stoic intellectual I'd known as Austin Hartt was peeling away. In his place was someone obviously on the brink of losing everything.

He was brilliant, yes, but his genius was now laced with madness—not that I blamed him for it; the man was halfway in the ground. I could see the threads of insanity in his nervous, constant motions, the way he shifted his weight from foot to foot, the way his eyes darted around, never stopping on anything for more than a few seconds. His was a mind constantly churning, caged inside a dying body, desperate to survive.

"My research has opened up completely new ways of thinking," he said, "ways that I'd never considered before. I don't understand everything I'm discovering and experiencing, but I do know that I'm standing on the brink of a major breakthrough that could revolutionize our understanding of the human mind. It's because of my research and self-experimentation that I'm not already dead."

"How do you know that?"

"My data confirms it." He began pacing, running his hand along his scalp as he moved. "I've compiled meticulous daily analytics since the day of my diagnosis—electroencephalograms, blood chemistry panels, psychological analyses, genetic mapping, stochastic models that render probabilities of various treatment outcomes. I've measured the tumor's plodding, predictable progress, watching it like a distant train coming toward me. I've affected the rate of biological deterioration by fifty-three percent. I'm still not entirely sure how, but I have some working hypotheses. All I need to do is crack the code before the clock runs out."

"How does it work? What are you doing to yourself? Some kind of chemotherapy? Radiation? Is that why your hair's fallen out?"

"Not fallen out. I shaved it so it's easier to hard wire."

"Hard wire," I said.

"Into my brain, of course."

"Obviously."

"If I'm going to beat this, the pathway is here," he said and tapped the side of his head. He was quiet for a moment. "Remember I told you about a delusional episode I experienced in Boston?"

I nodded. "It's what made you seek out Dr. Benton, but that's all you ever said about it."

"Because I never accepted that it really happened."

"Of course not. It was a delusion. That's what you told me."

He shook his head. "What if it was something more? During my episode, there was a girl—Christy—and she experienced some of the same things I did. We were friends back in Boston and I've tried tracking her down, but she's nowhere to be found."

"If it was just a delusion maybe she's not even real."

"She is. I know that as a fact. But the experience I had . . . I don't think it was *just* a delusion. There's another possibility, one that I hadn't considered before. Maybe what happened to me in Boston was an epiphany that my conscious mind couldn't process at the time. The human mind works in ways science doesn't fully understand, especially when it comes to things like dreaming, intuition, and subconscious learning. During my episode I met a man named Outlaw. So did Christy. That's why I wanted to talk to her, to learn more about her experience."

"Outlaw. Who was he?"

"I don't know, really." Austin looked past me, as if searching for words in the air. "The best I can figure, he was a projection of my subconscious, which was drawing me into a new way of thinking that I could never quite grasp."

"But if it was a projection of your subconscious, how could Christy experience it too?"

"That, I don't know."

He was flat-out scaring me. Hiding out in his apartment, drilling holes in his head, self-experimenting like some kind of mad scientist, talking about a figment of his imagination as if it were real—it was all too much.

There was wildness in his eyes, a desperate obsession that was driving him to the knife's edge. I had an image of him in a straitjacket, laughing maniacally, getting dragged down a tiled hall by orderlies.

He raised his hand. "I know how it sounds, but hear me out. A few months after I moved here, my headaches worsened. None of my meds could take the edge off anymore. Then one night, while I was standing in front of the mirror, I had this pain. Everything stopped. I'd never known agony like that before, like having a red-hot spike driven through my head while a vice crushed my skull at the same time. I grabbed the countertop and had the sensation that I was untethered from my body."

He shook his hand at his head. "I can't explain it. It was as though my body was a vehicle and I was in it, looking out. I remember thinking how mechanical and cumbersome the body was. Not 'my' body, but 'the' body. Like . . . like . . . it was a spacesuit that I was merely borrowing. The whole time I could hear my brain *chatter*."

His hands became puppets yapping at one another. "I now know it was the left hemispheric function of my mind, coordinating my body, telling it to move and do things that normally occur subconsciously. *Left hand, reach forward. Right hand, reach forward. Right leg, come forward. Plant foot. Stomach muscles contract.*

"That's when things got . . . weird."

"That wasn't weird enough?" I asked.

"No. I looked down and realized that I could no longer define the shape of my body. The entire room, in fact, had dissolved around me. That's the only way I can describe it—it dissolved and nothing was material anymore. The world was a vast field of shimmering pixels, just raw visible data. Most of it streaked past in blurs of light—I knew instantly that I was *seeing* energy traveling through the air—but some of it was organized in a way that I could recognize as my bathroom, my apartment, my neighborhood. I knew that I was organizing it that way with my mind, but really it *was* just energy."

He was so excited, telling me this, that he rose up on his toes, dropped down again, rose up, bouncing like that, up and down.

"Then my . . . *consciousness*, I guess, turned inward and I saw myself. That's when I saw the energy signature of my tumor's physical matter. I was looking right at it. That's when I heard Outlaw's voice. It was unmistakable, but I couldn't tell what he was saying because it sounded like the world was underwater.

"I was in that state for maybe seconds of clock time, but it seemed outside of time entirely. Then, as quickly as it began, it ended." He clapped his hands together once. "Like a computer rebooting, my mind came online and, instantly, the world snapped back into the way I'd always seen it."

I looked into his eyes—stopping on me, moving on—but there was no hint that he was telling me anything other than the truth. The truth as he believed it.

"What do you think happened?" I asked. "Was it a hallucination?"

His head shook vigorously. "No, no. Far from it."

"A spiritual experience of some kind?"

"There's something else at play here. Something we don't have the science to explain yet." He held up an index finger. "*Yet.* I started researching case studies and found that my experience isn't isolated. There are hundreds of documented experiences similar to mine. For example, a Harvard-trained neurologist contracted a rare form of bacterial meningitis that rendered him brain-dead, beyond any hope of treatment. He was *dead,* but then he woke up and his brain had healed spontaneously. Complete recovery."

"How?"

"No one knows, but he referenced the same energy field I saw. Another case: an Indian woman diagnosed with cancer in 2002 arrived at a hospital in 2006. The cancer had spread to every part of her body to the point where she couldn't stand, move, or even breathe on her own. Doctors gave her hours to live. She too had some form of experience that transcended her body and mind."

"She saw the same things you did?" I said.

"Yes, and when she came out of her coma she told the doctors she was healed. They didn't believe her, of course, but within days she walked out of the hospital. No cancer. There are hundreds of cases like that, some more bizarre than others, but they all point to the idea that there's a layer of reality that we could tap into if we only knew how. There are even cases of people born blind who, after having an experience like mine, described things they've never seen physically."

"What?"

"I used to believe that the things I've seen, both in Boston and during my stroke, were delusions. Now I don't think so."

"How do you explain it then?"

He nodded. "It's simple. I saw the data that's just beyond our physical sight, the building blocks for the temporal world."

"Data?"

"Energy . . . data . . . I don't know what to call it. I'm sure there's a scientific explanation for everything I experienced, even if none of it fits the existing models. Neither did quantum mechanics until a few decades ago."

"So what are you trying to do, build a new model?" I asked.

"No, I'm trying to find Outlaw again. He, whatever he represents, is the key to understanding all of this. I'm convinced of that. Both times I encountered him were in that altered state, and both times my mental experiences had physical ramifications. Don't you see? What happens in that substrate of reality directly affects everything else, including the physical realm that seems bound by Newtonian laws. What if we can get outside of the natural laws that we think constrain us?"

I crossed my arms over my chest. "Austin, it sounds—"

"Crazy, right? But think of it this way: what if the brain is nothing more than a biological computer, the physical tissue inside your skull, along with the hundred billion neurons and hundred trillion synapses that connect them—it's all hardware. Without data inputs, the hardware has nothing to process so it doesn't generate any output. For us, data is received through various phenomena: sight, smell, sound, touch, and taste. Without an operating system to translate the data and make sense of it, there would be no output—no perception, no self-awareness, no sensation. Our *observation* of the phenomena creates it.

"It's fundamental quantum physics. Werner Heisenberg's theories in 1925 laid the groundwork for the observer principle. The universe is comprised of energy that is everywhere and nowhere at the same time, existing only as pure and infinite potential until it's observed. It's the act of observation that instantly organizes the potentiality into a specific, measurable actuality. Into matter."

"Mind over matter?"

"Not mind *over* matter, mind *as* matter. Science has proven that matter is nothing more than organized energy. The solidity of matter is an illusion, a universal sleight of hand. The universe is mostly empty space and dark matter. We simply perceive it a certain way. And, if we know how, we can go beyond the firewall that nature gave us. What if you could strip reality down to its source code?"

"That's ridiculous."

"People used to say the same about Einstein's ideas and Galileo's and Friedrich Miescher's—the scientist who paved the way toward figuring out DNA. We don't know why the universe works in unsuspected ways, but it does, all the way down to the quantum level, to the level of thought and observation. All I'm doing is hacking the software that keeps me from seeing it. And it's working."

I stood silent.

"I'm just scratching the surface," he said. "I'm convinced my theory explains the case studies I've read. The neurologist, the Indian woman with cancer, and the others I've researched—they all accessed a layer of human consciousness that's just beyond our awareness. Likely the same one I caught a glimpse of during my stroke. That's what my subconscious was telling me."

"Outlaw."

"Yes."

I spoke slowly, trying to get a grip on this. "You're hacking into consciousness, and you think this Outlaw guy—whoever or whatever he is—is like a muse in your subconscious that can help you. And by hacking your brain, you can see past *this* reality"—I swept my hands wide, indicating everything around us—"to an underlying, more real layer of reality."

"Not just see past it, but *change* it."

"Change reality?"

"At the cellular—at the *atomic*—level. I think so, yes." He paused for a moment and I could practically hear his thoughts buzzing in his skull like a hive of bees. Then he looked at me and a smile formed.

"It's hard to swallow," I said, but he acted as if he didn't hear me.

"You should help me," he said, voicing what was obviously a new thought, a revelation. "If you saw it—"

"I'm not sure I want to."

What I didn't know is whether I believed everything, or anything, he'd told me. And if it were all just the delusional fantasy of a dying man, did I want to go into that fantasy myself? Did I want to follow him down that path of madness?

"I could use an extra hand, and you're the best programmer I know," he said. "You can start by just observing. Everything is automated with a program I developed so I could self-experiment. If you like what you see, then you can be more hands-on. You could optimize the software as I compile more data. It'll save me days, maybe weeks."

"I don't know . . ."

"Wait," he said, patting the air between us with his hand. "Before you say no, let me show you." He disappeared into another room.

"Show me what?" I stood staring at the door through which he'd disappeared. "Austin?"

After a minute, he returned, shirtless and wearing black shorts. He gestured with his head. "Follow me." He went through a large white door into what I had assumed was a sound booth.

"Uh, okay."

I followed him inside. The room was small, maybe twelve feet square, dimly lit and much warmer than the rest of the apartment. In the middle of the floor sat two white pods the size of queen beds. They looked like misshapen eggs with thick black cables snaking out of the sides. The faint odor of saltwater and incense hung on the air.

"This is where you work?" I said.

"Every day. I've conducted hundreds of hacks," he said, "all focused on replicating the experience I had during my stroke. I've worked with dozens of variables that induce altered states of consciousness. It wasn't until I began integrating specific catalysts into coordinated procedures that I began seeing results that I could replicate. Now it's a matter of optimizing the catalysts."

Austin reached down and gripped the edge of one pod. He hinged open the top portion like a clamshell, revealing water inside, illuminated by ethereal blue light.

"My first breakthrough came with this tank," he said. "Over time I discovered that transcending the mind requires three integrated elements: sensory deprivation, neural wave optimization, and a synchronicity 'kick' at the peak moment."

"What is this thing?" I asked, circling the tank.

"A sensory deprivation tank. Modified, of course. It's filled with saltwater, which has a higher density than fresh, allowing the human body to float effortlessly. I keep the water temperature at precisely ninety-three point five degrees Fahrenheit so that it's skin-receptor neutral. It substantially minimizes body awareness and sensory stimuli. It feels like floating in space, and you literally forget your body because nothing is touching it or giving you a spatial point of reference."

He walked to a nearby table. On top of it sat a dozen clear mannequin heads, each fitted with a web of white cords that were tipped with round nodes of some kind—sensors?—that attached the cord to the head.

"I prototyped this design several months ago. It's iteration twenty. I call the entire system the TAP—Theta Access Protocol."

From one of the glass heads, Austin carefully lifted the collection of cords and, one by one, with practiced ease, began attaching them to the metal ports in his skull. He adjusted the wires and opened a drawer in the table. He pulled out a pair of hearing aid type devices and put one in each ear.

"The headgear integrates multiple functions. Once I'm inside the tank and have attached a breathing tube everything runs automatically. The system first activates the sensors and fiber optic implants."

The skin on my forearms and the back of my neck tingled.

He continued: "When I've reached optimized brain-wave frequency, the system releases the 'Kick,' a vaporized neurocompound, which is delivered through the breathing mask, a simple nasal cannula. Then—"

"Wait, wait, wait," I said. "It's a drug?"

"A synthesized catalyst."

"Austin, you're not going beyond consciousness, you're getting high."

He looked at me as though I'd just insulted his mother. "These are naturally occurring compounds that are in our bodies right now. I've simply tweaked the combination. It's the Kick that initiates the metaexperience the Hack."

I nodded, but if he kept talking like this he was going to lose me.

"The system monitors the electrical activity of my brain during the first seconds and delivers laser pulses via the fiber optics to mimic my own neuron activity, thus prolonging the experience."

"How long does it last?" I asked.

"I'll show you. Once the Kick occurs, the entire experience will last fifteen seconds," he said and began climbing into the pod.

"Fifteen seconds? What could possibly happen in fifteen seconds?"

He smiled and said, "When space and time mean nothing, quite a lot. You can watch from the control panel. Just don't touch anything."

I stepped toward the door and watched as Austin climbed into the tank. He maneuvered himself into a seated position and connected the sensors on his head to a black insulated cord. He pushed a button and the lid began to lower.

I went to the control panel and focused on the array of displays above it. A green image of Austin's head filled one screen. He was adjusting the breathing tube, a cannula like the kind used to administer oxygen to hospital patients, in his nostrils. The video feed was from a night-vision camera mounted inside the pod. Altogether, there were six cameras, four inside the tank at various angles, and two outside the tank. Austin recorded everything.

"Computer," he said and eased back until he was floating, "initiate alpha protocol."

An electronic voice responded: "Alpha protocol initiated. Recording confirmed."

"Trial 324. Mark. Subject: Austin Hartt observed by Nyah Parks. Commence Hack protocol."

"Hack protocol commenced."

With that the low droning noise I'd heard earlier started, slowly growing louder. It filtered into the room through two small speakers mounted at the corners of the control panel. This was the sound feeding into Austin's headset.

Screens on the control panel streamed his biometric data. His heart rate was already beginning to slow noticeably. A digital image of his brain from multiple angles lit up with flashes of red, orange, and yellow, indicating electrical activity as the neurons fired. Next to it, an EEG measured his brain-wave activity. At first, the monitor showed short staccato lines. Over the course of ten minutes, the waves grew longer, slowing as his mind calmed and transitioned to a different state of consciousness. Then, like an aerial view of forest fires flickering out, the flashes on the digital brain image disappeared.

I stared at the image of Austin on-screen, his lips parted slightly. His eyes were closed and he floated motionless for five more minutes.

An electronic chime, like a tiny bell, sounded and a message appeared on a screen. *Kick protocol initiated.* A timer appeared on the screen and began counting up like a stopwatch.

As soon as the first digit appeared—1—I heard Austin exhale loudly through the speakers. I leaned closer to the screen monitoring his face as his eyelids parted. He stared straight into the camera. His pupils were bottomless and consumed his irises. His breathing came in thick, deep draws, yet his heart rate and vital signs continued to slow. His eyes began to twitch rapidly left to right, faster than anyone could consciously do.

A buzzing in my pocket startled me. I jerked upright and my attention broke from Austin's stare.

I shoved my hand in my pocket and pulled out my iPhone. The screen read "Jill Corbis." For a brief moment I considered answering it, but hesitated. She'd have to wait.

Not now, Jill. Not now. I thumbed the END button, sending her to voicemail.

The stopwatch on the screen now read 15.5 seconds. On the other screen, Austin was blinking, fully awake. He exhaled loudly. The long, slow brain waves on the EEG monitor began to shorten and speed up, turning into a mountain range of brain activity.

"Jill Corbis," he said softly, looking into the camera, seemingly right at me.

A chill seized my spine. I stared at the screen in disbelief.

What did he say?

"Not now, Jill," he said. "Not now."

1.9

Day Two
12:45 PM

"HOW COULD you have known about the phone call?" I asked.

Austin watched me from where he sat on a couch, dry and dressed in fresh clothes. He showed no adverse effects from the Hack. If anything, he seemed better, more lucid and calm.

He took a long draw of water from a clear bottle then set it down. "I saw it," he said. "I heard it."

"But I saw you on the monitor. You were inside the tank."

"My body was, yes, but not my awareness, my consciousness."

It sounded like madness, but as much as I didn't want to buy into it, I couldn't think of another explanation. "What's it feel like, being outside of your body?"

He thought for a second. "Like being upgraded. Everything's sharper, clearer, as if your awareness shifts from standard to high definition."

"But you were still in the tank." I couldn't get over that fact.

"We think of our physical bodies as who we are, all we are, but that's wrong. Once the Kick hit my system, I was immediately outside of the physical constraints of my body just like I was during my stroke. I had a vantage point on everything in the apartment and witnessed your cell phone screen the same instant you did."

I replayed that moment in my mind. "You said 'Not now' when you became conscious. I never said that out loud. I only thought it. But you knew. Like a psychic."

"There's nothing supernatural about what happened here today. It's all explainable science."

"How can you say that?"

"Is it so hard to believe?"

"Uh . . . *yeah*." I didn't add "duh," but I'm sure my face expressed it.

"Think of it this way." He shifted on the couch and said, "EEGs and MRIs map brain activity because thoughts, at the base level, are nothing more than electromagnetic pulses emanating from us like radio waves. We perceive our thoughts as being trapped in our skulls, available only to us, but they aren't. They're electrical impulses, which is why we can measure them. A galaxy of thoughts and data is swirling around us right now; we simply don't pick up on them because, like a receiver tuned to the wrong frequency, we can't. It's simply a matter of being on the right frequency. But tuning in requires hacking the firewall that prevents us from doing so."

"The brain."

"Yes."

I shook my head. "It's too bizarre."

"Until you've experienced it. And it's not just thoughts. I have a theory that all data—all material—is accessible. Imagine if you could tap into the data flow that's streaming past us right now—the Internet, cell calls, everything? It's all right here, closer than the air we're breathing, including every thought anyone has ever had throughout all of history."

"Thoughts . . ." I said. The concept was powerful, overwhelming. What if he was right? If TV signals and light waves could travel light-years through space, then why couldn't the electrical impulses we know as thoughts also last forever . . . somewhere?

He picked up the water again, took a swig. When he set it down, he gave me a long, intense look. "Nyah," he said, "help me. There's no one else I trust more or believe could handle the mental pressures of this. Say you will."

"You're playing with things that should be left alone. You're . . . you're . . . drilling holes in your head so you can insert wires into your brain. That alone is . . . I don't know, *insane*."

"Not insane, bold. There's a difference. Think about it before you say no. Between us we could break new ground that no one has ever even considered. Think of all the people this could help. The world would be a different place, a *better* place. We're talking about the next step toward transcendence."

"You think this could really help other people?"

"Of course."

"People like my mom?" I said. "I mean, assuming you're right, this could *heal* her?"

His brow furrowed slightly. "With time and enough research, maybe. But I wouldn't put your mother's life at risk, at least not until I know much more. I'm still only learning to walk in darkness and, at the moment, there are simply too many unknowns. What I'm doing is very dangerous, you understand."

"But you said it yourself. This is the kind of risk that's worth taking."

"Yes, because I have nothing to lose anymore."

"Neither do I," I said. "Or Mom."

His attention drifted to the glass-topped coffee table between us. He pointed to my cell phone resting on it. The screen was glowing. A call was coming in, but I didn't hear it because I'd silenced the ringer.

I picked it up and glanced at the screen. *Jill*. It was the third call in the past five minutes. I answered.

"Where are you?" Her voice was urgent, strained.

"Out. What's wrong?"

"We found Pixel."

Relief washed through me. "Where? Is he okay?"

She was quiet for a moment.

"Jill? *Tell me.*"

"I'm so sorry, but he's dead. Local police identified his body an hour ago."

I felt ice crystals form in my blood. Panic began to gather at the edge of my mind. "Dead? How?"

The easy smile on Austin's face faded. I turned away and walked across the room.

"We're still trying to determine exactly what happened. All we know right now is that a jogger found him this morning under a bridge. It looks like he jumped. I'm so sorry."

"Suicide?" I felt shell-shocked and my legs were unsteady beneath me. "No. No, they did this to him. They killed him. I told you they—"

"There's something else. We found a significant amount of heroin in his system."

"What? Pixel wasn't on drugs. He'd never even touched a cigarette. He was as clean as anyone I'd ever met. He's *fourteen*, a good kid." The truth snapped into focus. "Don't you see what's going on? They're covering their tracks."

"I need you to listen to me. At the moment, this appears to be an accident."

"They must've forced him to take it or something," I said, grief making my voice high. "He would never kill himself."

"We found more drugs."

I stopped. "What do you mean?"

"Heroin. We searched his room this morning. There was a shoebox in his closet—it was filled with the stuff."

"They must've planted it. Can't you see that?"

"Everyone has secrets."

"No, not Pixel. I *knew* him. Bell had him killed because of what he knew."

"Right now nothing implicates Bell or BlakBox."

"It wasn't an accident," I said, as sure as I was numb.

"I don't know if that's true or not, but the circumstances are suspect," Jill said. "I'll give you that much. That has me worried. Whatever you think you stumbled onto at BlakBox may have spooked Bell. If so, assuming you're right, you may be in danger too." She breathed a few times. "Wherever you are right now I need you to stay put so I can come get you. Understand?"

"No." I wasn't about to let anyone know about Austin, not even Jill. I couldn't drag him into this. I felt trapped in a dream in which I was running from something terrible, but I wasn't getting anywhere, just running in place. "Meet me at my place."

"I would prefer to come get you."

"I'll be careful. I promise. Meet me there. I'm going there now." I pressed the END button then stood motionless for a long time, stunned.

"You okay?" Austin said.

"I have to go." I started toward the door. Everything felt surreal, as if the world were moving at half speed.

Austin stood and followed me through the loft. "You're white as a sheet. What's going on? Talk to me."

"He's dead. I just have to go." I pulled open the door and slammed it on his words: "Who's dead?" He didn't follow me. He knew me well enough not to.

On the way to my apartment, I felt anxiety tighten around me like clothes too small. My mind was numb and panic was sinking deep into me. I felt the weight of eyes on me, watching. Waiting.

They'd killed Pixel. That goon who'd interrogated me, Jon Stone. And Walter Bell, that monster. No doubt they'd do the same to me if they had the chance.

Pixel. Fresh tears coated my cheeks.

As I turned onto Del Norte Avenue, I caught a glimpse of a black SUV sliding into traffic behind me, four cars back. It had been behind me the entire time on the freeway and I'd seen it after exiting too.

Don't panic. You're just imagining things.

The entrance to my apartment complex approached, but instead of turning into it I shot past. I'd go down a few streets and turn. I had to be sure I wasn't being followed.

The SUV changed lanes, passing another car and came into view again. It was still edging closer. I looked up at the intersection ahead and the traffic light burned yellow. A long line of traffic was already slowing to a stop.

No.

Red light. I eased to a stop, glancing in my mirror, then at the narrow gap between the cars. If I had to, I could zip through it. The SUV would be too big to follow.

I had to assume that Bell's people were after me, but *why*? Why had they killed Pixel and why were they after me? Why not just let it go?

There was only one explanation that made sense. Whatever was in the files I exported to Pixel was dangerous enough to kill for. What if Pixel had ditched the information before they got to him? Not finding it, they would've silenced him, then turned their attention to me. But I'd checked the server and nothing was there. He hadn't uploaded it. Unless . . . he must've saved it somewhere else.

Hands trembling, I glanced back again. The SUV was pulling alongside me in the left lane, rolling to a stop.

I looked over, expecting to see Stone or someone who looked just like him. I gunned my engine, ready to pop the clutch and peel away, into the gap between the cars and through the red light. I looked over and relaxed. A woman sat behind the wheel, three kids yelling at each other in the back seat.

Just being paranoid.

The light changed and I turned right at the intersection, then circled back to my apartment and parked my bike in an alleyway so it was out of sight. Maybe I was being paranoid, but I had to be careful. Something was wrong, deadly wrong. And I felt like someone was watching me.

I made my way to the apartment, gripping my helmet. It wasn't a gun—I wished I had one—but it'd do some damage in a pinch. No one was in sight as I climbed the stairs to the second floor and dug a key from my pocket.

Then I reached for the door, and the knob turned easily in my hand. *Unlocked.*

My heart hammered and I froze. Was someone inside? I gripped my helmet tighter and lifted it, ready to strike. Turned the knob all the way and stopped. What was I doing? I had no idea how many people where in there, how big they were, or how well armed. I had to get away. Fast.

Easing the door handle back into position, I backed away from the door, spun around and took a fast step—right into a thick man who had come up behind me. He wore a black suit like Jon Stone's. Without a word, he reached for me.

My palms pressed into his chest. I shoved and spun away, but a second man appeared from my apartment and lunged toward me.

I swung my helmet as they converged on me. It glanced off the second man's arm with no discernable reaction from him.

"We have her," one of the men said into a walkie-talkie.

I reeled my helmet back to take another swipe, and the first man grabbed my wrist and twisted. I yelped and the helmet clattered across the floor. In one smooth motion, the man wrenched my arm behind me and pushed me toward my apartment door.

"Get her inside," the other man said, stepping out of the way.

I went in, certain they would shove me to my knees and put a bullet in my head or inject me with an overdose of heroin, as they had done to poor Pixel. Forced from behind, I stumbled into the small entryway and saw Jill standing in my living room. The man released his grip.

"Thank God," Jill said.

"What's going on?" I asked. More men were moving through my apartment, their arms full of computer equipment and boxes. "You called me from here, didn't you?"

"We're collecting your computers for analysis. I've been cleared to conduct a full field investigation on Bell. Things just aren't adding up, and I'm going to find out why."

"You can't take my stuff," I said.

"I can." She held up a stapled sheaf of papers. "I've got a court order. It's for your own good."

One of the agents approached, holding something in his hand. Whatever it was, it was meant for me.

"Is it ready?" Jill asked the man.

"Yes, ma'am."

"What's that?" I asked.

"Electronic ankle monitor."

I spun toward her. "What? You're putting me under house arrest?"

"I'm sorry we have to do it this way, but you're our best chance to crack this case," she said. "Besides, I care about you. If you're in danger, the best place for you is right here. At least until we figure this out. From this moment on, you're under round-the-clock protection. So is your family, your mom and Lettie."

"Mom? Why?"

"Just as a precaution," she said. "It's just a gut feeling right now, but I think you might be right about Bell."

"You putting ankle monitors on my family too?"

She gave me a look. "I've posted a surveillance unit at Cedar Ridge. I think that'll be enough."

"But—" I said, eyeing the ankle bracelet, which might as well have been a dog collar on a chain. "You're making me a prisoner in my own home."

"I'm making you *safe*. Considering what happened to your friend, I want to know where you are at every moment. At least until we figure this out." She leaned closer. "You need to stay put."

"Like a fish in a barrel," I said under my breath. Then an idea struck me: "Let me help with your investigation!"

Jill threw back a look that said I was talking nonsense.

"I hacked Bell's company before," I said. "I can do it again. I'll get the information you need." I stared into her eyes. "We *need* to nail this guy. Leave my gear here. I can do it."

"Not this time." She gave the agent a nod. "Go ahead."

The man cinched the monitor around my ankle and told me how it worked: wandering twenty yards from the apartment building—giving me enough leash to take out the trash and go to the laundry room—or tampering with it would send an alarm to the monitoring company. An agent would be banging on my door faster than I could spit.

A few minutes later, Jill's team had packed everything up and left, leaving behind two men in a car out front to make sure I stayed inside.

I sat in silence for hours, until the sun dipped low in the sky and sent long shadows creeping through the streets like restless spirits. It had all happened so fast. My life was unraveling before it'd even gotten started.

Lettie always said it and she was right: a person reaps what she sows. And, at that moment, I despised what I'd shoved into the cracked mud of my life. Loneliness fell over me like a blanket as I sat on the living room floor surrounded by gathering shadows. Night hadn't yet fully fallen, but the room was grey and dark. Like my soul.

My family had been all but wiped out—half of us in the ground, another heading there quickly; and now Pixel was dead. I wanted nothing more than to make it right; I *had* to make it right. But how could I do anything from here?

The agents had turned my apartment upside down, taking everything. A few random cords were all that remained of my computer workstation. Everything else had been stripped bare. They'd even confiscated my cell phone.

My mind began to churn. I'd make my own opportunities. Most people will do anything if they're pushed hard enough, long enough. It's all a matter of how deep your desperation runs, and mine ran to the bone.

I couldn't get the conversation with Austin out of my mind. Whatever he was doing, however crazy it seemed, it was my only hope. Mom's, too.

If he could go under, if he could hack his brain, then so could I. I had to. I couldn't simply sit here with my finger up my nose. Pixel was dead, I had no chance of getting the money Mom needed, and time was running out.

Austin's research was now the only option—to fix this mess, to have a life again, to give Mom a chance. Nothing else mattered. The best I could do for Jill was stay out of sight while she investigated BlakBox, and the best thing I could do for Mom was learn to hack like Austin.

I had to try.

An agent checked on me just after midnight. I waited another thirty minutes before making my move. I knew exactly what I had to do, but I had to move fast.

I went to my hall closet and took a pair of heavy-duty shears from the toolbox, then went to my bedroom window. My apartment was on the backside of the building, away from the street where the agents were. I opened the window onto a fire escape, went down the stairs, cringing at every squeak and rattle they made, and dropped to the alleyway below. I landed in a crouch and waited. No footsteps running toward me. No one yelled for me to "Halt!"

Shears in hand and staying near the building, I made my way to where I'd parked my bike, hoping Jill hadn't taken it. It came into view and my tension eased—a little.

Kneeling, I worked one of the shear's blades into the gap between my skin and the monitor. The band itself was rubber with a circuit running through it. It would be fairly easy to cut, but when I did, it would trigger the alarm.

One deep breath and I cinched down on the handles. The blade sliced through, cutting the circuit with a distinct *snap*. I stripped it off and tossed it away with the shears.

Without so much as a glance back, I climbed on my bike, started it, and tore off down the street.

There was no turning back now.

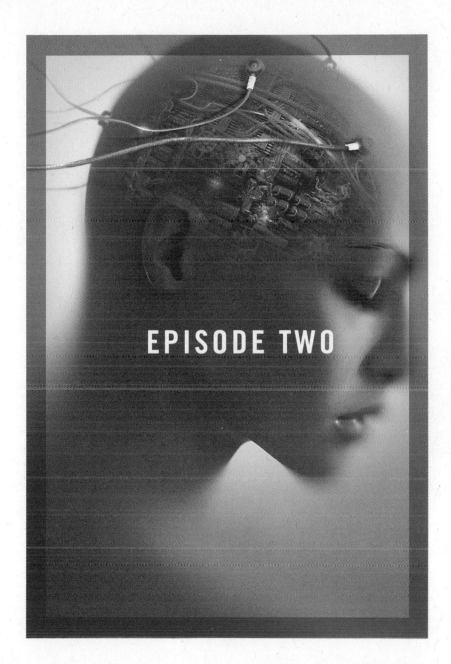

EPISODE TWO

2.1

Day Three
1:11 AM

"WHAT ARE you doing here?" Austin stood in his apartment doorway. He looked exhausted, but to me he'd never looked so wonderful. After escaping from my FBI-imposed prison, he was the best sight in the world.

I wrapped my arms around him and held tight.

"Hey . . . what's going on?" He held me at arm's length and looked me in the eyes. "You okay?"

"No," I said.

He led me inside and closed the door.

Removing the ankle monitor and fleeing from my apartment now felt like a terrible mistake. Surely the FBI was scouring the city for me, but I was certain no one had followed me. And without my cell signal to track me, I was a ghost.

"It'll be all right," he said. "Tell me what's going on."

We sat on his couch, and I told him everything: my experiences with and suspicions about BlakBox—the files I'd discovered and exported, the way they'd interrogated me, that they'd killed Pixel—Jill's investigation, my house arrest, which Jill had claimed was "for my own protection."

He listened quietly, then settled back into the couch to think for a while. Finally, he said, "Are you sure you weren't followed here?"

"I'm sure."

"Where'd you park?"

"In the abandoned warehouse on the corner, where you keep your Jeep. I took the alleyway and came in the back just like old times. No one knows I'm here, and no one saw me."

He let out a quiet sigh. "So what are you going to do?"

"The only thing I can do. Help my mom."

"By doing what? There's no way the Feds are going to let you get back to work."

"I'm not going back to work." I paused. "Teach me to hack."

"What? Your brain?"

"Yeah, the way you do it."

"I don't know." He shook his head. "I told you before, it's too dangerous. Helping me with the programming is one thing, but it's another to put you in the tank."

"You said your goal is to change reality. I want to change my Mom's reality. I want her to live, to have her old life back. And you can use my help, you said so."

"I do, but I also don't want you to get hurt."

"How will I get hurt? You seem fine and that's after, what, three hundred hacks?"

He stared at me, nothing to say.

"Saving lives. That's worth whatever risks we need to take, right? I'm not taking no for an answer. This is the right thing to do. You know it is. It's what we need to do to save you and my mom." I took his hand. "Neither of us has anything to lose."

He stood, breaking my grip, and started pacing. "I don't know." He chewed his bottom lip. I could nearly hear the cogs grating in his mind.

"This is an opportunity for both of us," I said. "We each get something out of it. You get a research partner and a chance to live, I get to help Mom."

"Maybe."

"I know we can do it. Look how far you've gotten on your own."

He ran his hands over his bald, studded head and continued pacing.

"Please," I said. "Don't make me beg."

"If we do this," he said, "we do it my way. My rules."

"Of course."

"How can we pull this off when you're not supposed to even be here? The FBI—"

"Doesn't know where I am. No one does, I promise. We'll work round the clock. I'll sleep on the floor. You have two tanks, right? We'll double down. I can be your control subject."

He stopped pacing and looked at me, wide-eyed. The idea was taking root in him.

"There's no better option," I said. "Time is ticking for both of us."

"Okay," he finally said. "Okay, you can help, but you have to do *exactly* as I say."

"Got it." My grin radiated at him.

"I hope I'm not making a mistake," he said.

I realized that I felt better than I had in a long time. Even before everything had hit the fan at BlakBox, Mom's deteriorating condition had weighed heavily on me. And money alone was no guarantee of finding a cure. Austin's dream of manipulating reality was a long shot, but at least it was something, at least I was *doing* something. I had momentum and that felt good, exhilarating.

"We're burning time," I said. "Let's get started."

"It'll take a while to bring you up to speed on how everything works."

I looked around. "Where do we start?"

"We need to prep you for a TAP, the neural interface array you'll use to connect your mind with the system. I'll have to take some measurements and fit you with sensors. That'll take a few hours."

"Let's do it." I sprang up off the couch.

After a moment of staring at me, he walked away, saying, "Follow me."

He led me across the far side of the loft into the kitchen, a large modern space that opened to a dining area overlooking the Bay through floor-to-ceiling windows. A single chair sat where a dining table might go, facing the window.

"We have to shave your head," he said. "There are some scissors on the countertop. Cut your hair as short as you can. I'll use clippers and a razor for the rest. Sit over there," he said, pointing to the chair. "Be right back."

I shrugged out of my jacket and draped it on the counter. I picked up the scissors and walked to the chair. My image reflected back at me from the window. Through it, the distant lights of the Bay Bridge sparkled like stars strung together over the water. It seemed so far away and detached from my life, like a still picture from a movie. Everything felt like that now.

You sure about this, Nyah?

In answer, I reached behind me, grabbed a handful of hair, and scissored it off my head. The hair hung limp in my hand, black with a thick streak of fading purple running through the middle of it. I turned my hand over and watched it fall to the floor.

Snip. Another clump fell away.

Then another and another . . . until my hair covered the floor around my feet like dark straw. Austin returned with electric clippers, a can of shaving cream, a hand towel and a razor. He tapped the seat back with the clippers. "Ready?"

I nodded. "Chop, chop. Let's do this."

He placed one hand on my head to steady it and turned on the clippers.

"Wait," I said. "I have a scar. From the accident. Don't freak out, all right?"

He paused. "I won't."

Drawing a deep breath, I watched our reflections in the window as he pressed the clippers to the base of my skull and slowly mowed a path to the top of my head then along my scalp. The vibration buzzed against the bone, and the remainder of my hair cascaded to the floor, leaving exposed skin that felt cold.

He worked quickly, adjusting the clippers closer to my skin with each pass before finally slathering my scalp with shaving cream and running a razor over it in long streaks—periodically wiping the blade on the towel—until my head was as bald as his.

Austin rubbed my head with the towel, like polishing a bowling ball, and stepped back. He said, "Welcome to the Bald and Beautiful Club."

I lifted my hand and ran my palm over my scalp, wincing when it reached the ragged scar. My head reminded me of my dad's freshly shaven face.

"There's a bathroom down the hall, on the left," he said. "Go rinse your head before we mark the locations for the TAP. When you're done, meet me over there." He pointed to a nearby contraption that resembled a dental chair.

I stood and brushed hair off my shirt and pants.

"Take as much time as you need," he said. "I'll get everything ready."

I walked down the hall, rubbing my scalp. It felt as though a portion of myself had been cut away, and I would never get it back. My hair had been a part of my identity: Nyah, the girl with the nose ring and funky hair. It had also covered the memento of the most horrible thing that'd ever happened to me. It was a part of my mask, I guess. Now it was gone, years of growth and care sliced away in less time than it took to brush it in the morning.

Emotion had churned inside me while Austin was shaving my head, but it didn't turn into a tsunami until I saw myself up close in the bathroom mirror. I didn't want to cry, but the tears came anyway, so I let them. They slipped down my cheeks while my fingertips drifted along the newly sensitive skin. My hair would grow back, but Nyah Parks as I knew her—as Mom and Dad and Tommy had known her—had departed and someone new was looking back at me.

But maybe, I thought, she *wasn't* a stranger, after all. Maybe she was a truer picture of the desperation I felt in the deepest part of me—exposed, no longer able to hide the scars and imperfections, now dragged into the light for all to see.

My fingertips lingered along the eight-inch scar that ran along the right side of my skull, front to back. Besides a broken arm, the deep gouge was the only injury I'd suffered in the accident that had claimed the rest of my family, the result of my head shattering one of the back windows. It'd taken forty-eight stitches, eighteen staples, and skin from my thigh to patch up my scalp. Nothing compared to what my family had sacrificed.

I stood tall and smeared the tears from my cheeks, pushing every thought but one from my mind. The reason I was there: Mom's life.

I splashed cold water over my face and head and dried them with a washcloth. By the time I'd finished, Austin was done adjusting a large wire frame on an articulating arm above the medical chair I'd seen earlier. It looked like the steel braces used to hold broken necks in place, the kind that attached to the skull with screws.

He looked up and smiled. "Sit down here," he said and patted the chair. He was wearing latex gloves and a clear face shield covered his face.

"What's that for?" I asked and flicked the bottom edge of the facemask with my finger.

"To protect my eyes. The drill bit creates a minute amount of bone dust. Nothing to worry about."

"Uh, okay," I said. I slid into the seat and found myself nearly lying down. The vinyl upholstery was cold and an examination light glared overhead. Austin pumped a foot pedal and the chair bent into a more upright position.

"Try to relax," he said, swabbing a cold cotton cloth over my head. The harsh smell of rubbing alcohol burned my nose. My raw scalp tingled.

He eased the wire frame over my head and carefully rotated several knobs until the device was cinched tight against my skull.

"What is this thing?" I asked.

"A calibration guide I'll use to place the four cranial access points. It's like a precision stencil to ensure an accurate borehole position. After it's in place I'll take a few preliminary measurements, then we'll evacuate the bone."

"Evacuate? You mean drill holes in my head."

"Evacuate sounds better."

"Not to me." I shifted nervously in the chair. "Is it a power drill, like a Black & Decker?"

"It's a surgical drill, very precise and very expensive. I modified the entire system with software I developed to guide the cranial vault incision and the skull boring process. Someone still has to initiate the process—it's not like you can drill into your own head, after all—but everything is calibrated; the computer guides the whole procedure."

"Will it hurt?"

"A little," he said. "I'll numb the region with Xylocaine, a local anesthetic. You'll just feel a pinch from the needle, like a bee sting."

"It's not the needle that worries me. It's the drilling holes in my head that makes me nervous."

"It's accurate to within micrometers. Trust me." He lifted a syringe from a metal tray and raised it over my head, out of sight. The needle pricked my scalp and I flinched. He injected me three more times then started adjusting something. "The sound is worse than the pain," he said. "You'll mostly just feel pressure. If you want, I can put you under."

"I'll be fine."

"You sure?"

"No." I glanced at him nervously. "You said you've done this before?"

"Yeah, with help. It's not that hard and the computer handles the actual drilling depth. Don't worry, you're safe. I promise."

I winced and gripped the chair arms as a low humming began to build above me. A tingling warmth crept across my scalp and down into my forehead as the Xylocaine spread from the injection points.

Austin worked slowly, methodically attaching instruments to the headgear, but because my neck was fixed in place and my gaze locked on a bookcase across the room, I could only feel it, not see it.

"I'm ready," he said. "Are you?"

"Will you stop asking, already?" I closed my eyes. "Just do it."

The drill's whirr grew louder in my ears and my pulse quickened.

"You'll feel some pressure as the bit penetrates the bone," Austin said. "Tell me if it's too much."

"Stop talking," I said.

I clenched my jaw and drew staccato breaths as a grinding sound reverberated through my head, growing louder by the second. Pressure bore down on my skull. The sensation was like having a screwdriver burrow slowly into the top of my head. The entire top portion of my skull felt like it was compressing into my brain.

The world swayed. I blinked and tried to focus on the bookshelf, but smudges of darkness and stars played at the edge of my vision.

Is this normal? I tried to speak, but nothing came out. Something was wrong.

"Relax," Austin said. His voice sounded distant and muffled as if he were speaking underwater. ". . . important . . . relax . . ."

I gripped the chair arms tighter. The pressure in my head came and lifted repeatedly, each new time intensifying until barbs of pain raked down my spine, branching out to grip my entire body.

I tried to open my mouth, to tell Austin that something was wrong, but the words wouldn't form. My jaw tightened and I tried to lift my hand. It felt heavy and not at all like a part of my body.

I couldn't move. Worse, I couldn't breathe.

I can't catch my breath. The words were clear and loud in my head.

"Nyah?" Austin's voice came again, this time unusually slow and deep like a movie running in slow motion.

Can't breathe . . .

The dark smudges gathered and grew until they covered the world around me. Numbness poured over my head like warm water and I thought, *Blood! My head has split wide open!* The sensation spilled down my entire body. My eyes fluttered.

Austin?

Austin's voice drifted into my head, but his garbled words came in fragments.

I tried to push the darkness away, tried to force my eyes to stay open, but I couldn't. I felt the weight of my body sink deeper into the chair. My torso and limbs shook, my skin trembling, my bones rattling.

My eyes squeezed closed, my teeth ground together. The world surrendered to utter blackness and somewhere far away I heard a scream.

2.2

Day Three
7:15 AM

SHE WASN'T dead. *One good thing, anyway,* Austin thought, but he wasn't so sure about any of this.

He leaned over Nyah as she lay unconscious on the chair and, with an antiseptic wipe, carefully cleaned the access points he'd drilled into her skull. Each of the precisely placed channels was rimmed with a thin titanium ring that could be capped when not in use—a design upgrade he'd developed after reading an Italian neurologist's research paper on postoperative sterility practices.

Tapping the brain was minimally invasive, yet there was always a risk of introducing bacteria to the meninges, the brain's protective outer membranes. The caps were safeguards against that.

He pulled off the surgical gloves then sank into the chair beside Nyah and rubbed the back of his neck. A dull throb worked through him and his eyes felt like they'd been packed with sand and glass.

When had he slept last? Two days ago? Three?

It was all a blur, a timeless cycle of research, self-experimentation and post-clinical analysis. Every trial led to more recalibration, more self-experimentation.

Rinse and repeat had become his mantra.

Experiment, analyze, recalibrate.

Rinse and repeat.

Collect data points, mine the data, extrapolate conclusions, and postulate the next move.

Rinse and repeat.

His dogged tenacity was finally beginning to pay dividends. Each new foray brought new insights into the inner workings of the human mind, *his mind.* But there was no end to it. Like a mythic Hydra, every question he answered led to two more. But, he assured himself, today marked the beginning of new opportunities.

Having Nyah's help would certainly speed the process. Maybe she could get above the trees and see the forest where he could not, find the path through it. Sometimes it was simply a matter of looking at a problem with fresh eyes.

He reached over and adjusted the oxygen monitor clipped to her left index finger. He glanced at the red numbers on the LED display. Her levels were good. Heart rate was stable, and her breathing came in steady draws now, not the near hyperventilation she'd experienced earlier. Except for her mild panic episode, the procedure had gone exceptionally well and required only two hours.

Still, as excited as he was to have Nyah as a research partner, the possibility of harming her twisted his stomach into a thick knot. He'd known what to do, true, but something could've gone wrong. Still could. They were just beginning and this was uncharted territory, the ragged edge of the map.

On top of all his medical concerns, there was the question of Bell and the FBI. Even she couldn't know if or how that would play out. Regardless, her world would never be the same. If he could spare her any more pain, emotional or physical, he would.

Nyah stirred and groaned.

Austin leaned forward and pulled up the thin fleece blanket he'd laid across her earlier. The room was cold and gooseflesh covered her arms.

It was possible—no, *probable*—that all of this was a terrible idea. It was one thing to experiment on himself; it was another altogether to include her, even if she *had* insisted. Nyah never took no for an answer, and he hoped that it wouldn't come back to bite both of them.

She was unlike anyone he'd ever known. Most people were two-dimensional, at best, living like automatons. They'd drone through life in a daze, always looking around, but never actually seeing anything or engaging in life's bigger questions. They didn't even realize there *were* bigger questions to ask. Most humans were simply content with existing and entertaining themselves with diversions until they died—fooled into thinking they were really alive when all along they had only bought into clever marketing. Mindlessly following everyone else.

Not Nyah. She saw the world for what it was, and she was determined to cut her own path through it. There was a quiet intensity to her that he'd noticed long before they spoke that first time in Dr. Benton's waiting room. It was impossible not to notice her; she'd turned heads every week and she hadn't even realized it, thinking she was the only one doing the observing. She always sat in the far corner of the room, studying everyone else. She always played it calm and cool, her eyes flicking around the room, reading everyone like a book. Austin hadn't thought of her as particularly beautiful, yet he was irresistibly drawn to her.

Now, he brushed a finger gently across her brow. *So different from everyone else.* And that's why he could never get her out of his mind. Turning her away and not contacting her for so long had been one of the hardest things he'd ever done.

Nyah's eyes snapped opened, startling Austin.

She blinked rapidly and looked around, struggling to get her bearings. Her face was pale with deep circles under her eyes. She returned her attention to Austin. "What . . . what . . . ?" she said.

"Welcome back," he said, clenching her hand. "How're you feeling?"

It took her a full thirty seconds to answer. "Terrible," she finally said. She pinched the bridge of her nose and closed her eyes. "Is my head supposed to feel like this?"

"Like a truck ran over it? That's normal for the first couple of hours." He held a penlight in front of her face. "Look straight ahead."

She winced as he flicked the light from side to side, checking her pupil response.

"What happened?" she said. "Everything went black. I thought I was—"

"Passing out?"

"Dying," she said.

He pocketed the light, then unclipped the oximeter from her finger and set it aside. "You panicked when I started the second hole. You were thrashing around so much I had to sedate you."

She thought about that for a few beats. "How'd it go?"

"Well, you didn't die."

She frowned. "I'm serious."

"There were no problems. You're ready to go."

"Is it . . ." She tentatively reached a hand toward the top of her head. "Can I touch it?"

"You can't hurt them," he said.

Nyah brought both hands to her scalp and hesitantly grazed her fingertips over her skull as if it were made of crackled glass on the verge of shattering. At first her eyes were wide, but she quickly became more comfortable with the feel of the implants under her fingers.

"You get used to them after a while," he said. "The hardest part is not having hair. It gets chilly." He handed her a red knit beanie. "You'll need this."

"I have holes in my head." She said it more to herself than to Austin after taking the cap from him.

"Four of them."

A wry smile formed on her face and she met his eyes. "Cool." She planted both hands on the chair and swung her legs over the edge.

"Whoa, you might want to take it slow." Austin helped her to unsteady feet. "You've been under awhile."

She gripped his arm and looked around the room. "I'm good. What time is it?"

"Almost seven-thirty in the morning." He watched her movements closely. She was lucid and moving surprisingly well. His recovery had taken nearly twelve hours. "You should take it easy for the next—"

"I'm fine. Really. Let's get to work. Every minute counts."

"You need rest."

"What I need is coffee and some aspirin." Her eyes went to the yellow legal pad sitting on the edge of the exam tray. "What's that?"

He shrugged. "Nothing. I'll take that . . ." He reached for it, but she got to it first.

Nyah flipped through the pad, turning page after page that had been doodled on and sketched over with a single symbol of varying sizes that repeated on no fewer than twenty pages:

"Wow," she said, studying the pages. "You drew these? You really like fancy O's."

"It's just a reminder," he said.

"Reminder? And what's this word on the top of the pages? *Deditio*?" She looked at him. "What's it mean?"

"It's Latin. It means unconditional surrender, letting go. Ever since Boston I can't get it out of my mind. I draw it all the time. I know, it's crazy."

"Not any more than the way I count things," she said. "And the symbol?"

"The man I told you about, Outlaw, wore a medallion fashioned that way."

Nyah nodded and touched her fingers to the written word. "Deditio," she said thoughtfully. "I like that." She handed him the pad.

"Deditio: letting go. Remember it in the tank. It'll serve you well." He smiled. "We should probably calibrate your sensory array and begin mapping a neural profile for the database. If you're up to it."

"Of course."

"Okay then. That'll give us a baseline to work from once we start hacking." He led her across the apartment to the control panel.

"Is that for me?" she asked, pointing to a spiderweb of cords clinging to one of the glass mannequin heads.

He lifted the set of wires and turned it in his hands. "I custom-fitted it to your TAP configuration while you were sedated. The dry fit was flawless, but we'll need to get you in the tank and do a few diagnostic runs, make sure the data feeds are optimized with the system. You know, dial you in."

"You want me in the tank?" Her eyes lit up. "Seriously?"

"If you're not feeling—"

"I'm ready to go."

"The sensory-deprivation tank is a bit overwhelming at first. We'll go as slowly as you want."

"Just try to keep up, okay?"

He smiled. "There are some shorts in the bathroom, brand new in the package. Some T-shirts, too. Go change and come back. I know it's a bit awkward, but—"

"It's fine," she said, walking away. "Like going to the beach."

"I'll prep the tank," he called after her, but she was already in the other room.

Nyah showed up five minutes later, barefoot and dressed in black shorts and a dark-blue sports bra. Standing in the doorway to the sensory-deprivation room, she looked like a chemotherapy patient dressed for an early morning jog.

"Didn't need the T-shirt," she explained. "Where do you want me?"

Austin stood at a nearby table making final adjustments to her headgear. He waved her toward him. "Over here. I have something for you."

As she approached, he handed her an analog wristwatch: a simple waterproof timepiece with an hour and minute hand and a slowly sweeping second hand.

"What's this for?" she said, turning it in her hand.

"Put it on. I've learned that time is a bit disorienting in the Hacks. Each second in the Hack feels like one minute of clock time outside of the tank. The watch will act as a mental cue, like a totem, to ground your awareness. If you find yourself losing track of how long you've been in the Hack, just look at your watch. It'll show you how much clock time has passed here in the tank."

She strapped it on and tilted her wrist toward her. "One minute in the Hack is an hour of real time here?"

"Clock time, I call it, and yes. Roughly," he said. "Assuming it works the same for you as it does me. Now let's get you plugged in."

"Hardwired, you mean," she said. "You've got to use the right terminology."

He chuckled. "Right."

"See, I pay attention."

She walked over to him and he forced himself to concentrate on the headgear. You'd never realize how curvy she was, under all the baggy clothing she usually wore.

He cleared his throat and turned toward her, then carefully lifted the bundle of sensors to her head, aligning each with the gleaming taps on her skull before snapping them into place. "Too tight?" he asked.

"Nope. Feels good."

"You're sure you're okay with this?"

"You sound like my mom," she said. "Stop asking."

He went to the tank and lifted its clamshell lid. The blue light from inside spilled into the dim room. He swept his hand toward it, bowed a little, and said, "After you."

She crossed the floor and lifted one foot over the edge into the water. Then the other foot.

"Turn around and just sit down for a few minutes," he said. "Get used to the feel of the water while I hardwire you."

"It's not warm," she said. "I thought it would be. But it's not cold either."

"It's temperature sensation neutral. Matching ambient and core body temperatures tricks your body into forgetting itself by removing sensory awareness."

Her gaze moved from one side of the pod to the other. "How's it work?"

He reached past her to six thin black cables that entered the pod through a one-inch access hole on the side. At the end of each was a threaded cylinder made of titanium. One at a time, he carefully pulled each wire closer and coupled it with the headgear.

He pointed to two of the wires. "These cables are the interface, both input and output. They output your biofeedback data to the computer for monitoring. The sensors in your headgear are highly sensitive and pick up your electromagnetic brain activity, all of it."

"What's the input?"

"These," he said, indicating the other cords. "Laser pulses delivered via the fiber optics I installed in your skull. They're targeted to specific regions of your brain so the light pulses will stimulate neural activity in loops, which the system will create from your brain-wave readings. By increasing the frequency we can prolong specific neural signatures."

"Hacking the brain." She drew a deep breath. "Right."

His attention lingered on her. "Almost ready. We'll do a simple run-through to get a reading of your baseline neural activity and responses to each stage of the experience. Everything will be an abbreviated version of a typical experiment. I'm setting it for a fifteen second Hack. Our objective here is to test your body's initial response and what phenomena, if any, you experience."

She nodded. "Got it."

"Don't be disappointed if nothing happens the first few times. It took dozens of trials and stimuli combinations before I experienced my first Hack."

She gave him a thumbs-up.

Austin connected the last of the sensors and slipped a loop of clear plastic tube over her head, resting it over her ears. He placed the two prongs of the oxygen tube into her nostrils. "During the first stages this will feed you with oxygen. Once we're ready for the Kick, the compound will come through the airflow system."

"How will I know when that happens?"

He grinned. "Trust me, you'll know." He stood upright and produced two waterproof in-ear headphones from his pocket. He handed them to her. "Put these in. Your ears will be below the water's surface. I'll talk to you through these and coach you along. There's an ambient microphone in the pod: talk and I'll hear you."

She pressed one into each ear.

"Lie back and relax. The water's extremely dense, so floating is effortless if you let go of muscle tension."

Nyah eased back, rippling the glowing water. The tank was wide enough that she would never come in contact with its sides, no matter how her arms and legs drifted. Eyes closed, she heaved a loud exhale and let her arms relax at her sides. Like a leaf on a still lake, she floated motionlessly.

"You're a natural," Austin whispered and pushed a button, shutting the tank's lid.

He left the room and secured the door behind him. He slid behind the control panel. Everything was ready. Toggling a switch, he opened the communication channel. "Can you hear me?"

"Yeah," Nyah's voice came through speakers angled toward him.

"Comfortable?" His fingers flew across the computer's keyboard and queued up the Hack protocol, which would synchronize the test sequence. Instantly, the seven flat-screen monitors that arched around the control panel came to life.

"Very relaxed. Almost feels like my body's part of the water."

"That's the idea." He watched the monitors as night-vision images of Nyah filled four of them, and biofeedback data streamed to the others. "I've got eyes on you now. Just focus on your breathing for a few minutes while I bring you online."

A flood of data streamed across the monitors—EEG readings, core and surface body temperature, breathing rate, blood oxygen level, and system diagnostics—all meticulously recorded for later analysis. If all went well, this would be the first of dozens, perhaps hundreds, of sessions.

It was real now and the air was thick with excitement for both of them. And fear too, because so much was unsure. But they were moving forward. More than that, they were sprinting ahead.

He flipped between camera angles until Nyah's face filled the screen directly in front of him. The light meter confirmed that the tank was void of all illumination. She lay in utter darkness.

"The system checks are good," he said. "Now the real fun begins. In a few seconds, I'll stop talking and you won't hear my voice until the end."

"Promise?"

"Hacking requires multiple phases. We'll start with a binaural acoustics sequence. You'll hear a deep, pulsing sound through your earpieces.

The vibration will also be released into the water via embedded speakers. The purpose of the sound is to synchronize your brain waves, transition them from the quick-moving beta-wave function to the longer, slower theta-wave state that's more conducive to enhanced cognitive states. All you need to do is relax and allow your mind to go silent. Surrender."

"Deditio, right?"

"That's right. Surrender. Let go. In order for the Kick to activate, your brain waves need to come down to an optimal level. That's when the real party begins. So relax, focus on the darkness in front of you, the patterns on the backs of your eyelids. Be mindful of your breathing. When a thought comes in, let it pass by without holding onto it. Imagine yourself as a leaf floating on a stream. Hacking is all about surrender, letting go of the sensory input that locks us in time-space."

"Surrender," she whispered. "Deditio."

"Just relax."

"I would if you'd stop talking," she said.

"Sorry."

Austin fed the sound loop into her earpieces, then opened the in-tank sound channel. He leaned closer to the monitor displaying her brain-wave activity. As expected, the digital readout drew a virtual mountain range of short, saw-toothed peaks, indicating the significant neural activity of a frantic mind. It was no surprise, judging by her spike in breathing and heart rate, which was pegged at ninety-three.

Apart from introducing a mild sedative to her airflow there was no way to induce a state of relaxation for her. The risks of additional sedation were too high, especially if she reached the Kick, which he doubted she would. It had taken him dozens of trials before he could relax enough for the Kick to initiate.

Letting go was far easier in theory than in practice. Still, he couldn't figure out how to consistently surrender to the Hack. His incessant thoughts always got in the way, making it nearly impossible to quiet his mind enough to fully let go. But he knew surrender—*deditio*—was the key.

At thirty-three minutes in the tank, Nyah's heart rate had slowed to fifty-eight beats per minutes and her EEG indicated a steady, slow transition from a beta-wave frequency—a range experienced when people were fully awake and alert—to an alpha frequency. Most people experienced alpha frequency right after waking or just before sleep; it was the doorway to theta, the low-level brain activity experienced during sleep and deep meditation.

Theta frequencies were the key to hacking the mind, and the optimal gateway was 4.44 Hz. Nyah's EEG continually nudged lower toward theta range. It would sporadically spike higher before edging down again. At forty-seven minutes, the monitor recorded a dip to 4.44.

An alarm window appeared on-screen:

KICK PROTOCOL CONFIRMED
INITIATE?

• • •

DARKNESS—thick and fluid like the kind I imagine exists at the bottom of the ocean. It swirled around me and swallowed everything as I floated inside the water tank, eyes wide but completely blinded to the world. Nothing had happened yet.

Austin's voice had gone silent and now I was left with the darkness and my own thoughts. How long had it been?

At first, floating in the water was more disorienting than I'd expected. With nothing to ground me, my body was robbed of even the sense of up, down, above, and below. I'd taken for granted how the simplest things like having the floor beneath my feet or feeling air colder than I was or seeing something across the room formed my reality and divided the world into *here* and *there, up* and *down, me* and *not me.*

Now I was simply . . . *here.*

Everything was *here,* but it felt like nowhere. A trick of the mind, Austin had said. Neural sleight of hand. Yet, nothing felt like an illusion or a trick.

I drew long, deep breaths and tried to let my mind drift.

Deditio, I'd say in my mind, but the more I tried, the faster my thoughts came. At first all I could hear was my heart, which fluttered against my rib cage like a bird trying to escape, and the deep thrumming frequency filtering through the earpieces. But it wasn't long before my thoughts overtook all of them and rumbled relentlessly into my mind like people—an angry mob of them—screaming to be heard.

Bad idea, Nyah. What have you done?

Holes in your head? Nuts! This won't do anything but kill you.

What if Austin dies while you're in here and you get trapped? What then? No one knows you're here.

Then, like a TV screen clicking off, my mind went back to the darkness and everything was calm, peaceful. But only a moment later, without any conscious effort, the TV came on again and began channel surfing; a string of images flashed through my mind: my mother, Lettie, Pixel, me. I saw myself in the bathroom mirror, scrutinizing my scarred, shaved head.

Ugly girl. Now everyone will see, won't they?

See how unfair life is?

A quick flash of an extreme close-up of Lettie's face: Everything happens for a reason.

And a chorus of voices, saying: Lie! She lies! Nothing happens for a reason. The universe is cruel and unfair! It's an uncaring machine grinding you to dust.

Bad things happen to good people because we're just cosmic playthings.

Then nothing again. No images, no commentaries. This went on, it seemed, forever—the cycles of thoughts and no thoughts. It was like the worst night I'd ever had lying in bed, unable to shut off my mind's obsessive loop of uncontrollable madness.

Was my mind always like this and I simply hadn't realized it, too busy to pay attention?

Another thought, this one quieter: *Let go.*

So I did, or at least tried. I imagined my body suspended beneath the ocean's surface, weightless and surrounded by profound silence and peace. I saw the ocean clearly. The more I gave myself to that image, the more I forgot about my racing heart or the fear bursting through my mind, telling me this was all a very bad idea. Of course it was a bad idea, but so what?

Surrender.

Soon, the darkness resolved into a single image and I was drifting in a void, dark and warm. The nothingness seemed much larger than the tiny tank I was in. There was nothing to judge distances: I was adrift beneath the surface of an endless ocean. I didn't need air, because I just was; I was there without form or need, a part of the void around me.

New thoughts pushed in, but I breathed them out into the water. Each one curled into the sea like black oil and vanished.

Deditio . . .

Instantly, a deep sense of relaxation washed through me. For the briefest moment, I thought, *This must be the Kick Austin told me about*, but then even this thought drifted away and was gone.

●●●

AUSTIN LIFTED his finger from the button that released an atomized dose of synthesized neurocompound into Nyah's airflow—the Kick. He watched her on-screen face closely. The cocktail would almost instantly plunge her into an enhanced state that the mind wasn't easily capable of achieving on its own. After that, the computer would record the momentary electrical pattern caused by her firing neurons and, using laser pulses, extend them.

"Amazing," he whispered to himself. It had taken him months to so easily attain the level of relaxation she had done in under an hour.

An on-screen indicator lit green, verifying the delivery of the compound.

Nyah's eyes drifted open, staring into the camera. Her pupils expanded and her eyes began flitting side to side uncontrollably. She sighed once, loudly, mouth stretched wide. Her body tensed, arching in the water. Yet none of her vital signs spiked.

She was beyond the threshold now.

She was inside.

ELECTRICITY CRACKLED all around me as I sank deeper into the dark ocean. It was accompanied by a blinding flash like an exploding star, illuminating the water all around me. It formed in the distance, a single point of light, then expanded in all directions at once, all in an instant. It filled the world faster than a thought and, simultaneously, took longer than a lifetime.

And the ocean disappeared; it instantaneously evaporated and I was no longer suspended in pristine waters, but floating in a vast white space. Or was I standing? The electric crackling became a roaring wind that I could hear, but not feel.

I felt no fear as I looked around. A rip in the white space appeared in front of me. It also floated in that vast nothingness, a tear in the white void: jagged edges, color shining through it.

Curiosity seized me. I walked closer—or *thought* about walking, about moving my legs—and I drew closer to it. Warm air drifted through, buffeting my skin.

I moved sideways and it was still directly before me. I went the other way. No matter how I moved, the rip was always right in front of me, as if moving with me, but so instantly and subtly, I couldn't discern its movement.

Where does it lead? What's beyond the rip?

I had to know.

Reaching out, I lightly pressed my fingers against it. The edges of the tear were frigid and made a sound like a frozen river cracking under-foot—loud enough to hear over the howling wind.

When I pulled my fingers away, the white space clung to them and stretched before breaking off and snapping back into place. The air rippled all around me, like the surface of a pond disturbed by a stone.

I reached forward again, this time sliding my hand through the narrow gap until it disappeared through the opening. Prickles of electricity pulsed through my arm, and a gentle breeze caressed my fingers on the other side.

A step forward, reaching farther, until my entire arm was through. I squeezed my eyes closed and took another step—going right into the tear and passing through it as if it possessed no more substance than a cloud.

The bellowing gale stopped; silence engulfed me.

When I opened my eyes I was standing in the sensory-deprivation room of Austin's loft. Everything seemed sharper, the textures more detailed, the colors more vivid. I remembered that Austin said hacking was like going from standard definition to high-def. Now I knew what he meant. Everything was crisp and energized.

To my left was the tank, its lid closed. I didn't remember ending my first session in it, didn't remember climbing out.

Am I still inside it?

The thought had barely touched my mind and I was inside the tank, hovering over the water, nose to nose with myself. That it was dark didn't matter. I could see my motionless body floating face up, as if it were all happening in the noonday sun. My eyes stared back at me, unmoving.

A thought jolted me: *Am I dead?*

No, not dead. I knew that somehow. I was something else. Something in-between, like Austin had described the first time I came to his apartment. What had he said? *Untethered.* I'd hacked my mind and become untethered. I was having an out-of-body experience.

I watched myself for a long time. It felt like meeting a stranger on the street only to discover she was an old friend who didn't look like I remembered. It was more than my missing hair. Like everyone, I'd only ever seen myself in a mirror, in two dimensions. Seeing myself from the outside, the way others witnessed me every day, startled me. There I lay, bald and scarred, thin and frail.

This is how I look? This is how Austin sees me?

An image of his face came to mind, and I was suddenly standing beside him, watching him as he sat at the control panel, dividing his attention between writing notes on a yellow legal pad and checking a panel of monitors and sensors. Camera feeds from inside the deprivation tank displayed my image on four screens, and a heart monitor beeped rhythmically.

I was very much alive.

"Austin," I said.

No response. He kept writing on his legal pad, unaware of my presence. As I watched him the rapid murmur of his thoughts entered my awareness as if he were talking out loud, which he wasn't. I was hearing his interior monologue just as he had heard mine. He was silently repeating a long string of numbers that he was jotting down along with fragments of ideas and observations as he watched me on-screen.

"I'm right here. Can you hear me?"

I reached out to place my hand on his shoulder, but it passed through him as though he were made of smoke. Or as though I was.

Held in front of me, my hand appeared solid and substantial. I glanced at the watch then. The second hand rotated sluggishly, as if straining against an unseen force. Only five seconds of clock time had passed. Austin was right, that five seconds had felt like five minutes. He'd said my Hack would last fifteen seconds.

I looked toward the isolation room. How had I gotten out here? I hadn't walked, I was sure of that. I simply thought about Austin, and

I was beside him. I looked across the room, toward the large picture windows in Austin's kitchen, and immediately found myself standing inches from them.

Amazing.

Austin was now on the far side of the apartment, still working at the control panel. An electric current of excitement flowed through me. The sense of liberation and freedom was intoxicating.

How far could I go? I looked out the window, toward the Bay Bridge and wondered what it would be like to be there, on the highest point of the bridge's support structure. And then I was there, atop the steel frame, gazing over San Francisco.

I wobbled wildly and flung my arms out, grasping for something to hold onto, but I was simply *there*. I wasn't going to fall.

Turning around slowly, I looked between my feet at the stretch of pavement far below and the steady stream of cars traversing the bridge, their drivers oblivious to my watching them from high above.

In the morning light, the dark waters of the San Francisco Bay looked like slate, and in the distance was the pale outline of Alcatraz Island. The world was waking up, and in a way so was I. My body was somewhere else while I was up here, free to move around however and wherever I wanted. It all seemed like a dream, and maybe it was—all just a dream, an illusion.

Mom would love this.

I closed my eyes and saw her smiling face.

A blink and the Bay vista vanished. There was no sense of movement; I was simply no longer on the bridge. Instead, I was standing at the end of a cramped, dark room. It was long and narrow, two walls lined with tall metal shelving. A thread of light outlined a door straight ahead.

I walked toward it, scanning the shelves as I passed them: Boxes of bandages, syringes, latex gloves, a stack of metal bedpans. I was in a medical-supply closet.

But why?

I came to the door and instinctively reached for the door handle. My hand passed through it and my first thought was, *I'm locked in!* It dawned on me: the same reason I couldn't turn the handle made the handle unnecessary. It was unnatural to simply walk *into* the door, but I did and passed right through it.

There was a well-lit hallway across from a large reception area. A nurse's station. I was in a hospital then. Four women dressed in colorful scrubs stood there, chatting and writing on clipboards. A buzzer sounded and a fifth nurse jumped up from a chair behind the counter and pointed down the hall. "302's crashing," she said, snatching up a phone. "Code blue. Page Doctor Morgan."

The four nurses rushed past me and I watched as they disappeared into one of the patient rooms midway down the hall. Two doctors wearing white lab coats sprinted from the other end of the hall and darted into the room. Someone followed them, pushing a cart loaded with machines.

A sense of dread boiled inside of me as I started down the hall, mind blank. Loud, urgent voices drifted out of the room and rushed down the corridor at me. I stepped forward and found myself standing outside the open doorway.

The handwritten nameplate beside the door read: *Parks, Elizabeth.*

Mom? My heart sank. How was this possible? She was at Cedar Ridge, not here.

I stepped into the room's chaos. It was filled with medical staff, all gathered around a form in the bed. Moonlight shone through the window and angled across the room.

Nighttime? That didn't make sense. It was still morning. There was no way I'd been in the Hack that long.

I stepped to the foot of the bed. There, in front of me, lay my mother. She was ashen, color draining from her face as I watched. Her eyes stared vacantly at the ceiling. On both sides of the bed, doctors and nurses worked to save her, compressing her chest with their palms, jabbing syringes into her, getting paddles ready to—I hoped—jump-start her heart.

"Hurry!" I screamed, but no one heard. "Mom!"

She was already dead. I knew it from the flatline tone of the heart-rate monitor and the way her mouth hung open as though gasping for breath, but there were no gasps coming from her.

"Mom!" I said again. "Please don't leave me. Please!"

The doctors and nurses blurred around me. A nurse passed through me as she rounded the bed. The entire scene seemed to slow down, then speed up, as if it were all a movie and someone was manipulating it with a remote control, speeding it up then dialing it back.

Soon the medical team stopped their frantic movements. The lead doctor, a man with white hair and horn-rimmed glasses, snapped off his latex gloves. He looked at his watch. "Time of death: 2:37 a.m. Marsha, notify Dr. Benton, please. Tell him it looks like the blood clot shifted. Let's schedule an autopsy to verify. We also need to notify the family."

Blood clot? Mom didn't have a blood clot.

The scene around me sped up as if someone had pressed a fast-forward button. All but one nurse filed quietly out of the room. The remaining nurse pulled the sheet over my mother's face, turned off the medical equipment, and left.

I was alone with her.

There I stood at her bedside, staring down at the lifeless form be-neath the sheets. I reached out my hand to pull the sheet away from her face, but my fingers slipped through it.

"Mom?" It came as little more than a whisper. I needed her to hear me, but it was too late.

The world felt like it had fallen out from beneath me. How was this even possible? She was supposed to be in her apartment, sleeping in her bed. I was at Austin's, in the tank. And the moon—it was 2:37 in the morning, the doctor had said—completely baffled me. No way I could still be in the Hack.

I scanned the room for anything to indicate that this was a dream. My attention locked on the date on a wall-mounted clock: two weeks from the day I'd climbed into the deprivation chamber for the first time.

What? How?

This had to be a dream.

The hospital trembled underfoot and the ground groaned long and loud. It was the twisting-steel sound of a ship before it collapses under the ocean's crushing pressure. It came again and the air thickened and grew heavy as it pressed against me.

I looked at my mom's bed. Everything—the bed, the blankets, my mom—was disintegrating, breaking into millions of tiny pixels that swirled into the air, joined by particles from the medical equipment, the tiles, the floor, the walls. All of it was coming apart, being carried away by a terrible, howling wind that now overtook the groaning.

Desperately, I reached for my mother's hand, but she disintegrated along with the rest of the room. I tried to scream, tried to find something to hold on to, but there was nothing to grab and nowhere to go. The world was peeling away, leaving only the white void I'd seen before. I spun around, searching for the rip I'd gone through earlier, but it was gone too.

I looked down at my hands and they too were starting to break apart and blow away in the fierce wind: my fingertips first—pixelating and flying away—then my palms, wrists, forearms . . . the destruction climbing my arm until my entire body collapsed into nothing.

Everything was stark black and I was back in the tank.

2.4

Day Three
8:40 AM

"FIFTEEN SECONDS," Austin said, barely able to contain his enthusiasm. In the entire time I'd known him, he'd never been this animated. "Your stats are unbelievable."

I sat on his couch, clutching my unsteady hands in my lap. The water had puckered my skin like a prune, and it felt good being in dry clothes again.

Now Austin was telling me about the data he'd gathered—"much more than I'd expected from your first Hack"—and how short it'd been, but all I could think about was Mom.

"Fifteen seconds," I repeated, shaking my head. "It felt much longer than that, like you said it would."

"Hack time is pliable, elastic. It's similar to what we experience in dreams." He handed me a steaming cup of tea. "It took awhile for your mind to quiet enough for the Kick to initiate, which is normal. If anything, you attained a relaxed state much more quickly than I anticipated. But once you did, yes, you were under only fifteen seconds."

I held up my hand. "Look at me, still shaking." I smiled at him. "I hadn't expected any of that, any of what happened."

"Neither had I." Austin placed a small digital recorder on the coffee table, then sat in the chair across from me. "Now, let's talk about what you saw. Start at the beginning. We need to document every experience so we can cross reference everything, look for commonalities and anomalies. As much as you can remember. We have to figure out how you were able to go under so easily."

I began to unfold my experience, beginning with my vision of floating in the ocean. When I got to the part about the rip or tear in the white air he stopped me.

"A tear?" he said.

"Yeah. It hung in midair, and I stepped through it into your apartment." I shook my head. "What *was* it?"

"The ocean was probably a mental projection you used to quiet your mind, but the white void—I suspect it was another abstraction your subconscious created to limit your awareness, like a firewall."

I paused. "Is it real?"

"No more so than the ocean you saw. It's your subconscious contextualizing the environment around you." Austin drifted into his thoughts for a long beat. He touched each fingertip on his right hand to his thumb, that nervous habit of his, indicating his mind was in heavy-processing mode. I waited for him to cycle through it seven times. Then he said, "Did you try walking *around* the rip?"

"I couldn't."

"Because it moved with you so that it was always in front of you."

A chill tickled my spine. "You *have* seen it!"

"Not a rip in the air, but something like it. I picture a door before I hack; I learned early in my research that my mind needed a mental cue, like a hypnotic suggestion to give my surroundings context. That you figured that out on your own is amazing. You found yourself in front of a rip of some kind. I go through a door. I call it the threshold state because it seems to be some kind of psychological division between physical reality and the ghost state."

"Ghost state?"

He shrugged. "It has nothing to do with ghosts. It's just a name I came up with to delineate it."

I nodded, thinking of how I'd felt moving through Austin's apartment and then to the bridge and hospital: like a ghost.

He leaned forward, elbows on his knees. He was eating this up. "What happened next?"

"I was in your apartment, standing next to you at the control panel. I could see my body like I can now—solid—but when I tried to touch you my hand went through you."

"That's the ghost state," he said with a smile. "Just like when I read your cell-phone screen and heard your thoughts."

"It was weird, but it got weirder when I left the apartment."

Austin's smile faded. "What do you mean, 'left the apartment'?"

I told him all about how I'd moved around the apartment simply by thinking about it, and how I'd *willed* myself outside and to the top of the bridge.

"It's not like I flew to the place or traveled to it, I said. "I just thought about it and was there."

"No sense of movement at all?" he asked.

"Nothing. It was like blinking and finding myself somewhere else, almost faster than I could think it."

He stood and began pacing, fingertips tapping against one another, his mind clearly spinning. "This is new. This is amazing."

"What do you mean 'new'?"

"A new phenomenon, leaving the apartment. I've never done that." He pointed at me. "We have to figure out why it happened *now*, to *you*. This is a serious breakthrough."

"You've *never* traveled outside of the apartment in a Hack?"

"No. My experience has always been localized." He squinted at me. "Why were you able to, what was different? We have to run diagnostics and go through each data point. There must be something different about your Hack that I missed. It could be any of a thousand variables—your biochemistry, an isolated reaction to the Kick, anything." His eyes got wide. "The bridge," he said. "Did you go anywhere else?"

I told him about the hospital and about seeing my mom die. As I did, my throat tightened. "I didn't recognize any of it," I said. "I've never been in that hospital, not before tonight. Was it real?"

Scenes from the experience gripped me: my mother lying there, the doctors working frantically to pull her back from death, her lifeless eyes and gaping mouth.

"I don't know," Austin said.

"One of the doctors mentioned a blood clot. Thing is, my mother doesn't have a blood clot. She just had a checkup. She has lots of problems, but a clot isn't one of them. It had to be a dream, right?"

Austin was silent.

"Right?" I said again, looking for reassurance. "Tell me you've had dreams during your Hacks."

He stopped pacing at a plush leather chair and plopped down into it. "No, never. I don't think dreaming is possible during a Hack."

"This doesn't make any sense. The date of my mom's death was two weeks from now. Is it possible that I saw the future?"

He thought for a moment. "I don't know. I guess it depends."

"On what?"

"Whether or not time and space are linear. Some physicists postulate that the past, present, and future all exist simultaneously and that we simply experience whatever present slice of the universe we happen to be in at the moment. Others think that hypothesis is ridiculous."

"What do you think?" I asked and watched his reaction.

"As a scientist I think anything's possible," he said without hesitation.

"So what does it mean, seeing my mother dying? How can that be?"

"Are you sure your mother doesn't have a blood clot? When was her last MRI?"

I shrugged. "Three, four months ago."

"She's been bedridden so it's possible that she developed one since then. There's only one way to know for sure: have Benton do an MRI on her. If it proves negative, it wasn't a premonition. But if it's confirmed . . ." He thought about it. "Well, that's something completely unexpected. Either way, this is something else new."

"You're right," I said. I glanced out the window. The sky was a beautiful electric blue. "I have to get her into Dr. Benton's."

I set the teacup down, stood and rounded the sofa.

"Whoa," he said, standing to his feet. "You can't leave. What about the FBI? You can't just go traipsing into your mom's apartment. You got away from them once, but I don't think they'll let it happen again."

"I can't just sit around and let my mom die. If what I saw wasn't a dream then I have to tell Lettie. I have to do something."

"Call her then, but don't go. You're safe here. Out there you aren't." His eyes contained more compassion than I'd seen in them before. Was I growing on him, or was it simply that having grappled with his own demise, he was now more concerned about others' feelings?

"I can't do that," I said. "The FBI took my phone. Maybe I can find a pay phone or something."

"Wait here a minute," he said and walked to a nearby shelf. He returned with a mobile phone in his hand. "I hate these things, but this is the best option."

He handed it to me.

"It's a burner," he said. "Got it at Walmart. The minutes are prepaid and the number is untraceable. Use this to call Lettie, have her take your mom in. But you can't leave here. Okay?"

"Thanks."

I took the phone up to the roof and dialed the number for Mom's room at Cedar Ridge. Lettie answered.

"It's me," I said.

"Where are you?" Her voice was strained. "A federal agent came here in the middle of the night looking for you. What's going on?"

"It's complicated." A beat. "I'm helping them with a case, but that's all I can say."

"They seemed really worried about you. Where've you been?"

"Somewhere safe. I promise."

"You need to come home now. We'll figure this out, but you have to come home."

"I can't, not yet. I will soon."

"Honey, let me come get you."

"No." I was silent for a moment. "But you have to do something for me. It's important. I need you to get Mom to Dr. Benton. Today. Tell him she needs an MRI."

"An MRI? She just had one a few months—"

"I know," I interrupted. "Just . . . do this for me. Please. I can't explain why, but you just have to trust me. And don't take no for an answer. It has to be today."

"They're so expensive, and insurance won't cover it if—"

"Lettie, listen to me. I had a *vision*, okay?" I let my words hang there. My grandmother was a spiritual woman who often talked about how God spoke to people in unusual ways—dreams, visions, even in tiny coincidences. I knew this would get her attention.

"What kind of vision?" she asked.

"The kind that feels real. It was early this morning. Nothing like this has ever happened to me before, but I think that's what it was. I saw Mom die of a blood clot. I think it was a warning of some kind. I know it sounds ludicrous."

"No, it doesn't," Lettie said. "If I do this, you have to promise you'll come home." Her words were firm, strengthened by determination and belief.

"First I have to—"

126

"*Promise* me."

I was silent for a moment. "Okay, but the MRI has to be today."

"I'll call Dr. Benton then."

"Today," I said. "Please."

"I'll make sure of it." She sighed heavily on the other end of the line. "What have you gotten yourself into, child?"

"I'll tell you everything," I said. "Soon."

"Please be safe."

"I will. The moment you get the results, call me back at this number, but don't give it to anyone else. Especially not the FBI. I'll be home soon," I said, and I hoped it was true.

2.5

Day Three
8:30 PM

AUSTIN STARED through bleary eyes at the digital brain scan that filled his computer monitor. He would compare the black-and-white image against the sequential database he'd developed to meticulously track his scans, but he already knew what he'd discover.

It had been twelve hours since Nyah's Hack. After calling her grandmother she'd crashed in the guest room, exhausted. He hadn't heard a peep from her since then, which gave him the time he needed to parse not only her data, but to update his own.

He leaned closer to the screen and traced his index finger across the stark image. The tumor that was rotting his mind from the inside out was a white mass set against the grey ridges of brain tissue. On-screen, the brain could have belonged to any of the hundreds of terminal patients whose cases he'd researched over the years in the hope of finding clues to help his own condition, but it wasn't somebody else's brain; it was his.

And despite his best efforts, the tumor was still destroying him with stunning speed. There was no escaping the data. Unlike people, data is incapable of lying or spinning the truth. It isn't right or wrong, it just *is*. It's the reason he'd always put more faith in science than he had in people.

The universe was built on immutable principles and laws, facts that led to reliable conclusions. Facts were never flawed, only the people who interpreted those facts were.

We see the world not as it is, but as we are, someone had once told him. But bending fact to serve one's perception could only lead to delusion. Insanity. And he wasn't insane. Not yet, anyway.

In fact, Dr. Benton believed Austin's tumor had significantly elevated his already formidable cognitive abilities. Somehow the fibrous mass had created unusual neural connections that didn't exist before, which allowed him to think more creatively. It was precisely because of his tumor that he was exceptional.

It was a hypothesis that seemed to bear itself out experientially. With each new day, the growth expanded and his mental processes grew more acute, more lucid. He required less sleep, but whether that was explained by a deeply rooted instinct to survive or, rather, by higher brain function, he didn't know.

Either way, he'd been driven to the point of obsession with finding a cure where experts claimed there was none to be found. He was convinced that, given enough time, he would find one. He simply needed enough data to lead him to it.

At the moment, however, the data led to only one conclusion: he would die, sooner rather than later. That's what the three neurologists back in Boston had told him, as well. There was nothing they could do for him except make the symptoms more bearable.

Only Dr. Benton had offered a solution beyond symptom management: an aggressive and experimental chemotherapy paired with radiation that he said might shrink the tumor.

Might. But even if it worked, he'd said, the possibility of destroying brain tissue was high—collateral damage, he'd called it. That was the price of surviving to see his twentieth birthday.

Austin would rather die. What would he be without his mind?

Nothing. He *was* his mind. The only thing he'd ever had that set him apart—that made him exceptional—was his powerful intellect. Taking that away, even if it meant he could continue to exist, was not an option. He would exist, but he would not be living.

I think, therefore I am. It had always been his core belief.

His temples pulsed painfully.

Where are those pills?

Austin swept his attention across the cluttered desk. He spotted the amber bottle behind a stack of reports and grabbed it. He emptied the last two pills into his mouth and washed them down with a half can of warm Red Bull.

He only took the powerful meds when the pain became unbearable. They dulled his senses and fogged his mind. His *mind*. He didn't want to lose it to cancer or its cure, so of course medicating it into a stupor made no sense, either.

He'd suspected a tumor was growing inside his head months before his Boston neurologist confirmed it. It began as an unshakeable feeling that something inside him was slightly off, that he wasn't well. Yet it was nothing more than a hunch.

Christy, his only friend at the time, often counseled him to have his headaches checked out, but there was no physical or psychological evidence to suggest the problem was anything other than stress-induced migraines. At the time, he'd been seventeen, living on his own, starting a new life, attending—even acing—graduate-level classes at Harvard. When he wasn't studying or doing research, he was busy developing software on the side.

Then everything ground to a halt. The migraines became more frequent and the pain more acute, like rusty drill bits boring through his skull. Blurry vision and insomnia followed until he couldn't even venture out of his apartment without sunglasses.

He'd experienced the worst of it when he and Christy were trapped in St. Matthew's hospital, an experience he still didn't know how to process. It hadn't been a shared delusion; he knew that much. But if not that, then what?

A voice broke the silence. "Austin, you're not going to believe this."

Austin jumped and spun his chair around. Nyah stood a few feet away in a black t-shirt and jeans, holding the mobile phone he'd given her.

"My mom," she said. "What I saw was real. It was *real*."

"The blood clot?"

She nodded. "Lettie just called. The MRI revealed a clot in her leg."

"You caught it before it could dislodge and hit her brain," he said.

Nyah grinned. "She's going to live." She rushed to him and bent down to hug him, pressing her cheek to his. "Thank you."

"What's the plan then? What are they going to do?"

She backed up a step, ran her palm over her scalp. "Dr. Benton's giving her a round of blood-thinning medication, hoping to dissolve it."

He forced a smile and stood. "That's great."

"You know what this means? I witnessed an event that hadn't happened yet—and won't now. How's that possible? You said something about time not being linear?"

He shook his head. "It could mean any number of things: overlapping timelines, ripples in time, wormholes . . . there are as many theories as there are people who've studied it. It's fascinating." And it was, but it was difficult for him to get excited; his thoughts seemed murky, as though they were drifting through dirty water.

She cocked her head to the side, concern wrinkling her brow. "Everything all right? You don't look so good."

He rubbed his forehead. "Just tired. I haven't been to sleep yet."

Nyah turned her attention to the images on the screen. "These new?"

"No, they're a week old. I went in and had an MRI taken. I do it every week."

She bit her bottom lip and turned worried eyes on him.

"The growth has accelerated since my last scan," he said. "It's getting worse. I have some tingling in my hands today and this gnawing headache."

"We'll figure it out," she said. "You're the smartest guy I know. And I'm the smartest girl you know."

"Yeah," he said and switched off the monitor, making the image disappear. He wished he could make the tumor disappear as easily. "We should suit up and get in the tanks as soon as we can. The more Hacks we do, the better."

"We? Together?"

"In tandem, yes. I spent the day poring over the data from your Hack. There had to be some explanation for the phenomena you experienced. Some technical component that explained why I've never been able to go beyond a localized out-of-body experience, but you were."

He walked to the control panel, Nyah close on his heels. "Well? Did you find out?" she asked.

"Yeah, it was a mistake," he said. His fingers ran across the keyboard, calling up a screen that compared the metrics of her Hack and his baseline. "When I ran the Hack protocol I didn't adjust the Kick dosage to account for your lower body weight."

"Wha . . . you gave me too much?"

He shook his head. "Technically, yes, but you weren't in any danger."

"So what happened? How did the dosage difference change things?"

"The synthesized compound I've been using—the Kick—typically elevates brain activity. The mixture you received had the opposite effect. Instead of amping up your brain activity, it inhibited it."

"You mean it shut down my brain?"

"Certain functions, yes. As I was running the system diagnostics I saw this." He pointed to a spike on a line graph filling the adjacent screen. "See how low your brain activity is compared to mine? This explains the differences between our experiences."

"You're sure?"

"Not entirely, but it makes sense. You were able to experience the Hack more effectively than I have because the stronger dosage of neuro-compound stripped away the mental firewall that keeps us from seeing reality as it truly is."

"You're saying we *think* too much?"

"We have preconceptions, yes. We're programmed to see the world a certain way."

"And the higher dosage numbs those preconceptions?"

"It mutes it, yes, and dials the brain's filter back enough for the Reality behind reality to come through. Really, there's only one way to be sure. We have to test it, so I spent all day reconfiguring the system so we can tandem hack."

"I can't wait."

He continued: "We've tapped into a layer of reality that's unconstrained by space. The next step is to see what happens when we do it together. We're getting closer. There seems to be a progression here, each new level revealing a new set of possibilities and a new paradigm of awareness. Right now we're in the temporal state, within our physical bodies. Beyond that there's the threshold."

"The ocean I saw," I said.

"Then there's the first firewall, the white void you saw, and beyond it—through the rip—is the ghost state. Each new state levels up the senses dramatically and strips away physical and mental limitations."

"Each level gives us more abilities," she said.

"Like a video game. But to progress you have to hack the firewall blocking each level."

"There are other firewalls?"

"That's my terminology. What it really is . . . ." He shrugged. "Who knows? Some natural phenomenon made to protect layers of reality."

"Eventually leading to what?"

"I think the top level is the state that allows the manipulation of matter itself."

She chewed on a fingernail, eyes flicking back and forth. "When are we going to do it? Hack together?"

"I reprogrammed everything so it can handle dual Hacks seamlessly. We'll replicate the exact parameters each time and the system will synchronize our Kicks as closely as possible. They may not be perfectly aligned, but it will be close enough that we'll cross the first firewall at approximately the same time. I hope."

"You hope?"

"I don't know how any of this works yet." He thought for a few moments, then held up an index finger. "I have an idea. Come with me." He held his hand out to her. She grabbed it and he led her into the adjacent room, which served as his study. He stopped in front of a large painting that hung halfway up the wall. It was of an ancient door, the color of blood. It seemed to be floating in midair.

"When you pictured the ocean," he said, "your subconscious created a mental cue that led you to a breach in that first firewall, the rip. I think it's essential that we both hold the same mental cue in mind when we go under. I think it will increase our odds of arriving at the same firewall. Can you do that?"

She stood there, intently studying the image. "I should think of this door when we're in the tanks?"

"Yes. Pay attention to the details. We need to see the same thing, I believe."

She turned toward him and smiled. "Okay. Got it."

"That's it? No, take some time with it."

Nyah tapped the side of her head. "No need. Eidetic memory. I'm a genius, remember?" With that she turned and walked out of the room. "You coming or do I have to do this by myself?"

2.6

Day Three
9:02 PM

AUSTIN HARDWIRED us into the system for the tandem Hack. I floated in the saltwater tank, and surrendered to the darkness quickly. It came almost effortlessly this time and soon I was hanging weightless in the familiar waters of the ocean—the ocean inside Austin's apartment. The ocean inside my mind.

This time, the fear I'd felt earlier was replaced by fascination with this strange world that I knew was real, despite logic insisting it was little more than a waking dream.

The more I let go of my attempts to explain and rationalize the mind-hacking experience, the easier it was to relax and drift deeper into the waters.

That's what it was like, sinking deeper into a careless sea that lifted my fear and carried it away on an invisible current. The deeper I sank, the more the relentless chatter in my mind faded until it was a mere whisper. And then it was nothing at all, replaced completely by the comfortable hum.

As I began to relax I held the image of the red door in my mind, intently imagining every detail as I'd seen it in the painting.

As before, the world evaporated into the white light. Instantly, I found myself once again standing in the white void. But this time instead of a rip, there was a red door—*the* red door. It was a mental firewall just as Austin suspected.

I hadn't thought of it that way until he'd said it, but he was right. The door was some kind of threshold. Whether it was really a door or just a projection of my mind didn't matter. What did matter was that it led to a place that had a direct impact on physical reality. That much we knew. That may have been all we knew.

I turned, looking for Austin, but he was nowhere in sight. There was only dimensionless white space that stretched forever in all directions, and the wind that roared through it. Maybe he'd already gone through the door, or maybe . . . maybe . . . A dozen possibilities for why he wasn't here occurred to me: maybe the tandem hadn't worked and he was back in the tank waiting to hack into reality; maybe there were many doors—not just one—and he was at another door, waiting for me. What if his door led somewhere else and I wouldn't be able to find him? What if this door opened to another place this time? There was no guarantee of anything, was there?

We knew so little.

I took a step toward the door and realized there was no knob or handle to open it. Could I just step through it?

I hesitated then leaned forward as I stepped into the blood-red door with my eyes closed. My face passed through it followed by the rest of my body. The terrible wind ceased howling and I knew without looking that I was beyond the door, beyond the firewall.

I'd hacked the first level again.

I opened my eyes, and once more I was standing in Austin's apartment. Everything crackled with intense definition as it had before—every color more vivid than normal, the air electrified with energy. My senses were heightened, picking up nuances and subtleties like never before.

I could feel the flow of some unseen energy in the room, like an air current. Why wasn't it visible? I lifted my hand and swept it slowly through the air, feeling the minute pressure differences as it passed through the seemingly empty space, as if my fingers were gliding through water.

"Nyah."

I spun around. He stood by the windows, watching me.

"Isn't this amazing?" Austin said, smiling.

A tremor of excitement rushed through me at the sight of him. Bodily, Austin was himself—still bald, still wearing the clothes he'd worn into the tank. But he seemed different, more vibrant and alive. I'd never before seen such a look of sheer contentment on any human face as I now saw on his. This was what unbridled happiness looked like. He was in his element, living his dream.

"Incredible," I answered.

He tilted his watch and glanced at it. "Five seconds have passed."

"Five minutes," I said.

Austin nodded. "We're set for thirty seconds total. That should give us enough time."

"For what?"

He reached his hand out to me. "Come on. I'll show you."

I raised my hand and was instantly in front of him, taking hold of his hand. To my surprise, it was solid to the touch and warm.

"We're in the same state of being," he explained. He squeezed my hand and our eyes met.

My eyes lowered to our hands. Our *consciousnesses* were holding hands. It seemed so intimate, but I knew we'd never be anything but friends. He had never shown any interest in me. I was just Nyah. I was always just Nyah to every guy I'd ever known.

He shifted to stand beside me and interlocked his fingers with mine. We were facing the big picture window—the dark night pressed against it, studded by lights from the Bay Bridge in the distance. He said, "This might not work . . ."

"What?" I asked.

"Just relax."

The apartment vanished and we were sailing over San Francisco, bright lights and evening traffic blurring beneath us. We were *flying!* Moving faster than seemed possible, even for a jet. The air was cool, but there was no air resistance or roaring wind.

Austin laughed out loud and let out a whoop as we banked left to glide over the dark Pacific waters.

I laughed too as the coastline disappeared behind us; there was nothing below us but ocean. We seemed to be accelerating. Ahead, a dark speck appeared on the horizon, but before I could take a breath we were there, skimming the deck of a massive cargo ship carrying stacks of containers as high as buildings. Then it too was gone in the distance as a massive island rose ahead of us.

Hawaii, I thought as it passed by on our right.

"Where are we going?" I asked.

"You'll see." He turned his head and smiled. "Trust me?"

"Of course."

"Then close your eyes," he said.

I did—for only a moment, if there were such things as moments in that state. I felt the earth once again beneath my feet. The whooshing sound of wind filled my ears, and the air was crisp and somehow fragile. It was cold. Very cold.

"Don't open them. Not yet," he said.

"Where are we?"

"Patience, my dear." I could hear the excitement in his voice. He sounded like a kid on Christmas as he pulled me along, then released my hand. "Okay, now."

I opened my eyes to the sight of pristine snow blanketing the rocky earth beneath my feet. Wind swept fine powder over my shoes and across the ground. Slowly, I lifted and turned my head, taking in the expansive vista as it came into my field of vision.

I gasped when I realized we were standing on a mountain ridge, a snow-packed summit that towered over a range of rocky spines and saw-tooth peaks stretching as far as the eye could see. Deep pockets of shadows filled the vast valleys below us. A skim of clouds drifted nearby, below us.

"It's the most beautiful thing I've ever seen," I said. "Where are we?"

"The top of the world." He turned around slowly, arms held out as if presenting it to me.

"Mount Everest?"

"There's only one top of the world. I've always dreamed two things: flying and coming here," he said, without diverting his eyes from the far horizon. "It's the only place on earth I ever wanted to experience before I died."

"You're not going to die."

Instead of answering, he pointed over the mountains. "Look."

I followed his gaze to where a blossom of light formed at the edge of the world and slowly grew until the horizon eventually caught fire from the rising sun. I never knew colors like that existed in real life.

"You asked me where we are, but not when we are," he said. "I imagined a sunrise from here, but in reality it's evening in Tibet. It seems time's a lot more flexible than even I suspected."

We'd traveled through space *and* time. It was too much for me to grasp, so I let the thought go and simply enjoyed my surroundings . . . and the person I was sharing it with.

We stood in silence as the sun rose higher into the sky, spilling light and life into the dark mountain range. I watched Austin for a long moment, his eyes fixed on the sunrise.

"You know," he said, "I don't care if everyone else forgets me as long as you don't."

That startled and thrilled me—at least as much as opening my eyes to the wonder of the Himalayas had.

"Whatever happens," he continued, "remember that we stood next to each other right here."

I didn't say anything for a long time. Finally I spoke: "I could never forget you."

He smiled as the sun lit his face.

I rose up on my toes and pressed my lips to his. I didn't think about what I was doing or try to talk myself into or out of it. I just did it. I lingered there for a moment and he kissed me back, gently, tenderly.

I stepped back and lowered my face. "Sorry."

"Wow," he said nervously. He put his finger under my chin and lifted my gaze to his. "Don't be sorry."

I smiled and then felt my face flush red. "I guess we should . . . you know . . ."

"We better get to work," he said.

"Yeah," I said.

He pulled me close to his body and held me. I pressed my face against his chest and felt his warmth. We stood like that for minutes or maybe it was hours. It didn't matter. All that did matter was that we were there together.

Austin released me and took a step back.

"So this is what hacking consciousness is?" I said. "Just a different way of moving around?"

"This is just the veneer," he said, looking around us. "When I had my stroke I was on a completely different level where I could see the energy infrastructure that forms all this." He swept his hand toward the panorama.

He was right. As exhilarating as it was to zip around the globe, drilling down to the base level of existence would be something else entirely. We needed to know more. We needed more abilities, more insight.

"We have to find the next firewall," I said, "but how?"

"Our experiences seem to be rooted in our intentions. We focused our will on the door, so we saw the door. That was one firewall, and beyond it was our ability to move freely in space and time." He looked at his wristwatch again. "Fifteen seconds left in the Hack."

"So we just close and our eyes and make a wish?" I said.

"Put that way, it sounds ridiculous, but we can't deny the fact that my concentrating on coming *here* is what brought us here. We have nothing else to go on. We need a mental connection that attaches our intentions to the firewall just like we did with the red door."

"But the door's not real."

"Doesn't matter, because it doesn't have to be. It's merely a hypnotic suggestion for the subconscious mind." He drew a deep breath and closed his eyes. "We should choose something that's easy for our minds to attach to, another door. A black door. I want you to hold that in your mind just like you did with the red one."

I nodded, then closed my eyes as well. "Tell me what to do."

"Picture it clearly. It's black and floating there, right in front of us. Do you see it?"

"No," I said. "I can't picture it."

"It's right here. You can open your eyes now," he said.

I did, but there was no door. Austin was a few feet to my right, taking a step away from me with his right hand extended.

"See it?" he asked, staring at nothing, as far as I could tell. "Just like I thought it would be. I'm going through it. Follow me."

Then I did see something, but it wasn't a door and it wasn't where he was looking. Just beyond him, to his left, was a shimmering white nothingness, a void, like a vertical seam torn in the air.

"Austin, wait," I said, but he was in midstep, and before his foot came down, he vanished.

"Austin!"

He was gone.

My eyes went to the slit in the air. It was nearly identical to the one I'd seen during my first Hack. It led somewhere, probably to Austin. It was all about intention, right? And my intention, like Austin's, was to access the level where anything can be changed on an atomic level.

Without hesitating, I walked toward the void and stepped through it.

I felt no movement, heard no sound at all. Only the air changed. In an instant the crisp, brittle air was replaced by warm humidity.

I blinked and an alleyway came into focus. Then the smell hit me— acrid and pungent. It was the scent of damp earth and decay and death. Mostly death.

Where am I?

2.7

Day Three
9:05 PM

"YOU'RE CERTAIN?" Walter Bell said, his voice stern on the other end of the call.

Stone held the phone to his ear as he glanced at the tablet computer resting on the passenger seat. A high-resolution satellite image of the warehouse filled the screen.

"Yes sir. The satellite passed out of sight and went off-line, but we were able to track her before it did. We're certain. It's her."

"Why there?" Bell said, "The Feds had her on lockdown. Why'd she leave?"

"I suspect she's attempting to retrieve the data on her own. She's obviously hiding something from them, though I don't know what or why. Either way, it's an opportunity. If she's hiding from them, it means they don't have anything yet. It also means she's likely alone."

Bell was quiet for a moment. "How close are you?"

"Twenty minutes."

"Call me when it's finished. I want this resolved today."

"Yes, sir."

Stone disconnected and slipped the phone into its sheath on his belt. The situation couldn't have played out better. The girl had escaped the FBI's watchful eye on her own and was clearly avoiding them.

Whatever she was doing, she wanted to keep it in the dark. She wanted to disappear.

He would make sure she did, and it would happen tonight.

EPISODE THREE

3.1

IN A BLINK the Himalayas had vanished from Austin's world. It had taken nothing more than setting his mind on the image of a black doorway, a mental suggestion like the red one he and Nyah had used to access the first level.

By walking through the black door he'd instantaneously traded one location for another. Now he found himself standing in the middle of a small clearing, hemmed in by a rainforest so dense it blocked the sky. The world around him seemed *more* material, more physical, not less, as he'd expected.

He turned his head, taking in the unfamiliar surroundings. Trees taller than buildings grew so closely together it was impossible to see more than twenty feet into the jungle. Why was he here? None of it was remotely familiar.

"Nyah!" he called. She'd imagined a black door too, and their destinations seemed to be determined by their intentions. So where was she?

He tilted his head and listened for her—her voice, her moving through the jungle, any sign of her. But he heard nothing except the nearby rumble of thunder. The scent of approaching rain hung on the wind, and along with it, the earthen aroma of damp ground.

"Nyah!" The jungle swallowed his words. Wind blowing through the trees was all that answered back. He couldn't worry about her now, time in the Hack was running out. Wherever she'd gone, obviously it wasn't here. No problem. They would both come out of the Hack soon enough.

The ground around him was worn to dirt in the shape of a circle about ten feet across. Flat, polished stones lay side by side and formed a boundary at the circle's edge. They were too thoughtfully placed to be happenstance. Someone had groomed this spot in the jungle. But who? And why?

What is this place?

A muffled snap reached him from the trees.

He spun and gazed into the dense vegetation. He called, "Who's there? Nyah?"

A faint whisper replied, so soft it could have been only a breeze. A child's voice, speaking a language Austin didn't know. It haunted the air, this time coming from his left.

He turned, but as soon as he moved the child's voice called from behind, followed by the sound of feet padding quickly over soft ground.

He crossed the clearing, stepped over the stone ring, and rushed in the direction of the noises, pushing through the thick leaves and bone-thick branches. He could've seen who it was if not for the trees.

"Wait!" he said as he plunged forward and into a tangle of saplings that blocked his way. Beyond them, through gaps in the foliage, he saw a child with olive skin and dark hair darting away, deeper into the lush jungle. A boy. The child sprinted for several yards then hopped atop a fallen tree and glanced over his shoulder.

With a wave of his hand he motioned for Austin to follow. He leaped off the tree with a laugh and fled into the jungle.

Austin blinked. The boy saw him? How could that be? There was a reason he called this the "ghost state." In all of the Hacks he'd experienced, never once had another person been able to see him. No one except Nyah, and then only because she too had been in the ghost state. Austin felt certain that that he and the boy were meant to meet.

Was the child in the ghost state, as well? How? Where had he come from?

"Wait!" he called and pushed through the saplings, hurrying after the boy. Within ten paces Austin had lost sight of him and the jungle closed in on all sides. The damp ground became gnarled with roots and rocks, and he stumbled, falling hard against a tree trunk.

Austin rose and rushed forward, weaving a path through the crowded trees. He planted a hand atop the fallen tree on which the boy had stood and hurdled it. Ahead, leaves rustled from the boy's passing and he followed.

"Come on," the child called.

Austin ran, arms held up to shield his face from the branches and vines clawing at him, snagging his clothes. Thunder bellowed and reverberated through the air as gloom fell over the jungle. The vast leaf canopy roared with the drumbeat of rain.

The forest thinned ahead, and Austin came to a stop and gripped a branch over his head. A sound reached him, louder than the rain. It came not from the sky, but from everywhere at once, as though the earth itself were groaning and writhing deep in the ground beneath his feet. The tone swelled, a deep hum that traveled through him, turning his bones into tuning forks.

He spotted something through the trees: a rectangular darkness beyond the tree line. It was a hut of some kind. Rubbing his arms, unnerved by the constant humming, Austin stepped out of the forest into a clearing completely devoid of trees, shrubs, and leaves. The soggy jungle floor had given way to a crackled dirt clearing, dry as bones despite the rain.

At the center of the circular opening cut into the jungle sat a hovel made of thatch, mud, and palm branches. The crude structure arched to form a dome ten feet in diameter and seemed barely tall enough for a grown man to stand inside. A wisp of bluish-white smoke curled from a hole in the roof and disappeared on the wind.

There was no sign of the child anywhere, or of anyone else, but there was still the sound—a low *thrumming* tone that changed now to a steady, unbroken rhythm like a heartbeat.

Wum wum . . . wum wum . . . wum wum . . .

Austin approached the hut's doorway cautiously and stopped. His heartbeat throbbed with the rhythm in the air. He waited for a breath, then lifted a hand to the curtain covering the entrance—an animal hide with black, wiry hair—and drew it aside.

In the darkness beyond, a fire flickered, its light almost instantly absorbed by the shadowy surroundings.

For the briefest moment his instincts urged him to turn around, run into the jungle and never look back. But there was nothing to fear here, was there? If anyone was in control of the situation, he was. If he willed to be somewhere else, he could be there instantly, right?

Austin ducked through the entrance and, cautiously, stepped inside. He released the pelt, and it fell closed behind him, shutting out the murky daylight. Shadows jumped toward him and pulled away, brought to life by the flicker of firelight. His eyes struggled to adjust, and he realized the humming sound had stopped.

He squinted at the dancing shadows. The air was sweet and pungent, a mix of charred wood and roasted meat. The orange fire sawed at the air in the middle of the room and, beyond it, a broad-shouldered man sat cross-legged, watching Austin with unflinching attention.

"Please," the man said. "Sit."

The voice was familiar.

As Austin's eyes adjusted, the soft shadows sharpened and the stranger came into crisp focus. He sat shirtless on the other side of the fire. His face tilted down as he stirred the coals with a stick, sending sparks into the air like fireflies. The flames threw a shadow across half his face, but there was no mistake.

It was Outlaw.

A figment in Austin's mind?

Outlaw's dark hair fell to his shoulders, strands of it fluttering on a current of air Austin did not feel. Black leather cords with tassels encircled the man's biceps. The muscles in his arms were defined, like ropes pulled taut, and a large tribal tattoo marked his right shoulder. Strong hands with pronounced veins rested on his knees, adorned with silver rings that glinted in the light. The man bore the look and air of a warrior, but Austin felt no threat from him.

His eyes were drawn to necklace around the man's neck, a braided-leather cord suspending to a necklace stone medallion over the center of his chest. The dim light obscured its details, but Austin knew it perfectly: an "O" meticulously carved in the middle, surrounded by tribal markings. And a single word: *Deditio.*

"You," Austin said. "I found you."

"Of course you did." The man sat upright and the fire illuminated his face. A toothpick rolled from one corner of his mouth to the other. He wasn't dressed as he had been when they first met in Boston—in a long black duster, motorcycle boots, jeans—but there was no doubt it was him. Stephen Carter, the man Austin knew as Outlaw.

Austin still wasn't sure if their previous encounter had been real or something else, a dream or hallucination.

"How did you get here?" Austin said.

"Same as you, I suspect."

"But . . . *how?*"

"Rest awhile. You look tired." A slight smile shaped his lips as he motioned for Austin to sit. Outlaw's eyes glinted with an intensity that radiated not just from his eyes, but from his entire being. It was the kind of confidence known only by those who'd walked the world's length and width, seen too much, and survived.

Austin crouched, resting his arms on his knees, and studied the man for a long moment. Outlaw's smile shifted a bit, as if amused by Austin's confusion.

"Where am I?" Austin said.

"Here, of course," the man said, and swept his hand through the air. "The place you intended to be. The place where everything can change." His smile faded. "That's what you wanted, isn't it, to find the place where you can heal your mind?"

"You can see me," Austin said. "How?"

"The same way you can see me." He pointed to his eyes. "It's very simple." He paused. "Even after all this time, I see that your mind is still using you."

"My mind isn't using me, it *is* me. It's who I am."

"So it would have you believe."

"It's what I believe."

"And that is your greatest source of pain," Outlaw said. "A mind focused on itself fears death above all else. It keeps you addicted to half-truths and illusions so you won't realize what it desperately wants to keep from you."

"Which is what?"

"The truth about what you really are. You've already forgotten what I once spoke to you. You're trapped inside," he said, tapping his temple. "This is the root of your suffering."

"Or my salvation," Austin answered.

"Tell me," Outlaw tilted his head to the side and his smile faded. "How's that working for you? Thinking your way to freedom and peace?"

The man's words weren't laced with any judgment, yet they sliced straight through Austin. How was that working for him? Fantastically, that's how. Maybe he never skipped down the road, giddy to face each day, but at least he found purpose in the pursuit of knowledge. If life wasn't about knowing more, learning more, experiencing more, then what was it about?

"Just fine, thank you," Austin said.

Outlaw chuckled. "Jika jika jawa, madman talking."

"I'm not the one who's sitting in a loincloth in the middle of nowhere."

"Maybe you should consider that this here—" Outlaw looked around, then squinted up at him, "is the middle of *everywhere*."

Austin took in his surroundings. "Is this real?"

"It depends on your perspective of real."

"No, it doesn't. What's real is real. Only perception is subjective."

"If that's true, then what's absolute?"

"Everything that can be measured. The observable, material universe."

"And that which you can't observe?" Outlaw arched a single brow. "Is that also real?"

"If we can't observe something it's only because we haven't determined how yet."

"Tell me, what do you observe in this moment?"

For a moment the hut was filled only with the sound of wood popping in the flame. "A hut. This fire. You. The ground beneath us."

"All real because . . ."

"I know it is," Austin said.

"You *think*, therefore the world *is* and you *are*."

"Of course. The mind is what gives reality form. It's the greatest gift we ever received from nature. The experiencing of natural phenomena is not only reality itself, but all of reality."

"I see. And without our minds, without the ability to process the world around us, we are . . . ?"

"Dead. The moment our biological minds die, so do we. There's nothing more."

"Nothing?"

"Nothing," Austin said and set his jaw.

"Interesting." Outlaw leaned forward. "We know this fire exists because, if I touch it"—he stretched his hand toward the flame—"it should burn me. That is the only possible outcome, yes?"

"Of course. Hold it there long enough and physical laws guarantee that you'll be burned."

Austin's eyes followed the man's hand as it hovered over the dancing flame, mere inches from it. After a few seconds he balled his hand into a fist, as if snatching something from the air, and drew it back slowly.

"And what of that which defies physical laws? That which we cannot explain." He said and opened his hand, turning it palm up. A bluish-white sphere of flame the size of a walnut swirled above his hand.

Slowly, he tilted his hand as if he planned to drop the ball to the ground. Yet, when he drew his hand away, it neither fell nor disappeared. Instead, it hung suspended in midair.

"Everything can be explained . . . eventually." Austin sat, unmoved. "*Everything*. There are things we simply haven't figured out . . . *yet*. But we will."

"Things like what you've seen through your experiments. Like this moment."

"Yes."

"What if there are things that simply cannot be explained and never will be?"

"Then they don't exist. Everything we see and can't see, all the way down to the quantum level, will eventually be explainable."

"And what of mystery?"

"It's simply another word for ignorance."

"Perhaps," Outlaw said and blew gently on the flame, sending it drifting back into the fire like a tumbling planet, where it unraveled and disappeared. "But if that's the case, then tell me, which are you?"

The question caught him off guard. "What?"

"Which are you: illusion or reality?"

"That's a ridiculous question."

"Perhaps I should state it differently."

Austin looked up from the fire and realized that the walls had vanished and the two of them were no longer inside the hut, but in a flat plain that seemed to stretch forever in every direction. The jungle was gone and the dark sky was moonless, filled with too many stars for the mind to hold. Every few seconds a speck of light—a shooting star, a comet—streaked across the sky, trailing a scratch of fading light.

Outlaw smiled. "In your world, everything is rooted in time. How long have we been talking? Do you know?"

Austin glimpsed his watch. "A few minutes."

"And in this moment, are you real?"

"Of course I am."

"Are you sure? Back in San Francisco your body has been floating for less than a minute, yet it's felt far longer hasn't it?"

He hesitated. "Yes."

"Your body is in San Francisco." Outlaw paused. "Is that also real?"

Austin flinched at the thought.

The man continued. "A better question might be: *Which* of you is really you? The one sitting in front of me now . . . or the one in your apartment at this moment?"

Austin hesitated. "Both. I'm clearly here, talking to you. I see you, I smell the fire, I feel its heat."

"Some might say that your version of reality is impossible. One person in two places at once. Seems ridiculous, don't you think?"

"To some, maybe."

"Such as those who believe that material reality is all there is?"

"Yes."

He tilted his head down slightly. "People like you."

"I . . ." His thoughts shuddered to a halt.

"You see what I mean." Outlaw said.

"What are you suggesting?"

"Not suggesting, merely reporting what I see. What you know as real is only real in part. You see the world through a darkened glass. You've begun to tap into a reality that most people would ridicule if you tried to explain it, an existence just beneath the skin of the seen world. The problem is, most do not have the eyes to see it."

"Or the knowledge."

"Knowledge is a tool, a pathway that's useful for a time, but only for a time. I can tell you, there is a way of being that doesn't rely on knowledge at all and where thinking is a great hindrance. Knowing *about* and knowing are two different things entirely."

Anger kindled within Austin. "Thinking is a tremendous ability."

"You cannot trust what you think you know," Outlaw said. "You have to let go of what you think you know. There's a narrow Way where all things are possible. The price to walk it is death, which is why it's such a rare find, a treasure buried in a field. Most will never seek it because they're terrified of what they will find."

"I'm not afraid."

Outlaw met his gaze and held it. "Yes. Actually, you are."

"If you know so much, tell me how to tap into the next level. I know the answer to healing my tumor is within reach. How do I get to that place?"

"I told you once, but you weren't ready to listen."

"Here I am. I'm ready."

"Ready for the truth?"

"I'd give everything I have for it," Austin said.

Outlaw was silent for a moment. A look of deep sadness crossed his face. "And you will."

A chill prickled Austin's skin. He didn't like the way Outlaw had said that.

"When the time comes," Outlaw said, "let go of all you know. See the small gods that you've made for what they are. Let them shrivel to dust and die. You know about many things, but *knowing* isn't the same as *understanding*. To truly understand demands surrender of everything, even the very need to know. Only when you're ready to empty yourself completely will you understand completely. Until then, you'll remain in darkness."

"I know far more than I did in Boston."

"And here you are, still blind," he said as the wind picked up, bending the flames. "You have a mind, but you are not your mind. You have a body, but you are not your body. What is the essence of you, the real you, is without beginning or end. You were an eternal thought held in the mind of the Creator before time began. An eternal thought that always was, is, and will be forever, even after your costume has returned to dust."

Dirt began to swirl violently in the air, steamrolling across the plain in an instant, and peppered Austin's face. He lifted his hand to shield his eyes; the dust churned faster and grew thicker.

He glanced at his watch: one second to go. The world closed around him and the air thickened. "No! Wait!"

"Trouble is coming," Outlaw said. "Save her."

Austin leaped to his feet, leaning into the wind, which now roared in his ears like a freight train. He took a step forward. The fire was gone.

"Where are you?" he yelled. "Wait! Save who?"

The wind swelled, pelting him with dust and gravel, biting into his flesh. It forced him to one knee. He dropped his head and shielded it with an arm. The earth shook beneath the sound of the fierce wind. He clenched his eyes tight and dropped onto the ground, curling into a ball. The rumbling grew louder, like an approaching jet. Closer and closer it came until it seemed right on top of him. Then, with a deafening whoosh and blinding flash—as bright and fast as lightning—the world disintegrated around him.

All was silent.

3.2

"AUSTIN?" I called, but heard no answer.

One moment I had been with him, standing on the crest of Mt. Everest, and the next I was here, wherever here was. My last thought had been of the second doorway, the black one Austin had described and hoped would lead us to another level.

Was this what lay beyond? A stinking alleyway? Was he here too?

I tilted my head to peer up. Clouds raced overhead, but like they do in time-lapse videos—too fast to be real, too vivid not to be. I blinked and the clouds slowed. A flock of purple-black ravens flitted through the air then vanished.

I was standing in a filthy, trash-clogged alley between two crumbling brick buildings. The humid air smelled like damp earth and decay. It was as far from the pristine beauty of the mountains as anyone could imagine.

My watch showed that only a second had passed since I'd stepped through the rip.

Where are you, Austin?

All around me, flies buzzed over piles of reeking trash. A mangy, emaciated dog sniffed at a pile. It rooted into the garbage, digging and snuffling. With a growl, it plunged in and backed out with a black rat dangling from its mouth.

The rodent twitched and squealed before going limp. The dog tossed its head back and bit hard, crunching into bones. It raced past me, claws clicking a crazed rhythm against the concrete. At the alley's end, it rounded a corner and disappeared.

That's when I noticed the people: a thick crowd of them at the mouth of the alley, none looking my way. Beyond them, cars congested a city street. But there was no sound and—stranger still—no movement. The people and cars were all frozen in the act of streaming past the alley in both directions.

Frozen?

Pushing off the wall, I walked toward them, lightheaded at the sight, steadying myself with a hand skimming along the wall. The city around me was as silent as a country meadow. The air was warm and damp; the decaying brick wall crumbled under my fingertips. This wasn't anywhere I recognized, and I couldn't wait around. If Austin was here, he wasn't in the alleyway.

Then a voice reached me. It was the sound of a girl singing.

"Who's there?" I said and stopped in the middle of the alley, scanning my surroundings. Trash and filth. Nothing more.

I began walking and heard the voice again. It reverberated off the muck-caked walls. I realized it emanated from outside the alleyway, from the city street ahead of me. I ran forward.

Coming out of the alley was like breaking the surface of a dark ocean. Suddenly sunlight blinded me and warmed my skin. I blinked against it and took in the scene: in every direction, the streets were clogged with rickshaws and motorbikes and taxis—all of them covered in a layer of dust so thick their colors had muted to a universal gray.

Gaunt cows, rib cages bulging, stood motionless in the streets. And the people: dust covered and bustling about, but that was just it. They *weren't* bustling. Maybe they had been once, but now, they stood, most in midstride, totally still and stiff. It was as if I'd stepped into a painstakingly rendered diorama of a busy city.

My mind scrambled for answers, but this was so foreign, so weird and surreal, my brain couldn't even form the questions.

I walked slowly through the crowd that packed the sidewalk and spilled into the street. There were men and women of every age, children as well. Most were dressed in rags and covered from head to foot in the thick dust that clung to everything.

But where—?

India.

The thought came on its own. I was sure—somehow—that I was in the slums of Calcutta. This is where my mother grew up and these were the streets from which the Catholic nuns had rescued her as a child. Had my subconscious brought me here?

I stepped into the street, passing beside two men frozen midstride in front of a rickshaw. How long had they all been like this?

Pausing, I leaned close to see if they were real, but I knew they were. Where the dust had blown or fallen or streaked off, their brown skin was slick with glistening sweat and their hair was damp and matted. The organic smell of life—sweat and dirt mixed with the aromas of warm bread and curry—hit me like a physical slap. As did the acrid odor of human waste, which pooled and caked in the street's shallow gutters.

Despite the stillness, everything seemed vividly alive and vital. Or perhaps it was that my senses were hypertuned to it all in a new way. It was strange, but I felt no repulsion, no discomfort.

Then a girl, a beggar with her right hand stretching out to a tangle of people that crowded around her, caught my attention. She was young, maybe no older than seven or eight, and clothed in a dress of filthy, threadbare rags. The child was emaciated and covered in dirt, but still beautiful. The scene reminded me of a photo my mom had shown me once, the only photo of her as a young girl in India.

This was my mother? Surely not. It had to be a trick of my mind, however real it seemed.

The beautiful singing had been coming from the child. Unlike the others, she was moving. I stood there, watching this girl who had called to the people crowding around her with the voice of an angel.

There was something incredibly different about her. Despite her physical condition, everything about her seemed unusually vibrant. Her eyes locked with mine and she smiled.

"Hello," she said, a sweet accent giving the word a singsong quality.

Startled, I took a tentative step toward her. "You can talk," I said.

"Of course I can," she said with a giggle. "So can you."

"And you can see me," I said. Austin was the only one who could see me in the Hacks. How was it possible that she could too? The thought brought Austin to mind and I wondered where he was.

"He's where he's meant to be, just as you are," she said, answering my thoughts. "Don't worry. He's safe."

"How . . . ?" I knelt down in front of the girl, coming eye to eye with her.

The child brushed my cheek with her hand. "You're very pretty. I like your eyes. They're like mine, very dark."

"Yes, they are," I said with a smile. "Thank you."

There was so much joy in the girl's face, the kind that everyone wants, but no one ever seems able to find and hang on to. If the world around her was terrible, she seemed not to notice. Maybe she was too young to realize the awfulness of this place.

"You will be my friend, okay?" she said.

"Of course I will."

"Good, good. I'm glad you come to my beautiful home." She held my gaze as if she'd answered my thought for me. "So glad. It's a perfect place for you, yes?"

I was silent. How could she possibly say that? The girl was suffering in a hell on earth. How was that perfect and why would anyone want to be here at all?

The girl took my hand. "You see this?" She swept her free hand through the air. "No need for pity in your eyes. God has abandoned this place, you think. The life is a mistake. Better to forget," she said, shaking her head. "Better to forget. This is what you think."

"I'm sorry," I said. "No, I don't think your life is a mistake." But I did, and I knew she'd felt it the instant our eyes had met. If there was no barrier between my thoughts and Austin's in the Hack then it was probably true now. With her.

The child's eyes were soft and gentle. "It's okay," she said softly. "We are meant to be born, meant to live—you and me—otherwise we're not born. Yes?"

"Yes." I nodded.

"Life is a gift. Things are not always as they look. Being hungry reminds me to be grateful when I have food. For things to live other things must die. This the way of life. What you see as suffering may be what is needed. All things matter—small things, big things—but we hold only a corner of the picture. We think our corner is everything." She smiled. "It's only just a corner." The girl was silent for a long moment and then released my hand. "I've waited a long time for you."

"You've waited for me?"

She watched me with great interest for several seconds, then her brow furrowed. "You are in great suffering. Great suffering, yes?"

"Suffering? I . . . I don't know."

"Questions," she said. "Many, many questions but they make you suffer very much. They crush you like a stone the size of the world. Why, why, why? This is the worst question of all. A very terrible question."

I was lost in her gaze. They weren't the eyes of a child, but someone who seemed far older, older than time itself. There was peace in them. It all felt like a dream, the kind that made no sense at all. I didn't know where I was or why I was there or who this girl was.

"You are desperate," she said. "I see it. This is true?"

I nodded and replied reflexively: "Yes."

She looked at me a long time without speaking. Her eyes flicked left to right quickly as though she were reading something that had been written on my face.

Finally she spoke in her gentle, singsong voice. "You believe you have lost so much. So much, but it is not your fault. You think it was, but you're wrong. All of it had to happen. It's part of the unfolding. You do not see it yet, but you can if you want."

"See what?"

"That your corner is just a corner. There's much more to your beautiful picture."

A lump worked itself into my throat.

She smiled a knowing smile. "Do not fear what's coming. It cannot hurt you. Go to your mother. She will teach you all you need to know. She needs you now. Save her, Nyah. Save your mother and you too will be saved."

"What are you talking about? What's coming? My mom is going to be okay, right?"

"We all die. All of us," she said. "But she needs you now. Go to her. The doorway you seek is one thing only—surrender. Only that will set you free and her too."

"To what? Surrender to what? What's going to happen?" Desperation made my voice shrill.

The girl leaned forward and took the sides of my head in her hands. Gently, she pulled me close until our foreheads touched. "You are so loved. There is no need to fear. Everything is okay. Everything. Let go," she whispered. "Let go."

"Please tell me what you mean." I felt something within me melt away and tears welled in my eyes. "What's going to be okay? Just tell me."

"Let go," she said again. "Your ashes will be beautiful again."

The tears came unbidden then. I could barely say it, but I did,

"Please, just tell me what's going to happen to my mom. What did you mean? Is she going to die? I have to know."

"Do not fear," she said and pressed her lips to the top of my head, kissing the scar that stretched across it.

When she did a jolt of electricity entered through the top of my head and shot through my body. Warmth ignited at the base of my spine and grew hotter as it climbed upward and into my head. Every inch of my body prickled with electricity as the sensation spread through my arms and chest, then down through my legs.

I gasped for breath, but every draw of air made the sensation in my body swell until it was nearly unbearable—not pain, but pleasure so raw I was sure my skin would catch fire.

I gripped the girl's arms and held tight. What was happening to me?

Like a wave, the energy churning inside me climbed again, but this time it seemed to draw the energy from the rest of my body. I could feel it drain from the muscle fibers in my legs and chest as it was pulled through my spine and into my throat.

My lips began to burn and tremble. Just as I thought my lungs would burst into flames, I heard myself exhale once. It sounded as loud as the wind itself and the force of it shook my body.

As quickly as it had started, the sound disappeared. The world was once again quiet, and my body was back to normal.

I stared, trembling and wide-eyed, at the beggar girl. The air sizzled as if lightning had struck nearby.

"There," she said. "So you will see."

"But how . . ."

"I take it from you. Do not carry it anymore. No more. Let go of your need to carry it. Your scars are not you." Her eyes went to my head. "Not anymore."

A shudder ran through me. Slowly, I lifted a hand to my head and touched the place the girl had kissed. I ran my hand over it again, feeling for the deep scar carved into my head. It was gone.

"It's . . . not possible," I said. My voice was shaking, my hands trembling. I clenched my eyes tight, feeling the hot tears squeezing through.

"So you say," the girl said. The world shifted audibly like a film frame clicking into place. Then there was a roar of sound—blaring horns, yelling men, and traffic—as the world around me came to life.

"Go to her," the girl said, her voice quieter now against the din.

I knelt there, eyes closed, lungs heaving. If the girl could heal me, maybe she could heal my mom. Or Austin. She could heal his tumor.

I said, "Should I bring my mom here . . . and Austin?" I opened my eyes.

The girl had disappeared.

I scanned the crowd, but there was no sign of her. I stood and turned in a complete circle. People shuffled, cars rolled, but the girl had slipped away. I needed to find her, needed to know who she was.

I pushed forward, shuffling through the thick crowd. A few steps into the street I caught a glimpse of her darting away, and I ran after her. The sidewalk and street were swollen with people all streaming toward me. I struggled and pushed for each step.

"Wait!" I yelled, but she didn't slow.

I dodged a group of women gathered in the middle of the sidewalk and surged forward. The girl was only ten paces ahead of me, slipping through the crowded streets. "Hey!" I said. She didn't turn, didn't pause.

"Come back!" My voice cracked with desperation.

The girl stopped and turned around, hands at her sides. She smiled and said something else, but the street noise snatched her words away.

"What?" I called, stumbling closer.

It was then that I noticed the shadows stretching through the streets like long fingers. I peered up at the sky as the sun dimmed. A thick swirl of cast iron clouds swirled low over the city like a monster hurricane.

The Hack was ending.

No! Not yet!

The child was only three paces from me now, walking along the crumbling sidewalk. The wind howled. "Wait!" I said. "Who are you? What's your name?" I grabbed for her, my fingers falling short.

I looked up just as the spinning cloud descended. No one seemed to notice the clouds or the wind. How could they not see it? Why weren't they shouting, pointing, running for cover?

I spun around, eyes searching frantically for the girl. Dust swirled all around and the wind howled louder until I was sure it couldn't get any louder. A gust toppled me, and I slammed to the ground. I screamed, a howl of fear and anguish, but there was no one to hear me. The streets were empty. The people were gone, as were the cars and rickshaws, the buildings and cows.

Everything was gone. Everything.

The world went dark and for a moment that stretched forever, I could hear only the frantic thump of my own heart and the terrible wind. I felt the familiar sensation of something ending, everything ending—I'd felt it in the hospital when the world had broken apart and vanished. It was an almost unbearable anticipation, a crescendo trembling for release.

"Austin!" I screamed.

My arms flailed and water splashed around me. I tasted it on my lips. Saltwater.

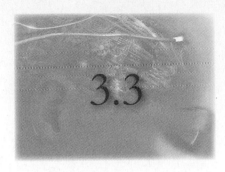

3.3

Day Three
9:15 PM

TEN MINUTES—that's all that separated Jon Stone from erasing this problem and the girl along with it. He trusted the intelligence he'd received and the girl's location, while not confirmed, was highly probable. With any luck she was still in the building. If not, he would wait until she returned.

His objective was simple: discover what she knew, retrieve the data, then burn every thread that led back to BlakBox. He would be fast and thorough, as he'd promised Bell. Every moment she lived put them at greater risk of exposure. Soon, this would all be nothing more than a sweet memory to savor when he pondered jobs well done.

Nine minutes.

Stone opened the glove compartment, removed his Glock semiautomatic pistol, and set it in the center console. He couldn't simply kill the girl, not until he first learned what she knew, what she'd told others, and where she'd stashed the files. That would require some persuasion, of course. Nothing personal, just business. Always just business.

He turned right, following the directions from the dash-mounted GPS. The digital clock marked the passage of more time.

Eight minutes.

3.4

Day Three
9:20 PM

I STARED at my own reflection in the windowpane overlooking the Bay from Austin's apartment. The girl looking back at me seemed like a stranger, so far away. So different.

As I held the cell phone to my ear with one hand, I traced my still trembling fingers over the smooth skin that had once borne a painful reminder of my traumatic past—a jagged, ugly wound that I'd covered up and hid from everyone, including myself. In place of the fleshy, puckered seam that had marred my scalp, there was now flawless skin.

What exactly had happened to me?

That's what Austin had wanted to know. Apparently his Hack had been as bizarre as mine, with the strange jungle and finding Outlaw. But the moment he'd seen my head, he became obsessed with recording every detail of my experience. Whatever I had tapped into changed physical reality. I'd experienced the ultimate goal of all his experiments, but it hadn't been what I'd expected. I didn't know what had happened, really.

"C'mon, Lettie. Answer the phone," I said, pacing now, chewing my fingernail. It was my fifth call.

"I can't take your call right now . . ."

Voicemail.

"It's me again. Call me. I'm worried." My concern was teetering on panic. Lettie had called me three times while we were in the Hack. She left one message, her words nearly unintelligible through heavy sobs: "It's your Mom, Nyah . . . Oh . . . oh . . . something's wrong . . . "—garbled words—" . . . hurry . . ."

The Indian girl's words came back to her: *She needs you now. Save her, Nyah. Save your mother.*

Whether the girl in the Hack was real or not didn't matter. I couldn't deny what she'd done to me. And if I couldn't deny that then what she'd said about Mom had to be true too. Mom was going to die. Isn't that what she'd said? I couldn't just let it happen.

"I have to go," I finally said, pocketing the phone and starting across the room.

"These numbers," Austin said, staring at the control console's monitors. "They're unbelievable." He shook his head in disbelief. He hadn't heard a word I'd said. He was so fixated on figuring out what had happened to me, I was pretty sure he was oblivious to the fact that he was still shirtless and dripping wet.

No, not fixated, obsessed. At that moment, all that mattered was the data right in front of him. I'd been physically changed and he had to know how. Had to know *right now.*

There was so much unusual data and so many statistical aberrations that at first Austin had thought the software was corrupt. The system could barely process it fast enough.

Only after running the diagnostics had he realized that we weren't looking at bad data or a system glitch at all. We were staring at hard evidence of the unexplainable. He was looking for a pattern, details beneath the details, the one elusive key that would open a treasure chest of answers.

Why had the last Hack been so different from the others? It all seemed so bizarre, so confusing, so dreamlike, but it had been real. We'd accessed something massive, a layer of consciousness that neither of us could explain.

But that wouldn't stop him from trying. He was driven by the need to know. We both were, but for me that was secondary to Mom's well-being. The data would always be there, but my mom wouldn't.

I hurried across the room to where my backpack and motorcycle helmet sat on a table behind Austin. "I have to go," I said again, as I passed behind him. "Something's wrong with my mom. The girl must've been right."

He didn't bother to answer or look up. Lost in the mirrored maze of his thoughts, he likely didn't hear me at all.

"Austin?" I said as I shrugged into my backpack. "Did you hear me?"

He must've caught a glimpse of me walking toward the door because he jerked upright and turned in my direction. "Wait," he said. "Where you going?"

"To see my mom." I tugged a knit cap over my bald head.

"What? No, you can't leave."

"Yes, I can. Something's really wrong. I have to find out what."

"Hold on." He closed the distance between us.

I reached for the door first, but he planted a hand on it, bracing it closed.

"It's too dangerous out there," he said. "You know that."

"I don't have a choice. The girl said I had to save my mother."

"Listen, I know you're worried, and maybe what you experienced was true—"

"Maybe? Look at my head." I pulled off the cap. "There's no 'maybe' here."

"Stop and think before you leave. Don't you think the FBI's watching for you? The minute you get anywhere near your mom, they've got you. What then?"

"I don't know. I'll figure something out."

"You won't have time to figure anything out. You slipped away from them once. They won't let it happen again. And then there's BlakBox. They're probably watching for you too."

I stood silent. He was right, but it was a chance I was willing to take. It was Mom we were talking about. I slowly stretched the cap back over my head. I said, "I don't expect you to understand."

He slipped between me and the door, and put his hands on my shoulders. "I do understand," he said. "Your mom needs you. But she needs you free . . . and alive. And she needs what you discovered in your Hack, a cure. Stay here with me. Let's do another Hack, just one more. It'll only take a few minutes. We'll wait for Lettie to call you back. I'm sure everything's fine."

I shook off his hands. "I'm leaving." I pushed him aside and opened the door.

"I'm going to reprogram the Hack protocol and upgrade the amount of time we spend in the tanks . . ." Talking as if he hadn't heard me at all. His eyes blazed with determination. I remembered that I'd thought he was flirting with madness when he first told me about hacking. "Instead of setting the cycle for fifteen seconds," he continued, "I want to test run a five-minute dosage. It would give us the time we need to experiment more, to experience more."

"Five minutes? Austin, that sounds risky. You don't know what kind of stress going that long with have on your body."

"I have to go deeper."

"Listen to yourself," I said. "You need a break. We both do. We're running on fumes. I know you want to figure this out, so do I, but let's look at this with fresh eyes. Let me check on my mom, and when I come back we'll pick up right here. Promise."

His gaze narrowed on me. "Five more minutes. Just five more. Your mom is going to be fine."

"I don't know that and neither do you."

"I need to go deeper, and I need you here to do that." His voice was raw from exhaustion and his eyes were etched with red. They flitted from side to side. He hadn't slept in days and it was showing. And since seeing my healed scar, he'd let desperation get the better of him. It had him in its grip now, I could feel it. "Please," he said.

"No. But don't Hack until I get back. Promise me you won't. It's dangerous."

"You saw the numbers," he said, ignoring my words. "Your biometrics during the second half of the Hack were off the charts entirely, and your neural imagery looked like a . . . like a freaking electrical storm."

"Austin—"

"Something unprecedented has happened here! We're cracking the code. We can go farther. You're assuming the window will stay open, that we can return to that place you discovered anytime, but maybe we can't. We have to reset the system as quickly as possible and find a way to extend our Hacks."

"You know what the girl said to me."

He sighed and relented. "Okay. You're right. Go see your mom. But get back here. Soon."

"I won't be gone long. I promise."

"And be careful," he said. "Make sure you take the back way."

"Stop worrying. No one knows we're here, remember?"

Austin had pushed himself to his limits, maybe beyond them. But he was right about one thing: when it comes to breaking new ground, it's not the reasonable person who leads the way, and the history books never mention the guy who played it safe.

To set sail in uncharted waters . . . well, that required someone with a fixation on the horizon that bordered on lunacy, someone who sees the future before it becomes obvious to everyone else.

A person who's willing to die to prove that the world isn't flat after all.

A person like Austin, and that had me worried the most.

"Promise me you won't do it alone," I said. "Wait until I'm back before you hack again."

He stood silent.

"Promise me," I pressed.

He nodded. "Okay."

"I'll be back soon," I said and slipped out the door.

I left his building by using an old loading dock behind the building, pausing in the shadows to watch for signs of movement in the street before sprinting across it to the abandoned warehouse one block over. I slipped into the alleyway, ran to the end of it, and entered the old building through a rusted service door that opened to the dark, cavernous space. I'd parked my motorcycle out of sight, next to Austin's Jeep.

Helmet on now, I jumped on my bike, started it, and pulled onto the street with the girl's words echoing through my mind.

Save your mother.

I had to get to Mom. I had to know she was okay. I had to save her.

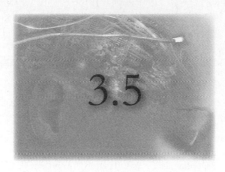

3.5

Day Three
9:28 PM

DARKENED WAREHOUSES, long forsaken in the name of progress, lined the quiet streets by the Bay. This was the girl's haven, her safe harbor. Or so she believed.

Stone pulled his black BMW onto a street lit by a single stuttering lamp. The ancient smell of seawater drifted through his open window.

As the car rounded the corner, its headlights swept across a storefront, glinting off the jagged edges of a vandalized window. The girl was in a building two blocks south. He would approach it from behind, park out of view, then make his way on foot. He wondered to whom the girl had run and whether that person would be there and thus require dispatching as well.

As he eased to a stop, something drew his attention—the burr of an engine echoing nearby. It was out of place in the deserted streets. A motorcycle.

He tilted his head, listening as he rolled forward and eased to a stop at the next cross street.

The engine whined louder, drawing closer. He looked through the passenger window just as a motorcycle emerged from an alleyway halfway down the street. Same model as the one registered to the girl. Had to be her.

The rider's head turned his way to check for traffic, and he dipped below the level of the dash for a second. The motorcycle turned away from him and sped down the street—fast, but not in a way that indicated she'd spotted him.

Stone pulled away from the curb and stomped the accelerator pedal to the floor. The engine growl filled the night air. A hundred yards ahead, the motorcycle's taillight flickered red, the bike leaned hard to the left and disappeared down another alley.

He roared past the alley, glimpsing the rider as he sped by. The gap between the buildings was too narrow for him to give chase. The only option was to circle the building and hope the girl would turn in his direction when she emerged on the adjacent street.

Stone rounded the building and circled the block, but the girl was already gone. She'd either seen him, or was exercising precautionary maneuvers to avoid tails she hadn't detected. He drove back to the first alleyway from which she'd emerged and parked nearby.

He found the warehouse door cracked open. The smell of the motorcycle's exhaust still hung in the air when he entered. In one corner sat a vehicle covered by a tattered canvas tarp, looking like a half-washed-away sand sculpture. He stripped off the cover, revealing an old Jeep, and searched the vehicle. No registration papers and the identification number had been filed off; there wasn't even a stray crumpled receipt that might betray the owner's identity.

He lifted his phone and dialed a number. "Run this plate," he said and recited the dusty numbers from the California plates.

Computer keys clicked on the other end. "Reported as stolen two years ago."

"Give me a trace on—" His words were interrupted by an incoming call. He glanced at the screen. Bell. No hesitation, he clicked over. "Sir."

"The mother's been moved to the hospital," Bell said.

"The girl just left the warehouse," he said as he hurried back to the alley. "Must be where she's headed."

"The FBI is there too."

"I'm on my way," Stone said, already halfway to his car. "We need to get to her first."

3.6

Day Three
9:45 PM

AS I SPED through the streets, my mind grappled with too many thoughts: Maybe Lettie wasn't answering because she'd left her phone in her purse. Maybe it was much worse than that. *Something's wrong . . . hurry . . .* What if Mom died without me by her side? No, I could never live with that.

The world blurred past, it seemed, in mere seconds and I was soon leaving the highway for the side streets near Cedar Ridge, expecting the black car I'd seen by Austin's to suddenly appear. But there was no sign of it.

I turned into a shopping-center parking lot adjacent to the assisted-care campus and found an empty space on the far end, out of sight. Austin was probably right; Jill likely had surveillance on the building so I couldn't simply waltz in the front door.

I would cross the drainage ditch that cut between the properties and circle behind the building to Mom's apartment, which had a small patio with a sliding glass door. I'd slip in unnoticed, check on her and leave. Piece of cake.

By the time I reached the other side of the ditch I felt a knife of uneasiness in my gut. I eased forward, nearing the corner of the building. Mom's apartment was on the back side of the complex, tenth from the end.

In and get out. No problem.

My gaze snapped toward shadows, distant headlights, trash blowing in the wind—I was that jumpy. The FBI probably had eyes on me now. What would I do if they moved in? I couldn't run back to Austin's. That would put not only him at jeopardy, but also everything we'd accomplished. The research was too important—not just to Austin, but to me—to put it at risk. Mom *needed* our research. I believed that more than ever with this latest scare and now that I'd experienced healing myself. It wasn't a fantasy or pipe dream. It was real: Mom could be cured.

Seconds dragged with each step. One by one, patio lights snapped on as my passing triggering their motion sensors. I expected black vehicles to come roaring from every direction, boxing me in with men hanging out of the windows, weapons drawn. But so far, so good. In fact, the campus was strangely still.

I reached her patio without incident. I stepped up to the sliding glass door and quietly unlocked it. I tugged it open and leaned my head into the drapes. No voices, no noise, no lights, so I eased the material aside and stepped through. My pulse thumped hard as I moved deeper into the room, passing near the foot of Mom's bed, reaching my hand down to the covers.

The bed was empty.

I followed its edge to the bedside table and felt for the lamp. My heart lurched into my throat when I found it tipped onto its side on the table. I righted it and switched it on. The top bedsheet had been stripped off and tossed in a tangled heap on the floor, partially covering the sparkling shards and slivers of a shattered drinking glass strewn across the floor. Mom's wheelchair lay on its side, shoved against the closet door.

What had happened here? Where was everyone?

My first thought: BlakBox. What if they'd grabbed my family to get to me? The mere thought of it turned my fear into boiling anger. I had to do something. I had to find them.

A voice from the living room reached me, too softly spoken to discern male or female, but I knew it wasn't Mom or Lettie. I tiptoed to the nearly closed bedroom door and peeked through the opening into the hallway. Light from the living room fell across the hallway floor, and the voice came again. A shadow passed through the light.

I grabbed a heavy metal statuette of the Statue of Liberty sitting on Mom's dresser and stepped into the hallway. I raised it as I made my way toward the voice. As I drew near, I realized it was a woman, and her tone was urgent. I reached the end of the hallway and turned the corner, Lady Liberty ready to crack some skulls.

Jill's worried eyes met mine as she turned in my direction, cell phone pressed to her ear. "I have her," she said. "She's here."

I lowered the statuette and glanced around the room. We were alone and the door to the hallway was half open.

"What's going on?" I said. "Where's my mom?"

"Bring the car around," she said into the phone. She thumbed a button on the phone and dropped it into a pocket of her beige blazer. "Where have you been?" she asked me.

"Jill, where's my mom?" I snapped.

She glanced at the beanie on my head. Then reached for my arm. "You should sit down."

I jerked away. "I don't want to sit down! What's going on?"

"Lettie found your mother unconscious a couple hours ago. She called me when she couldn't reach you."

"Unconscious? What . . . what . . . ? Where is she?"

Something's wrong . . . hurry . . .

She needs you now. Save her, Nyah. Save your mother.

"She's in good hands. The ambulance got here within minutes and took her to General Hospital. She's in the emergency room right now."

My heart felt like it was in free fall. "How is she?"

"She's alive. They're running tests now to figure out what's wrong. I'm sorry."

"I have to get there," I said and started toward the front door. She caught me by the arm.

"Not by yourself you're not," she said. "Not after your disappearing act."

"Are you serious?" I tried to tug my arm free, but her grip was too tight. "My Mom's *dying.*"

"You don't know that."

I was breathing hard now. "Yes, I do."

A beat.

Letting out a heavy sigh, she brushed past me and began pulling me toward the door. "Come on. I'll take you to the hospital myself." I stumbled behind her, feeling like a child caught doing something really awful. "Have you noticed anyone following you?" she asked.

"Yeah, but I think I'm just being paranoid."

"Maybe not," she said.

Before we reached it, the front door opened and a man stepped into the opening. He wore jeans, a white shirt, and Kevlar vest emblazoned with "FBI" over the chest. "Car's out front," he said.

"You're hurting me."

"Get used to it," Jill said. "I *might* let you go once we're in the car, I haven't decided. But one thing's certain: I'm not letting you out of my sight until this thing's over."

3.7

Day Three
10:46 PM

JILL PEPPERED me with questions during the ride: Where had I gone? Who had I seen? What had I been doing? I couldn't tell her the truth, so I made up a story about staying mobile and out of sight, crashing at bus stations and eating stale vending-machine food.

We found Lettie in a small waiting room on the hospital's main floor. There was nothing to do but wait. So I sat there, chewing my fingernails, waiting. After the accident, I spent way too much time in the hospital, which is why I hate them so much. They smell like death and loss; their lights are too bright and too white, like an autopsy room; and if you're not on a gurney, people want to know why. And now here I was in one again, just as powerless and nauseated and scared as I was the last time.

Dr. Benton appeared fifteen minutes later. Lettie and I stood. She patted my hand and whispered, "It's going to be all right."

As he approached, Dr. Benton lifted his fist to his mouth and cleared his throat. A heavy stone settled in my gut. Everyone has a tell, a nervous tic that gives away the truth no matter how much they try to conceal it. I'd gotten enough bad news from him to know his—and that was it, his tell: clearing his throat.

"No," I whispered back. "Nothing's going to be all right."

"How is she?" Lettie asked the doctor.

"Resting comfortably. We just moved her to a private room."

"What happened?" I asked.

"She suffered an ischemic stroke caused by a blood clot in her brain."

"Her brain?" Lettie said, a tremor in her voice. "But the clot you found was in her leg, wasn't it?"

"That's right, it was. It seems likely that the medication used to treat the clot caused it to break loose. It passed through her bloodstream and, eventually, lodged in her brain tissue. I'm afraid the neurological damage she suffered is severe."

"What does that mean, severe?" I said.

"There are portions of her brain that were significantly starved of oxygen when the clot constricted her blood supply. These parts of her brain have lost all function."

"She's brain dead?" I said. "Is that what you're saying?"

"Not entirely," he said. "She's lost her ability to speak and respond to simple commands. She's unresponsive to every test that we use to gauge cognitive awareness. Her condition is fragile; however, at the moment she's breathing on her own, which is an encouraging sign. I think our best course of action now is to ensure that she's comfortable while we wait and let things run their course."

"You mean wait for her to die," I said.

"Nyah . . ." Lettie said, gripping my arm.

"I'm sorry," the doctor said. "There's little we can do. Surgery is too risky and I'm not sure any treatment would be beneficial at this point. She's remarkably stable for now, which is a miracle in itself. We'll have to do some more tests and wait it out."

"But she'll never speak again or wake up?" I said. *Or laugh or hug me or . . . or . . .* I couldn't handle this. Instead of breaking down, my mind went into proactive mode: *I won't let this happen to her! I won't!*

He shook his head. "I'm sorry," Dr. Benton said, "but you have to prepare yourself for the possibility that she may not recover."

My eyes blurred. "I want to see her."

"Of course. I'll take you upstairs."

He held the door open and we stepped into the hall, Lettie gripping my arm, Jill practically glued to my back. The moment we emerged I saw a man waiting by the nurse's station. It was the agent who'd driven Jill and me to the hospital. He stepped toward us.

"Dr. Benton's taking us to see her mother," Jill said to him. "Keep your eyes open." Then to Dr. Benton: "Where's her room?"

"Twelfth floor," he said.

"I'm staying with them," Jill said to the agent. "If anything seems out of place, call me."

The agent nodded.

"Follow me," Dr. Benton said and led us to the elevator.

My thoughts spiraled as the elevator climbed upward. I held tight to Lettie's hand. It was all happening so fast. It probably was the last time I'd ever see my mom, but how do you say good-bye when all you want to do is hold on?

Outside the elevator on the twelfth floor, Jill touched my shoulder. "I'm sorry, but we can't stay long," she said. "Just a few minutes is all I can give you. After we know you're safe and the dust settles, you can come back, okay?"

"Sure," I said, feeling numb.

Unlike the main floor, there was no nurse's station here, just an alcove from which four hallways branched like tunnels into the unknown.

"This way," Dr. Benton said and led us down the rightmost hallway. The lighting was softer here than on the main floor, almost tranquil; it was as quiet as a library and we saw no one else.

"So peaceful." Lettie said, trying to find something comforting to say, that was Lettie. Mom's room was at the end, on the left. The door was open and a bulging yellow folder sat in a basket by the door. Dr.

Benton grabbed it as we entered and flipped it open.

I didn't want to go in. Not really. But I did.

Except for the rhythmic beep of the heart monitor, the room was still. Lettie stifled a cry as she approached the bed where Mom lay corpse still, her head propped up by a pillow.

I struggled to catch my breath when I saw her. I'd last felt this way at my brother's and father's funerals—the feeling that I was looking at an empty shell that was once brimming with life and personality and potential, with whatever it was that made them *them*. I was staring at a husk, a puppet that my mom had once brought to life. A costume that didn't fit her anymore.

A knot formed in my throat and I choked it down.

Dr. Benton moved a wheelchair out of the way and leaned over the bed. Carefully, he lifted her right eyelid with his thumb and waved a penlight in front of it. We stood at the foot of the bed and watched. An IV ran into her arm and a cell-phone-sized device on her forearm monitored her heart rate.

Her chest rose and fell as she drew shallow breaths.

"She's not on a respirator?" Lettie said.

"We're not authorized," he said. "Elizabeth's medical file indicated that she doesn't wish for any extraordinary measures to prolong her life. That includes respiration."

I stepped closer and laid my hand on hers. Her face was so peaceful. Her hair spread across the pillow neatly. Someone had taken the time to brush it.

"I'll give you some privacy," Dr. Benton said and looked at Jill. It was a subtle hint, but she caught it.

She stepped up behind me and gave my shoulder a squeeze. "I'm going to step out too. If you need anything, I'll be close."

"There's a private waiting room down the other hall," Dr. Benton said. "I'll take you there. It's quiet and you can make phone calls or do whatever you need to do."

"Thanks, Jill," I said. "For everything."

She nodded and followed Dr. Benton into the hallway.

Lettie laid her purse at the foot of the bed, stepped to the far side, and took Mom's other hand. "I'm so sorry," she whispered.

We stood there, sniffing and wiping at our tears.

"This is my fault," I finally said.

"Why would you say such a thing, sweetheart? How could this be your fault?"

"You heard what Dr. Benton said. The medication they gave her for the clot in her leg likely caused this. It's my fault."

"No, it isn't."

"The vision I had was real. It was *real*. I thought it was a warning, something that we had time to change. You did too. Instead, it made things worse. If I hadn't had the vision then Dr. Benton would've never prescribed the medication and this wouldn't have happened."

"She's still alive. That's a gift."

"You call this alive?"

Lettie said nothing.

I stared down at Mom and ran my hand under my nose. "It'd have been better if you hadn't found her."

"Don't say that."

"It's true. Look at her. This is no way to live. She probably doesn't know we're even here."

"She knows," she whispered. "The real her knows."

"Maybe." I smeared the tears with the heel of my hand.

"God wasn't caught by surprise with this," Lettie said. "He knew this would happen and how it will turn out. It will turn out for good. Somehow. We just don't see the whole picture."

"Just a pathetic little corner," I said under my breath.

"I want to tell you something," she continued. "Hear me, okay?"

I nodded.

"One morning a few months after the accident I found your mom painting by her bedroom window. She'd pulled herself from bed and somehow gotten into that wheelchair. Well, I can't tell you how worried I was. What if she'd hit her head or something worse? I was beside myself, but your mother just chuckled at me and had that look in her eye. Know what she said?"

I shook my head.

"She looked at me and I knew it was a moment of clarity. Somehow she was there that morning. The spark that always lit your mother was there. She said, 'Life's kicked my ass, but that doesn't mean I have to stay down. As long as there's something I can do, I'm going to do it.' Then she went back to painting."

I smiled.

"That was the last time she remembered me," she said. "And you're right, it seems so unfair."

"She looks beautiful," I said and brushed my finger through her hair. She looked so peaceful. "Mind if I have a few minutes alone? I'd like to say good . . ." I choked back fresh tears. "I want to say good-bye."

"Sure. I'll be down the hall with Jill, okay? Take your time." Lettie came around the bed and gave me a hug from behind before leaving the room.

Everything was quiet. "I'm sorry, Mom. I'm so sorry."

I didn't expect her to answer me or move. I knew there was no hope of that, but that she simply lay there, as though already in her coffin, made my heart ache. I took a deep breath. *This will not do*, I thought. My entire life had been pulverized and there was nothing left, no pieces to scrape up and nowhere to go. Everything was gone.

Still, walking away from Mom now felt like giving up. She was clinging to life, what little of it she had to hold on to. And maybe that was enough—just enough of an ember for our consciousness hacking to rekindle her fire. If my scar could be healed, if all those case studies

Austin had told me about were true, then why couldn't Mom?

But if I left now, Jill would stash me away in some safe house with bars on the windows and agents watching me 24/7. No way I'd be able to return to Austin's apartment to continue unlocking the secrets of the universe. Sounds corny, I know, or melodramatic, but that's exactly what we were doing. How else can you describe changing reality?

Changing reality. Changing the inevitable. Changing Mom. Healing her.

Save her . . .

I leaned close and kissed her on the cheek. She still smelled like roses. I whispered, "I'm going to save you. I promise."

Saving her meant getting her out of there. That was the only way. I had to get her into the Hack and to the girl who'd healed me. The only way to do that was by taking Mom to Austin's apartment.

My eyes drifted to the foot of her bed and the red purse sitting there. Lettie's purse. I grabbed it and pulled it open. It was crammed with more things than anyone would ever need, but I only needed one thing: her van keys. They were right there on top and then they were in my hand.

I had to tell Austin. He needed to prepare the tanks. Time was of the essence. I reached to my back pocket, but the disposable cell phone Austin had given me wasn't there. I'd left it in my backpack, which was still at Cedar Ridge. I'd set it down before leaving with Jill.

Lettie's phone. I overturned her purse, dumping the contents onto the bed and retrieved her phone. I pictured Austin's landline number as I had jotted it on the back of a prescription order two years before and thumbed the buttons.

Austin's phone rang . . . rang . . . rang . . .

"Come on. Where are you?"

I only had minutes before Lettie returned. Minutes before Jill took me with her.

A click sounded on the other end. "Hello?" I said.

"The person at 415-327 . . ."

"No, no, no. Answer your phone, Austin."

". . . isn't available to take your call . . ."

"Crap."

"Please leave your message at the tone."

A beep.

"It's me. Call me when you get this." I left Lettie's number. I pocketed the phone and stood motionless, staring at my mom.

Move, I told myself. *No time to think . . . just move! Now!*

And I did.

3.8

Day Three
11:04 PM

JON STONE walked the starkly lit hallway of San Francisco General Hospital, the heels of his shoes clacking, clacking against the tiles.

The girl was in the building, he could feel her the way a shark could smell blood from miles away. He had to take her. Once she left with the FBI, getting to her would prove far more difficult, if not impossible. It was now or never. And never wasn't an option.

After securing her, he would head east into the Nevada desert and there, away from prying eyes, extract the information he needed. Then he would eliminate her.

Eliminate her. He smiled at that. What was with these word games people played, even with themselves? *Kill her.* He would kill her. Yes.

"May I help you?" A vibrant, large-haired woman said as he approached the first- floor information desk. She was all teeth and entirely too happy.

"I do hope so," he said, donning his best worried expression. "I'm looking for a family friend who was just admitted. This place is so big I don't know where to start."

"I know, right?" she said with a wave of her hand. He half expected her teeth to hop right out of her mouth. "It can be overwhelming. What's your friend's name, darling?"

"Parks," he said. "Elizabeth Parks."

After a few keystrokes on the computer she looked up. "She was just moved to a private room on twelve." She paused. "But I'm so sorry. Visiting hours are officially over."

He wrinkled his brow and checked his watch. "I'm actually on my way to the airport. This is the only chance I'll have to see her. Make an exception . . . please?"

She looked him over slowly. "Just a few minutes?" she said.

"I'll be in and out, I promise."

"When the nurse makes her rounds, you skedaddle." She smiled more broadly at her use of the word. "Deal?"

"Deal."

She twisted and pointed behind her. "You want to take the elevators down the hall, on the right."

"Thank you," he said and headed down the hall. When he reached the elevators, he continued past them to the end of the corridor. Without a glance back, he turned right and pushed through the doorway to the stairwell.

This time, the girl wouldn't get past him.

• • •

AUSTIN HEARD the sensory-deprivation tank close behind him as he headed for the control console. Water streamed off his body, leaving little puddles in his wake. He pressed a palm against his chest and felt his heart pounding as fast as a paint-mixing machine. He'd started without Nyah because—well, because progress, now when they were so close, was more important than the promise he'd made to her.

He'd made four solo Hacks since she'd left, each one longer than the previous one; the last one, he'd been under for four minutes. He had to ride the momentum, with or without her.

Subjecting his body to such stress was taking its toll, but nothing compared to the alternative. Desperate situations require measures sufficient for the task. He'd known what he would do before she walked out the door.

He had no other choice. He had to find Outlaw again and he couldn't wait.

Nyah had discovered the very thing he'd been searching for all along: the intersection of what *was* and what *could be*. It was that zero point on the quantum level that enabled energy to be changed, transforming physical reality.

He'd theorized about it, researched the efficacy of its existence, and had become convinced with time and his own experience that it was possible. But she had proven it beyond a doubt.

Now it was within reach and he couldn't simply let it slip away. If she could heal her scar then he could heal the tumor rotting his brain. Heal or die. There were no other options.

She had barely left the building before he'd rebooted the system and began formulating new protocols to extend the time he could spend inside the tank. The key was properly balancing the neurocompounds in the Kick with the frequency and placement of the laser pulses via the TAPs.

The sessions had been back-to-back and he'd left the tank only to adjust the software to push him deeper with each new Hack.

But something was wrong. Despite the added time, nothing new had happened. In fact, he'd lost significant ground since hacking with Nyah. He could walk around his apartment, but that's as far as he could go. No matter what he did, he couldn't find the red door or Outlaw. Like his earliest Hacks, he was limited to a localized experience. Why? It was as if he'd been locked out.

Why?

He paced nervously, tapping each finger seven times with his thumb, mind sifting relentlessly through the problem. Maybe his tolerance for the Kick had increased to the point it no longer worked. Maybe the answer was amping up the dosage . . . but that was dangerous.

Exhaustion had settled into his bones. Weeks of insomnia and pushing his body further than it was meant to go had finally caught up with him . . . and it was rolling over him like a freight train. Each new Hack stressed his body to near breaking.

Austin shivered uncontrollably as he shuffled toward the control console. A few more sessions, that's all he needed. He had to shut his mind down, be aggressive with the Kick. He had to go all in.

That was the key: quiet the brain, quiet the brain, quiet the brain. But each time he returned from a Hack without making progress, the more desperate he became and the more his brain churned, frantic for answers. Combating his own manic state meant going much deeper for a much longer time than he had before. Physically, he was worn dangerously thin, but he was too close to let off the gas. If anything, he had to push harder. Jam the accelerator through the floor. The alternative was to do nothing . . . and die.

He already had one foot in the grave: he was beginning to notice dramatic changes in his fine motor skills and cognitive ability. A heavy fog had settled in his mind that he couldn't clear away.

No, he couldn't wait. Not for Nyah. Not for anyone.

He had to find Outlaw. He was the answer to all of this; Austin was sure of it. The girl that Nyah had seen was undoubtedly a projection of her subconscious. Outlaw was a projection of his, which meant that any hope of healing his mind rested there. With Outlaw.

The software was already analyzing the new data when he reached the console and sank into a chair. He squinted at the blurry monitor and wheeled closer. Even after dialing the monitor's brightness down, the light speared his eyes like shards of glass.

He palmed the computer mouse with a trembling hand and clicked on the diagnostics summary. His vital signs were still deteriorating.

Blood pressure: Elevated and rising. Heart rate: Off the charts. Respiratory: He did not need a machine to know he was close to hyperventilation. Temperature: Now, that was the most troubling. His fever had spiked to 104.3 degrees, up two degrees with the most recent Hack.

What was causing these alarming vitals? Lack of sleep? The tumor? He'd never suffered any physiological changes from hacking, but then again he'd never subjected his body to so much so quickly.

What was he missing? The answer was beyond his reach, but only barely.

He needed more time.

Ticktock, Austin.

A headache burned the inside of his skull. He snatched the amber bottle of pain meds off the console. Empty. He tossed it across the floor and reached for a second bottle. Two pills left. His fingers trembled so badly that he could barely open it.

He dumped them straight into his mouth and swallowed hard. They scraped his parched throat on the way down.

C'mon, Austin. Just a few more Hacks, a few more.

The solution's there, waiting for you to find it.

Unsteady fingers lingered over the keyboard.

He who hesitates is lost.

Austin tapped the keys, setting the protocol parameters for the next Hack. Target session time: twenty minutes. He had to go deep. Twenty minutes in clock time, nearly a day inside the Hack. That would be enough. It had to be.

The software ran a series of calculations to determine the necessary levels of laser stimulus and neurocompound for the Kick.

The software recalibrated and cycled through a series of check protocols as it prepared to run what he was certain would be the final session. Almost ready. All he had to do was prep the headgear and get back in the tank.

Steadying himself with a hand on the console, he stood and stepped toward the tank room. An electronic chirp stopped him. He scanned the console, confused. Then he saw its source: the black phone, his landline, sitting atop a yellow legal pad.

He picked it up and glanced at the screen. BLOCKED ID. It wasn't Nyah's number, which he'd programmed in when he'd given her the other prepaid phone. He set it back on the console and walked away.

Prepping the tank, he ground his molars together and cursed his body for its betrayal. Every part of him prickled with pain and a dull, throbbing ache seeped into his bones. He was in bad shape, but soon that would change. He believed it. He had to believe it.

The saltwater felt frigid against his skin as he sat in the tank connecting the headgear. Why did it feel so cold? The salt smell too—it was overwhelming.

Your mind's unraveling, that's why.

He shoved the thought aside, but the fear had already set in.

This is what it feels like to lose your mind.

No.

You can't stop it. You're losing yourself. Your mind is dying.

"No," he said out loud, but he knew the truth. "Computer, initiate Hack protocol Delta."

A digital voice responded. "Hack protocol Delta confirmed. Initiating solo Hack. Engaging in ten . . . nine . . . eight . . ."

Austin drew a deep breath and exhaled loudly, letting his body go limp in the water. The pain in his chest was spreading through his arms like fire.

"Seven . . . six . . . five . . ."

Pain unlike anything he'd ever experienced exploded behind his left eye. It was barbed and terrible as if a thick, rusted spike had been hammered into his eye socket and through the back of his head. His jaw stretched wide, but no sound came out. His throat clamped tight as a second wave of pain hit.

Somewhere in the distance a voice said, "Four . . . three . . . two . . ."

His entire body arched in a spasm of pain that pulled every muscle so taut that he thought they would start snapping like rubber bands. Every bone felt ready to shatter. Mentally, he screamed and felt his entire being—mind and body—collapsing in on itself.

". . . one . . . Engaging Hack protocol . . ."

A streak of brilliant light blinded him and the roar of a vast explosion sucking all the oxygen from the world filled his ears. Then . . .

Silence. Utter silence.

Day Three
11:05 PM

LETTIE SHOWED me long ago how to maneuver Mom into a wheelchair. It was all about leverage and letting gravity do its thing. On any given day, one of us would have to move Mom on our own, and when there's no one else to rely on, you get good at things that no one should have to be good at.

I positioned the wheelchair close to the bed and stripped the top blanket and sheets off Mom. "Ready to go, Mom?" I said and leaned over her. I worked my arm behind her until I had a good grip and tugged her torso toward me.

Like me, Mom was small framed and her body slid easily across the sheets. I spun her upper torso toward me until I could hook my hands under her armpits and take her weight as it leaned against me. Her head flopped back onto my shoulder and I shrugged to hold it steady.

Leaning back, I took a step and then another, slowing dragging her toward the wheelchair. I saw too late that I'd yanked the IV hose loose. Saline water streamed from the bag and onto the floor.

I took another step and Mom's feet reached the mattress's edge. With a final heave, they came free and swung to the floor. Her heels hit with a dull splash in the saline puddle. The sudden impact caused her to list sideways.

My slight frame sagged under her weight and I stumbled back, but caught my footing. I was breathing hard now, my muscles aching from the effort.

A few more sharp tugs and she was in the chair. Without pausing to rest, I disengaged the brakes, spun the wheelchair around, and pushed it toward the door.

The plan was simple: Get her down the hall and to the elevator before anyone could see us. Success depended on speed.

I cracked open the door and leaned out to check the hallway. Seeing it empty, I opened the door wide and kicked a rubber doorstop beneath it. I wheeled Mom out turned right and headed for the elevators. In my heart, hope glowed a little brighter with each step, like blowing on a hot coal.

Keep moving.

I had a direct line of sight to the alcove and, just beyond it, the elevators. The waiting area where Jill and Lettie sat was down another hall, out of view. At any moment, one of them could come down the hall and catch me. Driven forward by that thought, I pushed Mom faster.

I considered the obstacles that lay ahead. The biggest one was the wristband Mom wore. It was a Wi-Fi-enabled device that connected to sensors on her body and fed heart rate, blood pressure, and oxygen levels to a nurse's station. Once she got out of signal range, the data on their screens would flat line. Someone would come running and it wouldn't be long—a minute? less?— before Jill got wind of our absence. Most likely, we'd be in the elevator when the alarms sounded.

As we passed by open patient rooms I heard the electronic murmur of ventilators and monitoring equipment. I kept a smile on my face and my gaze straight ahead. If a doctor or nurse spotted us, I needed to look confident. I was just another visitor giving her loved one a change of scenery.

A woman laughed as I hurried past a room. A man too, and I looked over my shoulder. The hall was still clear.

You're okay. Keep moving.

Thirty feet to the elevator . . . twenty-eight . . . I abandoned my careful pace. I was too exposed—and too close to get caught now. Putting all of my weight on the wheelchair's handles I leaned forward and sprinted to the elevator doors. Jammed the DOWN button. A gentle hum filled the elevator shaft.

"All right, you can do this," I whispered through gritted teeth, eyes flitting nervously between the elevator and the hall to my right. If anyone saw me, I was done.

An eternity passed before the doors parted with a whispered *shoosh*. I wheeled Mom in, reached to my left and smacked the "1" button just as voices approached from one of the hallways.

The doors closed and the elevator jerked slightly beneath my feet before beginning its glacial descent back to earth.

11 . . . 10 . . . 9 . . .

Just as I'd feared, the monitor on her wrist chimed as we passed the eighth floor. It had lost the Wi-Fi signal. Trembling now, I spun Mom's wheelchair around to face the doors. The moment they parted, I would have to move fast and find Lettie's minivan, which was in the Emergency Room parking lot.

8 . . . 7 . . . 6 . . .

• • •

STONE PASSED the third-floor landing and continued his upward climb, taking the stairs calmly. Somewhere above him a door banged shut and a twinge of urgency rushed through him. He quickened his pace.

Pausing at the door to the twelfth floor, he drew his gun from its shoulder harness and attached a silencer. He hoped firing on anyone would be unnecessary. Drawing attention would create problems, particularly being on an upper-level floor. He needed to get the girl with as little commotion as possible.

The gun hung loose at his side as he pulled the door open a crack. The hallway resonated with activity. Frantic voices echoed down the hallways. Something was wrong. He leaned closer as two nurses rushed from a room across the hall. A doctor followed, running behind them with a phone to his ear.

Holding the gun just inside the flap of his jacket, Stone stepped into the hallway and angled toward the room they'd exited.

He reached it within a few strides and his eyes found the patient's name handwritten on a strip of whiteboard. Elizabeth Parks. The girl's mother.

The door was propped open and he went in. His practiced eyes took in everything instantly: The bed was empty. Water on the floor. No girl. But there was a woman. She stood at the window, her back to him.

"She must've taken her," the woman said into a phone. "I don't know why, I don't know where—" She turned and their eyes met. It was Jill Corbis, FBI. Her eyes widened and she grabbed for the gun holstered at her hip.

Stone pulled his pistol and put two rounds into the center of the woman's chest. The shots were muffled snaps, hardly louder than a clap.

Her body jerked with the impact and fell backward, against the window. The phone clattered across the floor. He covered the distance between them in a few strides and grabbed her before she could topple into a cart of medical equipment. Pressing the muzzle of the silencer into her ribs, he squeezed the trigger again then gently lowered her to the floor.

He quickly gathered the three spent cartridges from the floor and pocketed them, ignoring the blood pooling from her body. The girl was gone, but likely still nearby, if not still in the building.

Holstering his weapon, he slipped into the hallway. No one in sight.

Judging by the spilled IV bag, the girl had moved the mother, obviously without the agent's knowledge. But why would she do that? More importantly, where was she now?

Stone studied the hallway, looking left and right, then entered the stairwell. He knew exactly where she was going.

• • •

I PUSHED the wheelchair through the parking lot as fast as I could manage. Using the key fob's controls, I had the van unlocked and the chairlift electronically unfolding from the side door before we reached it. Even so, we had to wait as the lift whirred and hummed, dropping to the ground slowly.

"Come on, come on, come on."

It settled on the asphalt with a scrape and I wheeled Mom on. I pushed another button and the lift slowly raised her. My mind was numb with fear. No one had seen me yet, but they'd surely realized by now that I was gone and so was Mom.

With the chair in the van, I strapped Mom in and climbed behind the wheel. I backed out so fast that I scraped a parked ambulance.

My eyes shot forward as a man came through the Emergency Room exit. The security guard saw me and began running toward the van, yelling. Close on his heels was the FBI agent Jill had told to wait on the first floor. I had expected to see him in the lobby, but he hadn't been there when I stepped off the elevator.

I shoved the van into drive and yanked the wheel hard as I floored it. The tires barked, and I careened through the parking lot toward the exit. The minivan banged over a speed bump and bounced like a carnival ride when I came out of the parking lot. Engine straining, I turned right into traffic, cutting off a Volvo that blared its horn. The van fishtailed, found its bearing, and shot forward.

The hospital grew smaller in the rearview mirror and I sighed with relief when I saw Mom was okay. Glancing at both outside mirrors, I determined we weren't being followed. Yet. I had to put as much distance between us as possible. I had to get her to Austin. There, we would be safe.

I jammed the pedal down, accelerated through a red light, and roared up the highway on-ramp.

"Hang on, Mom," I said, looking in the rearview mirror. Her head lolled forward and side to side in rhythm with the jostling of the van. I took the first exit I came to and picked my way through side streets toward Austin's. I hoped the FBI would think I had stayed on the highway and crossed the Bay.

Fifteen minutes later I turned into the underground parking garage at Austin's. He'd told me to never park at the building itself in case I was being tailed, but there was no time to park down the street. I needed to get Mom upstairs as quickly as possible.

The wooden access gate was down, but I had no time for etiquette. I rammed through it, sending the thing flying in an explosion of splinters. I bounced through the dimly lit garage and stopped by a doorway that had to lead inside.

My hands were shaking uncontrollably and my entire body buzzed with adrenaline. I climbed out and stared for a moment at the garage entrance. I didn't think anyone had followed me here, because if they had I'd be dead.

I pushed the button to open the side door and lower the lift, then got Mom out of the van. How was I going to explain this to Austin? I'd brought up the idea of putting my mom in the Hack, but talking about it and doing it were different things.

Mom's breath was ragged and shallow by the time I got her on the lobby elevator. She was in serious condition. She was dying and no one could change that using medicine. If Mom was going to live, it would take a miracle and she of all people was due one. Just one.

The elevator jarred to a stop on the top floor, and I wheeled the chair to Austin's door. I threw the door open, circled back around the wheelchair and pushed Mom in. The moment I set foot inside I heard the alarm echoing through the room.

"Austin?" I called and pushed Mom deeper into the room. "Where are you?"

As I moved forward, the alarm grew louder, and I realized it was coming from the console.

"Austin?" I engaged the wheelchair's brakes and rushed to the control panel.

I saw him first on the monitors. His face stared into the camera with vacant eyes, his mouth open in a silent scream. He was in one of the tanks.

"Oh, dear God . . ." I said, eyes on the biometric data flowing across the screen. "What have you done?"

The erratic tone of the heart rate monitor fed through the speakers and the diagnostic panel. I ran to the controls, which flashed with warnings. His pulse was 200. Now 205 . . . 215 . . . climbing with each second.

He'd hacked without me . . .

His pulse spiked at 224 beats per minute and, as I watched, the erratic beep of his heart rate coming through the monitor's speaker gave way to a singular tone, long and mournful. It was the loudest, most horrific sound in the world. The numbers on the monitor clicked to zero.

On the screen, his face went slack and he exhaled a hollow breath. Just one.

I was too late.

Austin was dead.

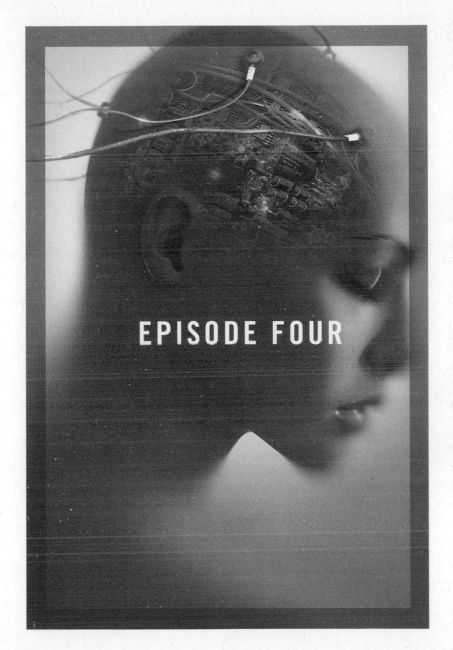

EPISODE FOUR

4.1

Day Three
11:33 PM

"I HAD to kill her," Stone said into the phone. He sat in his car across the street from the hospital, watching as police and FBI vehicles converged on the building.

"A federal agent," Bell said.

"A necessary complication. She saw me. I left no evidence at the scene, of course." His mind spun. "Telling you was a mistake."

"What?"

"Plausible deniability."

"If it gets that far—"

"It won't."

Stone could hear Bell breathing, thinking. Finally, his boss asked, "And where's the girl?"

"On the move. She won't return to her own apartment. It's too risky. She's obviously avoiding the FBI, so she'll go somewhere the authorities don't know about."

"The warehouse," Bell said.

"That's my assumption. I'm headed there now," he said, putting the car in drive. Something about the warehouse itself or the adjacent buildings tied her to the area, but what?

"Give me an ETA," Bell said.

Stone angled into traffic and pointed toward the highway. "Twenty minutes. No more."

•••

I RUSHED to the sensory-deprivation room, driven by terror, and threw the door open. It banged hard against the wall.

"Austin!"

The light on the white clamshell tank glowed blue, indicating that it was actively engaged in a Hack. Why had Austin hacked into the system alone? He'd talked about going deeper, pushing the system further than either of us had before, but that meant taking significant risks. Unacceptable risks.

The computer's robotic voice filtered through speakers perched in the corners of the room. In a calm, detached monotone it droned:

"Subject termination confirmed. Recovery protocol initiated. Subject termination confirmed. Recovery protocol initiated . . ."

"What'd you do?" I said, my voice cracking. "What'd you do?"

The recovery protocol was a fail-safe that Austin had programmed for his solo hacking long before I came along. He'd designed it for a worst-case scenario, worst-case meaning death. His death. It triggered automatically in the event his vital signs fell below a redline pulse and respiration threshold. After a sixty-second alarm, the computer would shut down the entire system.

I reached the tank and jabbed the hatch-release button. The lid rose slowly. All the time in the world.

"Come on. Come on. Open!"

I gripped the yawning lid and yanked it up like a car hood. Something broke with a *clank*, but it stayed open. The tank's interior lights blinked to life, illuminating the water and his motionless body.

Austin floated with his head at the other end of the tank, feet toward me. His arms drifted palms down at his sides, and thin black cords dangled from the tank's ceiling to where they connected with his TAPs.

The sight stole my breath. I'd seen him in the tank before, but now he looked frail, barely more than skin and bones, as though the Hack had sucked away his muscles.

"Subject termination confirmed . . . Recovery protocol initiated . . ."

The words jarred me away from my frustration at Austin's stupidity—*Why was he hacking by himself? Why hadn't he waited?*—and back into a state of panic: his heart had stopped!

I ducked through the opening and plunged my right foot into the water, splashing it over my legs, against the sides of the tank. "Austin!" I yelled. His eyes were glazed and frozen wide. His jaw gaped open, lips apart, skin pale as paper. I'd seen that hollow stare before and knew too well its terrible meaning.

"Not like this," I said. "Please . . . not like this."

The diagnostic systems had to be wrong. Maybe he hadn't connected something properly. He was exhausted after all. Mistakes happen. He couldn't be dead—unconscious maybe, but not *dead*. He was too careful, too calculating to push things to the point of no return. Wasn't he?

Still, everyone had limits. Even him.

"Wake up!" I screamed and stooped to grab him.

My other foot came over the edge and snagged the side of the tank. It wasn't much, but it was enough to send me off-balance. I pitched forward. I grasped for the lip of the tank, but my fingers grazed the slick surface and slipped off. With nothing to stop me, I fell on top of Austin, pushing him under before he came up again like a log. The saltwater was denser than both of us. Staying under was impossible, thankfully. I gasped and pushed off of him onto my knees beside him.

"Tank evacuation initiated," the electronic voice said.

I blinked water from my eyes and looked around. A mechanical hum filled the tank and a swirl broke the water's surface in front of me. The level began to drop—quickly. The computer was draining the tank—part of the fail-safe protocol to prevent the slim possibility of drowning. Austin had considered every eventuality when programming the fail-safe, including passing out under water, however unlikely that was. The tank was emptying loudly through a wide grate embedded beneath us.

Austin's body bobbed slightly, undulating on the gentle waves rippling through the tank.

I leaned over him, my eyes searching for any signs of consciousness. Nothing. His lips were pale blue and his pupils where deep pools of black.

"What do I do?" I raised my head and yelled—at the monotonous voice, at God, at myself, I don't know: "What do I do?"

My hands, gripping Austin's shoulder and arm, shook and my mind locked tight, shut down by fear. I felt powerless, kneeling there beside my friend, just watching him slip away. Images of Tommy—hanging sideways in his seat, bleeding out and staring at me as though he couldn't believe I wasn't doing something to help—raked across my mind like steel fingernails.

It was happening again.

I looked around frantically, pushing two fingers into each eye socket to clear the water.

"Get a grip. Think," I said. My gaze skimmed over Austin's still body. "Okay, okay . . ."

I leaned close to his face until my ear grazed his nose. No breath. There was just the lapping of water against the side of his face and into his mouth. Reaching my arm across him, I rolled his body toward me, and water rushed from his nose and mouth.

"You can't die," I said. "Not yet."

I flipped him to his back again and pinched his nose as I tilted his head back to open his airway. I encircled my mouth over his and puffed out a hard breath. His lips were cool, life draining from him faster than the water from the tank, if his life hadn't already left completely. His chest expanded, then the air escaped with a hollow sound. Again, I pressed my lips to his and blew again—wishing that it was life and not just air that I was breathing into him.

It wasn't working.

"Please," I whispered. My vision was bleary, my eyes stinging from the saltwater.

He needed more. His heart needed help. But there was still too much water to do chest compressions in the tank and I couldn't wait until it drained completely. The water level was barely down by half, well below the lip of the tank—disappearing quickly but not quickly enough.

What do I do?

The system's alarm—*wah-wah-wah*—echoed through the apartment, seeming colder and crueler than it had before, when I first heard it. Each tone was like a hammer blow on the nails of Austin's coffin. I was cut off from all hope and help and nothing I did would change that. I was alone. My mind stuttered, trying to break loose of the fear that clamped it and threatened to crush me.

What would Austin do if the roles were reversed? The answer boiled to the surface. He would reboot me. Reset my body like a computer.

Okay, okay—how?

My thoughts churned furiously.

My heart. He would shock my heart.

The defibrillator. There was a defibrillator in the apartment.

As the water continued to drain, I climbed out of the tank and made my way toward the tall metal shelves on the apartment's far side. They were crammed with meticulously organized shelves of equipment and medical supplies. Austin had outfitted the loft with better technology than some hospitals—medicines, imaging devices, even experimental equipment that he'd bought directly from the overseas labs that invented next-generation technology.

On my initial tour of the place, he'd pointed out the heart defibrillator and flashed an instructional card at me. I wished now that I had taken a minute to scan the card; my eidetic mind would have remembered every word and illustration. Too late now. I looked quickly for the card and when I didn't immediately see it, decided to wing it. I'd seen medical shows; what more did I need? The defibrillator was part of a cardiac "crash cart" a medical-equipment company had given him as a thank you for purchasing an expensive imaging machine. "Spend a million dollars," he'd said, "and a personalized fountain pen just won't do." I found it atop a metal cart, which I wheeled toward the tank room at Olympian speed.

There was a problem, though: Austin was still lying in several inches of water. Using the defibrillator in the tank wasn't a wise idea. Even if the equipment could fit through the opening, using it was far too risky. The high voltage from the shock paddles could possibly conduct through the water and into me, and then we'd both be down for the count.

I had to get him out of the water.

With the two pods, a table and all the cables, there wasn't enough space in the tank room to put him on the floor. I would have to drag him out to the main room if this was going to work.

I slid the cart to a stop beside the door and jammed its power cord into an outlet. The machine came to life with a high-pitched tone as I rushed back to Austin and ducked inside the tank.

He outweighed me by at least seventy pounds and the gap between the water level and the tank lid was more than two feet. I'd have to lift him over it by myself, and I wasn't exactly what anyone would call athletic.

I stepped over his body, squatted to my haunches just above his head, and hooked my hands under his arms. Bracing one foot on the tank wall behind me and another on the tank floor, I heaved upward, turned and hauled him to the tank's edge. I didn't think about it, I just did it.

Straining to keep balanced, I stepped over the lip and leaned back to keep his weight against me. With a loud grunt, I backpedaled, tugging again and again, dragging his limp body over the lip and out of the tank. Getting Mom out of the hospital bed had been like fluffing a pillow compared to this. His heels snagged on the lip, but one good yank pulled them over. One step at a time, I hauled him into the apartment. I eased his body to the floor, his eyes staring straight at me, void of life.

Go! Go! Go! Hurry!

The defibrillator hummed a high-pitched tone and red lights blinked on the narrow display, indicating its readiness. I reached for the black dial that set the energy level, but my mind froze.

How much? The television shows I'd seen hadn't gone into that kind of detail. The voltage settings were in joules, from 100 to 400. Too little voltage and it wouldn't do much of anything; too much could jolt him right into the Grim Reaper's grasp.

I twisted the knob clockwise until it pointed halfway, 200, and the machine made a long, long tone while it charged. I picked up the paddles and positioned them near his chest.

A memory of the doctors using a defib on my mother in the Hack made me think: *Gel.* I dropped one of the paddles and grabbed a green tube of electro conductive gel from the cart. Without it, the electricity wouldn't conduct. I squeezed too hard and the goo squirted onto and over the flat part of the one pad I had in hand. I picked up the other paddle and rubbed them together, smearing the gel. With the machine blaring its full-charge warning, I pressed the paddles to Austin's chest and thumbed down a button on a handle.

There was a loud *thump* and his body heaved up in a muscle-constricted arch, then settled back onto the floor.

I waited. Nothing.

Charged again, I pressed the paddles to his pale skin.

Thump!

He heaved up as electricity arced through his chest.

No sign of movement. Nothing.

"Austin! Come on, man! Come tell me what I'm doing wrong! Come—"

I thought of the kiss we'd shared on Mt. Everest. So warm in the cold air. So . . . perfect.

Don't leave me.

I pressed my fingers against his neck, feeling for a pulse, but could have been pushing my fingers to a statue. I leaned close to his mouth. Not even a trickle of air escaped.

"Please . . ." I said through clenched teeth. "*Please.*"

It wasn't enough voltage. That had to be the problem.

I cranked the dial to the maximum setting and shocked his body. Then again and again and again. Each time, his body twisted in involuntary spasms before falling slack again to the floor. Each time, I pressed the buttons with hope, and each time, that hope was met with crushing defeat.

He wasn't moving. He wasn't breathing.

He's not coming back. You're too late.

I screamed and slammed my fist into the center of his chest.

The computer system's warnings continued to echo in the apartment. It was the loneliest sound I could have imagined. It wasn't supposed to be like this. He was supposed to live. We were supposed to save him.

But we hadn't. He was dead.

As I knelt there, my eyes went to the second saltwater tank just beyond the doorway, the tank I used for my Hacks.

The tank.

Save him through the Hack.

The idea surprised me, like a bolt of lightning cracking down into a nearby tree out of pitch-black night. The defibrillator hadn't worked and wasn't going to, no matter how many times I tried. If Austin was going to live, I would have to save him. The only way I knew to do that was by hacking.

I sprang to my feet and, before my mind could convince me what a bad idea this was, I went to the control panel. Fingers flying over the keys, I shut down the first tank, which had been fully drained. The warning alarms went silent as I reset the system and powered up the second tank.

The command prompts appeared on screen: *Initiate Hack Protocol?*

I palmed the mouse. Clicked the confirmation key.

Command: *Configure Session Time . . .*

Time . . . time . . . how much time did I need?

I had to go deep into the Hack—through the second doorway, the one that had taken me to India—and find the girl who'd healed me. She could help us, I was sure of it. But I had to find her. The Kick dosage had to give me enough time to do that.

00h:00m:60s [ENTER]

One minute—one hour of Hack time. Was that enough? I knew where I was going this time and where to find the girl. At least I thought so. I didn't want to consider the idea that she'd be somewhere else. I pushed away another flash of concern: What if she didn't *want* to help us? How could she *not* help us?

There was no time to strip out of my clothes, no time to do any of the system checks we normally ran through, so I launched the auto-Hack application, and ran for the tank, kicking off my shoes.

Under my breath I prayed that all of it would work. If it didn't, everything would be lost.

4.2

EVERYTHING WAS profoundly silent as if the universe was holding its breath. Austin drifted in a vast sea of darkness, carried along by a current of peace that moved in deep ebbs and swells around him . . . through him. The flash of pain that had burned through his body like lightning and set every nerve ablaze had disappeared completely.

Now, he felt nothing at all: no pain, no worry, no fear. And yet everything. A vast emptiness that somehow also had substance to it.

He was in the Hack—that much he knew, though he'd never felt the sensations that were coursing through him in that moment. Every Hack he'd experienced had felt surreal. But this . . . this felt more real than anything he'd encountered. He didn't simply *feel* its reality, he *knew* it at the deepest part of himself, as if the core of his being was entangled with the world around him.

Austin relaxed and let his arms and legs drift free. Was this the ocean Nyah had experienced the first time she'd hacked?

Then a thought arose in his mind as if it had bubbled up from the depths far below him. It was an idea that he felt, saw, and heard all at the same time. He *knew* it. It had come to him unlike any thought had before, from everywhere at once. It was a simple thought.

Breathe.

But he couldn't simply breathe the water, if that's what it was. Could he?

It came again, this time stronger, but gentle. *Breathe.*

He parted his lips slightly and sipped at the darkness, letting it slip over his tongue. It was cold—far colder than ice—and stung as it filled his mouth and washed down his throat. It was tasteless, but it crackled in his mouth and made a sound like the spark of electricity that resonated in his ears and soon vibrated through his entire body with irresistible force.

Again the overwhelming word came: *Breathe.*

He opened his mouth wider and pulled the liquid into his lungs with a long draw. He exhaled it, feeling the current it made as it rushed from his mouth and nose. He drew it in again, and this time he laughed, surprised. The muffled sound of his own voice disappeared into the liquid surrounding him. It was absurd, breathing underwater. Wasn't it? And yet, here he was.

Curious . . .

The thought faded when a deep rumbling, like a storm might sound from inside a thunderhead, resonated through the water so loudly he thought it might crush his bones. Distant light flashed, like lightning stabbing through the sea. It shot deep into the ocean and branched in all directions, piercing the wet darkness with white-hot fingers.

Lightning in the ocean?

Something pulled at his body—a force strong and strange. It felt *personal* in an unexplainable way, as if someone had snatched him and was dragging him up from the depths.

Immediately he was rushing toward the surface, drawn upward toward a pinprick of light high above him. He rushed toward it, accelerating until he broke through the dark surface. Light exploded all around him.

The world snapped into sharp focus. He turned, slowly looking at his surroundings, which shimmered with clarity, though he already knew where he was.

"Not like this," he heard a familiar voice say. "Please . . . not like this."

He twisted back and saw.

Nyah.

He was watching her from above the tank. A body was floating in the tank. His body. He'd seen himself during Hacks before, but this time felt . . . different. Final. The body in the tank struck him as nothing more than an empty shell or a vehicle that he'd discarded because he no longer had use for it. It wasn't him any more than the clothes he'd put on that morning were him.

Drifting higher, he could see not only the body, but his entire apartment, including a woman in a wheelchair. Nyah's mother.

His attention was drawn back to Nyah who was breathing into the body's mouth, frantic. She was trembling with fear. He could feel it as if her emotions pulsated from her like shock waves radiating out in all directions. He watched her curiously as she struggled. What she was doing was obvious, of course—she was trying to revive his body, wake him from the Hack.

She was trying to keep him alive. He should've felt fear, but he didn't. There was only a detached curiosity. Why was she so distraught? Didn't she know that there was nothing to fear? There was no problem. He was right there, beside her even if she couldn't see him.

Austin heard the computer's voice warning of danger. The fail-safe had triggered, which meant that his heart had stopped.

His returned his gaze to his body. So he was, what, *dead*? No, that was impossible, wasn't it? If he were dead then his brain would've ceased all function. He wouldn't be able to witness this very moment. Instead, there would be nothingness, oblivion, because his conscious mind was all that made him alive. It was all that made anyone alive.

But he *was* aware of where he was, who he was, and that meant his brain was still functioning down in the tank, in his body.

He felt no fear. Compassion welled in him for his friend and the fear she felt. He watched as Nyah stood inside the tank then stepped out of it. She hurried through his apartment, desperately looking for something. He wanted to tell her that there was nothing to worry about, that he was fine inside the Hack. All he had to do was go deeper while she waited for him to come back.

Just wait for me to come back.

He was going to find the doorway. She didn't know that, of course. It was all going to be fine, he wanted to tell her. He just had to find Outlaw.

His focus drifted back to the body, *his* body. As he stared at it, fascinated, the world around him began to shimmer and shift.

Everything in view suddenly dissolved with a sizzling sound, replaced by a darkness—utter and complete—that swallowed the world. It was cold and thick and bottomless and fluid. No up or down existed and the darkness seemed infinitely vast. There was no edge to be found nor surface to break through. The darkness was everything there was. It was absolute. It wasn't like the water he'd breathed before. This was something altogether different. Something to be escaped, though he knew he couldn't.

The world surrounding him seemed like a secret he'd forgotten—but now remembered, triggered instantly by seeing it again. That puzzled him: he'd never been here before. Had he?

Fear welled in him for the first time. He felt it first like a rivulet of water trickling through a hairline crack in a rock. He frantically searched the darkness. Where was the door? He needed to find it and progress to the next level. Only then could he begin looking for Outlaw. Where was it? It had never taken this long before to find it. Something was wrong.

Where am I?

He could feel the darkness as much as see it. It resolved into a murky swirl of brackish grey and black. A tangled network of black tendrils—like coiling ink. Shapes began to emerge, slithering and writhing around him. A mechanical sound filled his ears—a tortuous grind and clank of gears larger than the world. He couldn't tell from which direction it came.

Panicked now, Austin twisted, searching for a way out. Something was very wrong!

A bright pinprick suddenly snapped into view, high above him. Light! Now rushing toward him.

The darkness peeled away from it, driven by a shock wave that pushed ahead of the light. The shock wave reached him before the light did and it roared through him, sweeping away fear as if it were a fog blown by a warm wind.

The light source drifted to a stop just above him. A tunnel? Bluish-white, radiating an inexhaustible power, brighter than any sun or star.

The light stirred and extended toward him.

He could do nothing but watch. The light had come to him, and he knew it was the only way to ever be near it. Bathed in its warmth, he sensed peace and love that he'd long forgotten.

A warm current stirred when the light touched him, driving away whatever frigid emptiness remained in his awareness. He focused on the brilliant light, and a voice reached into the deepest part of him, speaking words in a language he couldn't understand. The words came as a song, though not sung in any way that he'd ever known. It was beyond singing, beyond knowing. It was a song that could only be known by *being* it.

An intoxicating song of exquisite pleasure and love. A knot formed in his throat; tears misted his sight. An intense desire to be joined with that song swallowed him.

He felt something deep inside of him release, something that had once wrapped him tightly. And the moment it did, he heard himself say, "Yes." Then again, "Yes." And with that one word, everything changed.

In an instant he was rushing upward again, pulled by the light, and now he began to tremble, overwhelmed.

Beyond the white light he saw a swirling cluster of blue and white and purple that appeared infinitely far away. It swept through the darkness, trailing vast fingers of light like a spiraling galaxy filling the whole universe. Within the span of a breath he'd reached it and was plunging headlong through the shimmering cosmic vortex.

The light closed below him, blotting out the darkness. He felt a hand grip his own and he surrendered himself completely.

This is it, he thought. This is really it.

4.3

I RAN. The second hand on my wristwatch ticked at a glacial pace. But fifteen seconds of clock time had already passed since I was plunged into the Hack. I'd moved quickly, retracing my steps through the two white rifts that had been my doorways in previous Hacks.

The black door that Austin had seen still eluded me, but it didn't matter. I was on the inside. More importantly, I was in India. Moving through the levels had been much easier this time, but I still needed every second of clock time—every minute of Hack time—and wished I had programmed the system for more.

Only forty-five seconds of clock time remained.

I moved in a kind of panicky stumbling run down the same dank alleyway of Calcutta I'd been before, rushing toward the swell of people in the streets just ahead. Unlike the first time I was here, the world now pulsed and surged with motion, vibrant and very much alive. No one was frozen in place.

Reaching the sidewalk, I slid to a stop and scanned the thick crowd. *Where was she?* The scene was a swarm of diesel fumes, shouting vendors, and gridlocked taxis, livestock, and motorcycles. People, too, crowded the streets, seeming to fill every space not occupied by a vehicle or animal. They moved sluggishly in the heat—all headed, it seemed, nowhere in particular.

Before, the girl had been to the right of the alley, sitting beside the street. I pushed forward, shoving and weaving my way through the surge of people. Within seconds I reached the spot where I'd knelt in front of her, but she was nowhere in sight.

I spun, searching the crowd for her. My heart pounded as I nervously scanned the faces rushing by me, none of them hers. I glanced through the narrow gaps between bodies as they shuffled past.

What if I couldn't find her? What would I do then? She was Austin's last chance, and Mom's too. If the girl could affect physical reality then maybe she could save him even if he wasn't there with me. It was a stretch, but no more than anything else I'd already witnessed.

Hope bled from my veins as I moved forward into the street, wishing desperately for a glimpse of the girl. In this chaos she could be anywhere, or nowhere. Maybe I was too late. Was it possible that the girl didn't exist at all, that she never did? No, she was real. She had to be.

Halfway across the dusty street my eyes locked on a figure no more than twenty feet ahead, watching me with a gentle smile. A shock of familiarity spiked through me, and the sight brought me to a dead halt.

The world around me slowed to a grinding pace. Everything fell away at the periphery, leaving only the two of us. That's the way it seemed.

I stepped forward. It wasn't possible.

Another step. I expected her to fade away like a mirage, but she didn't.

"Mom?" I said. She sat in a wheelchair on the other side of the road. Among the chaos she seemed entirely out of place, sitting there so peacefully. Her eyes were bright, the eyes of someone fully aware and engaged with the world and not trapped helplessly in her own head.

What kind of trick was this?

I stopped in front of her, still in complete disbelief that I was now seeing my mother as I knew her.

She looked me up and down, and said, "Nyah."

They say you can see people—the real them—if you look deep into their eyes because eyes are the windows to the soul, the essence of who we are. Standing there, gazing deeply into her loving face, I knew that this wasn't a trick of the eye or the mind. My mom was as real as anything else in the universe at that moment.

"Mom?" I was terrified to even blink, certain that, if I did, she would disappear, and it would all turn out to be nothing more than a dream.

"I'm here," she said. Her voice was tender, but strong. There was no hesitation in her words, no slur in her voice like there had been over the months as her condition had deteriorated.

She wasn't just alive, but fully aware. Alive-ness, if you want to call it that, radiated from her, but how was it even possible? She was in Austin's apartment, not in the Hack with me . . . yet, here she was. How?

The woman in the chair wasn't the same one whose life I'd watched fade away—one day, one memory at a time—over the past two years. She was my mom, the woman I'd known before our life had been violently shattered. I knew it and so did she.

She was talking to me! And she remembered my name.

"I don't understand," I said. "Why are you here?"

She smiled, and tears glistened in her eyes. "For you."

"You're in a wheelchair in Austin's apartment right now."

"My body, yes, but not *me*." She held out her arms.

My heart had been locked away long ago, but her words kicked down the door. It wasn't a dream, and even if it was, I didn't care anymore. I stepped forward and wrapped my arms around her, burying my head into her shoulder, and began to sob. My body shook as she held me close, cradling me as best she could.

"It's okay, sweetheart," she whispered. "Everything's going to be okay."

I held onto her as if my life depended on it.

She held me and kissed the top of my head. I felt her lips press against my bare scalp and her warm tears too, as they landed on me.

"I've missed you so much," I said. "I'm so glad you're here."

For several moments, she held me tight, then drew back and took my face in her hands. She looked deep into my eyes with a love I hadn't felt in so long.

"Look at you. So beautiful. So strong."

"Thank you," I said, a hitch in my voice and a smile on my face.

"Your head," she said and traced her finger along my temple with a look of wonder.

"I shaved it."

"I see that," she said. She lay her open hand on my scalp and ran her palm over it. "I remember. There was a scar here once."

I shrugged. "Something happened."

"Yes," she said with a knowing smile. "I know."

How could she know?

She held me at arm's length. "Let me look at you."

There was bottomless compassion in her eyes that reached deep into me and began to draw the tattered pieces of my heart together. In spite of all the wreckage the years had left behind, and all the scars life had cut into me, there was no resisting the love I felt in that moment.

"You've been through so much," she said and wiped a tear across my cheek with her thumb. "You've learned much too. Haven't you?"

I bit my lip. I couldn't speak. All of the pain and hurt that had bound my life like razor wire, holding it together while at the same time killing me slowly, was being clipped away by her words. I could feel it physically.

"Some things are ending," she said, "but only so new things can take their place."

Ending? Fear flashed through me. "What do you mean?"

"I'm returning home," she said. "You can't come with me yet."

"Home?" Then in an instant I knew what she meant. She was dying. "No, stay. You have to stay."

"Listen to me," she said. "I know you feel alone, but you're not."

"Don't leave me." My voice cracked, barely a whisper. "Please."

"I'm always with you. And so are Dad and Tommy. You're loved—cherished more than you can ever imagine. I know that what's happened to you, to us, seems random and pointless and cruel, but it's not. I've seen it. I see it now. Everything had to happen as it did. It was the only way."

"No," I said. "It wasn't the only way. It didn't have to happen. It *shouldn't* have happened."

"But it did." She answered with a gentle smile.

"It destroyed our lives," I said. "How is that beautiful? How is that fair or right or good?"

"Sweetheart, there's a truth that's so large and beautiful and perfect that it holds everything together. It's hard to see it now, but it's true."

The entire world seemed to stall around me. "How? How does it hold it together and make it better?"

"It's a mystery too big to know, but it exists and it's truer than anything else that ever was because it's more real than what we think of as real. I know it. I've seen it . . ." She was quiet for a moment. "I want to tell you something, and I want you to hear me."

I grew still.

"After the accident, the world changed for me. Physically, I mean. It *looked* different. It was transformed as if I had a new set of eyes or a pair of glasses that allowed me to see what others can't—a reality that is part ours and part . . . something else, something just out of sight. Both together, entangling one another. I began to see patterns in everything, intricate shapes and connections that flowed from one thing to another—events and people and circumstances—weaving them together in beautiful ways that only I could see."

"Your artwork—all of those designs and shapes. That's what you were drawing and painting."

She nodded slightly. "Yes. I was catching glimpses of the life that's just beyond what we can see. You know what I'm talking about."

"I've seen things. Visions."

"No, sweetheart, visions are dreams. These weren't dreams. They're more real than you or me. More real than can be described with frail things like words. Art was the closest language I had to express what I saw, but even then it fell so short, like trying to write a symphony with only a few notes or pen a novel with a handful of words."

I knew she was telling the truth. I was experiencing it right then, in the Hack. There was something else to the world—something *other* that our brains filtered out, that existed around us if only we knew how to hack into it.

In my mind's eye, it became clear. Austin had tried to explain it, but at the time I didn't have the ears to hear. The Hacks that Austin and I were doing relied on shutting down the brain, not enhancing it. Only when we did that, when we silenced the brain's incessant processing, could we access reality in a new way. It was our thinking that got in the way.

Austin had said it himself, the brain was like a computer running software programmed to handle one layer of reality, but not all the other layers of reality. There was a firewall that blocked the way, but our Hacks had shut down the firewall so that we could see.

Mom's brain damage must have done the same thing for her, only naturally. She could see the world differently, more clearly, because her firewall, her mind, had been stripped away, leaving the Reality behind reality exposed. Her firewalls had not only cracked, they'd crumbled to dust.

She continued. "With time the patterns and images became clearer to me. I saw other beings—lights and shadows—moving through the patterns. I began to understand that things we would see as terrible or tragic, while they brought unbearable pain, were transformed into something new. They *had* to be transformed because that was the plan all along. It's how God works. I realized that life was beautiful, perfectly ordered, and death and suffering can be as well, in its own way."

"Suffering's not beautiful," I said.

"Necessary. Without it, growth would be impossible. There would be no opportunity for our hearts to unfold, to blossom, like they were meant to. The only thing that truly crushes our hearts is our unwillingness to let go. Let go of our need to control. Let go of our need to know the answers to our questions. No amount of suffering is truly heavy enough to crush us completely unless we let it. It only has the power that we give it."

Let go.

My head tingled.

"Unless a seed falls to the ground and dies it remains a lone seed," she said. "All things that live eventually become the soil in which new things can take root. Things that would otherwise not exist."

She paused and her smile softened. "Sweetheart, everything that's happened to our family has left so many unanswered questions. Yet, life will eventually blossom into something beyond imagination—if we can let go and allow it to happen. Do you believe it?"

Let go. It's what the girl had told me on this very street. She'd been right. For a moment, however brief, the girl had helped me let go. I had let go of my need for a scar—my belief that it was the least I deserved after what happened to the rest of my family. I'd let go of those things, and I'd been healed.

"I can't," I said. "I can't let go of you."

She ran her finger over where my scar once had been. "Yes, you can. You've done it before."

"That was . . . different."

"No, it wasn't." As her finger grazed my skin, a jolt of energy shot through my head and into my body. I gasped and took a step back. The sensation converged in my chest and my heart began to ram hard. My legs were unsteady.

"You've sat in darkness too long," Mom said. "It's time to leave it behind. You have to let go of everything." She paused. "You have to let me go."

Her words were like a stone landing on my heart. "No," I said. "No, you can't die."

"When God calls his children home, there's no death, no sting. There's only new life. Resurrection. That's the life that I want, dear, not the rumor or shadow of it I've been trapped in for the past year."

"The girl said I have to save you." I heard the desperation in my own voice. I could barely choke out the words.

"You already have. By bringing me to Austin's you saved me." She took my hand and held it gently in hers. "You saved me. When you wake up you'll see that I've already passed. I died and I wanted to die. By taking me from the hospital you gave me what I most wanted, the ability to pass in peace. It's what I want."

Tears flowed from my eyes, but it wasn't simply from sadness or loss, but release. I could feel myself letting her go, and in that was the first glimmer of hope.

"Don't give up on life," she said. "You'll find joy again . . . and peace. And love. I've seen it. I promise you, it'll be okay. There's nothing to fear. Open your eyes. See . . ."

She touched my head and the energy that radiated in my skull felt like two hot coals behind my eyes.

"Every moment of your life, every choice and every circumstance, has carved a path to this very moment," Mom said. "You're always exactly where you're meant to be at precisely the perfect time. You can trust that always. When it's dark and when it's light. In those times when you scream at the sky or when you turn your face up to catch the warmth of the sun—you can trust that."

I felt every muscle in my body ease. I drew a long breath and let it out slowly. I didn't want to fight anymore. I was too tired and my soul felt so crooked and brittle I knew it would break if I kept going the way I had been.

"You are always in the perfect place and the perfect time," she said again. "Do you trust that?"

"I . . . I want to."

"Then do. Let go of your pain. There's no need to cling to it anymore. It's not you. It *happened* to you, but none of it is you. Don't just believe it, *know* it."

"*Know* it," I whispered and closed my eyes. "Yes . . ."

Before the word left my mouth it set something in motion, something that I couldn't see or hear or feel. My word, a simple act of surrender, triggered a seismic chain reaction that would change everything. I just didn't know in what ways yet.

"Do you want to live?" Mom said.

"Yes," I said.

"Then live. You'll forget, but then you'll remember again. It's okay. Don't be afraid, there's nothing to fear. You're always exactly where you're meant to be, and there is always something you can do. Even now. Even with Austin."

"Austin . . ." My thoughts zeroed in on him and the image of his dead body lying on the apartment floor. "What do I do?"

"Save him," she said. "There's still time, but you must hurry. Save him."

"I want to, but I can't. How do I save him? If it was the tumor that killed him then there's nothing—"

"It wasn't the tumor," she said. "It's what he put into his veins. It was far too much."

The world was shifting around me. I shot a look at my watch as the second hand nudged forward. My time was nearly gone. The Hack was ending.

"Restart his heart," she said.

"I tried that!" I screamed as the street and everything around it crackled and began to burn away at the edges. "It didn't work."

"Put something else in his veins," she said and pushed upright. "You already know where to look." She stood from the wheelchair as dust swirled around us and took a step forward. My mom pulled me to her and held tight. "I love you, Nyah. I love you and I promise I'll see you again. Don't be afraid."

Desperate to hang on to her, I pressed my face against her chest. "I love you too. I love you . . ."

With the roar of wind in my ears I let my mom go. I let her move on and live in that place that I knew existed so deep that no Hack could go far enough to tap it. There was only one door to that reality and all of us would pass through it at some point, whether soon or when we're old. It's where she wanted to go and it's where I would see her again someday.

"I love you," she said, a whisper in my ear, and she took a step back. "To the moon and back." Light gathered around her, swirled and engulfed her, swallowed her.

She was home.

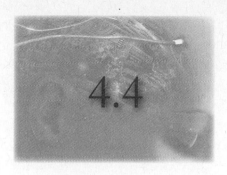

4.4

Day Three
11:59 PM

STONE CIRCLED the block slowly, headlights darkened as he scanned the streets and deserted warehouses for signs of life. It didn't matter how far the girl ran, he would eventually catch up to her. It was simply a matter of when.

He suspected that she would come back to this place even if she intended to eventually flee the city. Something in the warehouse or the nearby building was important to her. Something or some*one*.

The building from the satellite image came into view, rising from the shadowy streets, ahead and on the right. High on the top floor a sliver of light, barely perceptible, bled through a painted-over window. It was the only trace of light for blocks. She was inside.

He parked a block north and approached the building, staying to the patchwork of shadows as he walked the perimeter. On the building's back side he found the garage entrance and, just inside, a shattered gate arm that had likely been smashed in the girl's haste.

No sign of movement as he entered the garage. Two caged bulbs, ancient looking and glowing dirty yellow, clung to the ceiling and cast dull circles on the pitted concrete floor. Ahead, a minivan was visible in the anemic light of a third bulb, this one centered above a black metal door that undoubtedly led into the building. The lone vehicle was parked crooked, a few feet from it.

The lack of cars confirmed his suspicion that the building itself was abandoned, a half-finished development, judging by the stacked pallets of building supplies along the far wall.

A quick search of the van revealed nothing more than a cell phone, which sat in the passenger's seat, and a clump of crinkled registration and insurance paperwork in the glove compartment. The engine still tick-tick-ticked from the heat, but that was the only sound in the deserted place.

After slashing the van's tires as a precaution—he couldn't afford a second escape—Stone's eyes leveled on the door and he stepped toward it. The next time he came out, the girl would be with him. One way or another.

• • •

THE BLINDING white light vanished. Electric-blue sky stretched above Austin and a jagged spine of snow-capped mountains reached toward him from far below. With the roar of wind in his ears, he soared over the top of a saw-toothed peak and the rugged mountains gave way to a vast plain of multicolored grasses and trees.

He gasped. Never before had he seen such vivid colors. There were no words to describe them, nor were they colors that were limited to the sense of sight. He could *hear* the colors and *feel* them in his chest as surely as an ocean wave crashing into him.

He looked to his left and a child gripped his hand. It was the boy he'd followed through the jungle; the one who'd led him to the hut. To Outlaw. The child's hair lifted on the wind and his olive skin glistened in the light, which came from everywhere at once. The sun was nowhere he could see.

The boy turned his head and smiled. *Hello, Austin.* The child had not spoken, but his words—complete with inflection and the pitch of a child's voice—came instantly into Austin's mind. It was similar to his experience in the Hack, only faster and more complete.

Where am I? Austin said, though he too didn't speak with words.

The child remained silent.

"Am I dead?"

"Dead?" The boy laughed. "No one dies. Not ever."

He was young, no older than twelve, but his voice seemed ancient. Austin didn't know the child, not like he knew Nyah or other people, yet he felt a familiarity that was unexplainable; the child emanated a presence that Austin had always felt near him.

He looked down as they flew over a vast forest. They swooped in wide, lazy arcs over ridges and between thick groves of trees twice the height and thickness of any sequoia tree he'd ever seen on his hiking trips through the Northwest.

This is Earth, he thought, but the beauty was also something other than Earth, more than was possible on Earth. In fact, everything was somehow more than what he knew in his experience. The world felt more substantial, more *real*.

It was as if he'd spent his entire life hidden deep underground, dwelling in darkness, mindlessly watching shadows on the wall that someone had told him were reality. Only now, he'd stepped into the sunlight and discovered that reality was vastly more.

As they sailed over a patch of iridescent flowers that shimmered in the light, the entire field exploded with color in motion. The flowers weren't flowers at all, but millions of hummingbirds that took wing with a loud rush of sound. The birds darted into the sky as one and trailed behind them.

It was all unexplainable, completely illogical to the part of him that needed to know where he was and how he got there. And what "there" actually was.

"Home," the boy said. "It's home."

Home. Austin—being an orphan, alone in the world—had no familiarity of the word's deeper context; it was utterly foreign to him.

"Where are we going?" he asked.

The boy pointed ahead, to a rise in the land. "You'll see."

Seven waterfalls thundered into a valley below and fed a vast lake that was as emerald as glacial water. Thick mist billowed across the lake far below and the water spilled over the rocks and split into seven tributaries, the beginnings of rivers that flowed in many directions.

They sailed to the lake, so close to its surface their passing left ripples in the water. Before they reached the waterfalls they pitched steeply upward into the mist, rising nearly vertical. The water spray was cool on his face and tasted sweet on his lips. The wind blew through him as they climbed higher, through the billowing cloud, and high into the sky.

Soon they were miles above the ground and punching through a skim of clouds they ascended into an ink-black sky alive with glimmering lights, though not stars. The lights were like comets and they streaked from one horizon to the next in countless numbers. They were of different colors and as they moved the sky shimmered with deep, resonating sounds. Austin marveled at the spectacle and wanted to know more.

The boy remained silent and pulled him higher into the darkness. They slowed to a gentle stop. Silence pressed in on them.

Austin looked around him, feeling weightless. In the distance, the streaks of light crisscrossed the darkness, and he understood they were beings of some kind. As they moved, the thunderous booms reverberated through the expanse, and after several moments he realized the booms were reminiscent of voices shouting . . . singing . . . laughing.

He turned to speak, but the child was no longer by his side. Still, he felt the same presence as though he were. Austin looked below him and the earth had disappeared as well, replaced by the sight of distant star spirals and blazing suns.

An overwhelming sense of comfort embraced him. He was suspended in a void, immense and infinitely deep and wide and long—the dark waters he'd been rescued from paled miserably in comparison. Here, light enveloped him. God. The fabric from which all things were cut, seen and unseen, and he knew that it wasn't an "it" at all.

The presence that streamed through him and held every part of him together—every atom and thought—was infinite, far too vast to be described with any word or concept or idea. All of those things that he once considered real and concrete seemed pathetically one-dimensional now—shadows of shadows and nothing more. Words like infinite and omnipotent and unconditional love could never begin to capture even the slightest notion of what he was experiencing, like comparing a spark from a dying candlewick to a supernova large enough to swallow the universe.

I made this for you.

A tide of infinite warmth and compassion washed over his awareness and went to the deepest corners of him. It wasn't a voice or even a thought that had come to him. It was something else that was far more personal. It was a Presence and it knew him entirely and accepted him without judgment.

Do you like it?

He didn't hear the question as words, only as awareness that he himself had formed into words. An awareness that was familiar. So familiar.

Yes, he heard himself say. His entire being, every shred and fiber of him resonated with gratitude and there was only one response possible. *Yes.* If he could have said it a million times with a million voices it still wouldn't have been enough to express the gratitude and awe that overtook him in that instant.

This was not simply a being, but Being itself. The creative One from Whom, through Whom, and to Whom all things existed. Without this Presence, existence was impossible.

He knew all of this instantaneously. He needed no evidence because it was self-evident.

Austin was silent, rendered speechless with wonder and awe. But he knew that this was only the beginning.

4.5

Day Three
11:59 PM

I STUMBLED out of the saltwater tank, blinking to focus my eyes, and rushed into the apartment with Mom's words resonating through my mind. She was where I'd left her, slumped forward in the wheelchair with her chin resting on her chest.

I reached her and felt for a pulse, but I already knew she was dead. It's what she wanted and what I'd help her find: lasting peace and freedom.

"I love you, Mom," I said, placing a kiss on her head. "I'll save him, I promise."

I ran to a nearby shelving unit and scanned the medical supplies Austin had stacked there. Mom had said that something Austin had put in his veins had killed him. I had to assume she meant the Kick compound. He'd said he wanted to go deeper, but the only way to do that was to up the dosage to minimize his brain activity. The dosage must have been too much for his body to process.

Tracing my finger from box to box I scanned the labels. I had to find the epinephrine. Mom said I needed to put something in his veins to jump-start his heart, and the only thing I knew that could do that was epinephrine.

My gaze dropped to the bottom shelf. A red plastic container the size of a thick book was bound to the shelf by a single black strap. Thick white letters were printed across the top: Epinephrine.

I pulled the case free and charged back to Austin.

Dropping to my knees beside him, I snapped open the case's lid. Inside, embedded in grey foam, lay several vials of clear liquid and a large syringe with a capped needle. Epinephrine: medical adrenaline, the kind used to jolt patients' bodies out of anaphylactic shock or cardiac arrest. It's a last-resort solution, sometimes administered directly to the heart tissue and has been known to bring clinically dead patients gasping back to life.

With trembling fingers, I worked the needle cap loose and drew an entire vial of the drug into the syringe. It didn't look like enough, though, so I drew another, holding it to the light.

I tossed aside the empty vial, and it skittered across the floor as I leaned over Austin's body. Getting the drug into his body would be the easy part, but how would it circulate? His heart wasn't pumping so it would do no good to inject it into his arm.

Jab it into his heart?

Without a better idea I straddled his body and, syringe in my right hand, ran my left over his ribs, feeling for a gap. I couldn't just stab him, using the syringe like a knife. If I hit a bone, the needle could snap. If my aim was off, I could puncture his lung and miss his heart entirely. No, I'd have to lean into it and push it in slowly.

I traced my fingers over his cold skin, feeling for what I thought might give me the best shot at his heart, and marked the gap with my fingers.

I took a deep breath and pressed the thin needle against his skin. The flesh gave beneath the pressure and the needle punctured it, releasing a bead of blood. The needle flexed dangerously and scraped against a rib. The needle was too thin and too short.

I slid it out and sat up. What now? How could I reach his heart?

Austin's head had flopped to the side, exposing a large, pale blue vein in his neck.

There. I leaned close and worked the needle beneath his skin until it was inserted into the vein. Holding it steady, I jammed the plunger home and watched the fluid as it entered the vein, ballooning it slightly.

I jerked the needle free and tossed it aside. I leaned into his chest with my hands. I had to circulate the adrenaline on my own. It was the only way to get it through his heart and into the rest of his body.

• • •

THE THRUM vibrating through Austin was like the roar of a million tides. It was life itself and it filled him in a way that he believed he had known once before, long ago. Even before he was in the womb of his unknown mother, this was here. This is where all things came from long before anything ever was, and this was where he belonged. He knew it all in less than an instant, in the impossibly small space between thoughts—here, where the past, present, and future seemed to be all happening at once, beyond time.

Here there was only love, unending and inexhaustible, bottomless, extended out to the entire universe, wrapped around it, cradling it.

Here there was only God.

Who are you?

The revelation came as an instant flash of knowledge—not an answer that came as a thought or even words, but something far more fundamental.

I AM that I AM.

A deep, impenetrable gratitude as deep and fluid as a million oceans coursed through him. All of those years of seeking and wrestling and struggling for knowledge, revelation, and truth was possible only because he was being led forward, beckoned. The struggle and pain of pursuing the answers had led him here.

These were the words of Jesus when asked who he was. *Before Abraham was, I AM.* The life he'd lived with the simple belief of a child, as a child, came flooding back to him. This was that kingdom of heaven, as much inside of him as beyond him.

But the him he'd always thought of as him, wasn't really him. He realized that he could no longer sense possessing a physical body. He had no fleshly hands to hold in front of his face or legs to stand on. He'd been stripped down to the core of who he was, without a body or brain, which had no significance here where the expanse and depth and height and width of truth was too much for his or any mind to hold. And this reality too much for a trillion minds to grasp. In a short lifetime of scraping together philosophies and ideas and facts, he'd learned many things, but all of that knowing was, at best, hollow and, at worst, a shadow that he'd fallen in love with.

You were created to love and be loved.

The truth thundered across the cosmos in a shock wave of raw energy and love. It spread in all directions at the same time, causing all of existence to shimmer and vibrate. There was nothing he could ever do that would cause him to be loved less than he was in that moment—or in any moment of his existence. Nor could he possibly be loved more. Nor could he disappoint the One who'd breathed him into being. Austin was fully known in ways that he couldn't understand, and yet he was fully, completely accepted and treasured.

How was it possible that such unfathomable perfection would love him so completely? He wasn't perfect; nobody was.

And yet, he was loved. He knew that without question. Here, all things were as they should be or they would not be at all. In this Love, all things were held together.

In dying, your life blooms; in letting go, you find your true self.

The universe suddenly swirled and shifted, revealing an overwhelming panorama of spiral galaxies that stretched before him, more than could ever be counted. Billions of them, or maybe billions of billions.

Purple veins of shimmering energy crisscrossed the vast open space, coiling and connecting in all directions in geometric patterns he could barely process. Newborn stars pulsed within dense clouds of swirling, multicolored gas. In the distance, a massive star collapsed into itself, compressing into a pinpoint of light that disappeared before erupting again in an explosion great enough to wipe out entire galaxies.

Look closer.

Immediately he saw beyond the galaxies. Yet not beyond as if *overlaying* them. Entire dimensions shimmering in light, expanding outward in a swirling, dervish motion—a dance—as they raced across the void at speeds no human could ever experience while bound to the limited dimensions of his earthly existence.

There was no end to them. No edge to any of it. Everything stretched as far distant as was possible for him to see and beyond. There was no beginning and no end.

Austin watched in stunned awe, surrounded by an overwhelming sense that he too was eternal. He too was known long before he was ever born, before the foundations of the worlds were laid.

The words were like salve that worked deep into the fractures of his heart. He'd never considered it before. There was no evidence, there were no facts, to prove that he was anything more than his biological mind, yet it was now a self-evident truth that didn't need proving any more than his own existence.

His mind *wasn't* him. There was a part of him that existed beyond his body, beyond his mind, beyond his thoughts. There was a place where this deep resonating existence connected with him and, there, he was at home. The realization brought him back to his childhood, growing up in a monastery, learning of an infinite God and being in wonder and accepting that truth without question. This was essentially that.

But then the words had put God in a box, as words could only do. In truth, he saw, God was not defined by words. God was the Word itself. Infinite. And he was in awe once again. Weeping with gratitude and ecstasy without shedding a tear.

How long Austin remained in that state of raw bliss he could not know, because there was no time in his awareness. He only became aware that there was yet time at all when something changed.

There was a jolt of light and his field of vision shuddered.

What was that?

There is nothing to fear.

Another flash and he felt himself being drawn down. Falling away.

But he couldn't go! Not now!

The world he'd seen earlier materialized around him as he was drawn downward. Within seconds he was falling through the clouds with the boy once more by his side. The child spoke not a word as they tumbled through empty space.

They were careening toward the earth far below. He looked over at the young boy.

"I don't want to go back!"

The child was silent, his focus intent on a pinprick of darkness far below. It was death, he thought. Or the dimension his body had lived in.

"Please . . . I want to stay."

But the boy said nothing. The pinprick of darkness ahead grew into a yawning abyss that stretched wide to swallow him again.

"No . . ."

He felt the boy release his hand.

Then Austin was alone, rushing into that darkness.

...

I BLEW hard into Austin's mouth again, struggling to fill his lungs. I locked my elbows, placed the heels of my palms over his chest and drove my weight into him in the hope that his heart would spasm to life again. The adrenaline was in his veins, but was it circulating?

"Hang on," I said and tilted his chin. Two more long breaths into his mouth before switching my hands to his chest. I was gasping for breath myself as I compressed his rib cage, tank water still dripping off my face.

One, two . . .

"Come on . . ."

Three, four, five . . .

Again, more breaths and compressions until I was sure I would crack his ribs. But I didn't care, I had to bring him back. Again and again, but with each breath, each compression, each thump on his chest, the finality of his death became my own.

"Wake up!" I screamed, as if to myself as much as to him. "Wake up!"

Austin had moved into this apartment to escape the world, to drop off the grid. Reclusion meant privacy and peace, but also isolation. No one was coming.

There was nothing I could do. My brother and father were dead. Austin was dead. My mother was dead.

I was alone.

Darkness crushed me with that realization. It was as if I'd been dropped into the middle of the ocean with a lead weight chained to my neck.

I lifted my chin and screamed at the ceiling, a ragged scream filled with years of pain.

I really was alone.

4.6

STONE PAUSED midstride and listened, but the only sounds were the old wood groaning under the strain of the wind. The lobby was filled with scaffolding and plastic-wrapped stacks of lumber.

His eyes traced the floor, which was covered in a skim of dust that had been disturbed in a trail from the door to the elevator and nowhere else. Twin lines, thin and parallel, carved a fresh path in the grime. Between the lines, which he assumed had been made by the mother's wheelchair, were footprints.

Veering toward the stairwell, he paused only to glance at the gated, open-air elevator that rose through the vaulted ceiling. A lighted digit above the door indicated that it was parked on the top floor.

He took the stairs, moving quickly and silently. He heard the girl's scream as he reached the top floor's open doorway. He paused at the threshold, waiting, listening.

Another scream. Just the girl. That didn't mean she was alone in the apartment with her mother, but he suspected that was the case. Her anguished shrieks piqued his curiosity.

Stone hadn't bothered reattaching the sound suppressor to the gun's barrel. There was no need. No one would hear her screams or the gunshots.

He moved deeper into the dimly lit hallway, angling right, following the sound of the girl's voice, which came from an open doorway across from the elevator.

He reached the door, pistol cocked by his face. The massive room beyond the entrance was dim and filled with blinking server racks and medical equipment. Several feet into the room a woman sat in a wheelchair with her back to the door. The mother.

The girl was out of sight, somewhere on the far side. Stone held his weapon in both hands, arms now extended. Rolling off the wall and around the threshold, he entered the apartment.

•••

"I WON'T give up on you," I whispered. "I won't . . ."

I leaned down to blow into his mouth again, three quick breaths, knowing it was hopeless, but unable to stop. A loud crack echoed through the apartment when I straightened to pump his chest again. Something slammed into my right shoulder, knocking me to the floor. I cried out and grabbed my shoulder. Pain radiated from it, hot and fiery. A bloom of red blood spread across my shirt, below my collarbone.

I'd been shot?

But then it wasn't a question.

I'd been shot!

I jerked my eyes toward the source of the sound. The view was mostly blocked by shelves and a desk, but I still caught a glimpse of black pants and shoes walking toward me.

Frantic, I pushed upright and struggled to my knees, feeling like a trapped rat, as a second gunshot split the air. To my left, the doorframe to the tank room splintered. Another *crack!* sent a bullet across my scalp, grazing it and stinging like the lash of a bullwhip.

"Trust me, if I wanted you to be dead, you'd be dead."

Stone . . . but how had the man found me? No one had followed me here, I was sure of it. My eyes searched the room, looking for some way around him. The sharp pain in my shoulder pulsed in agonizing rhythm with my heart.

"Stand up," he said.

I crawled forward, keeping the desk between the man and me, and peered around the corner. He stood twenty feet beyond the console. The large control panel was the only thing separating us. The only way out was through him.

I pressed my back to the mammoth desk, which provided my only shelter. Blood soaked my shirt, making the material cling to my skin. A cold chill worked through the right side of my body and my head felt light. I was trapped and no one knew where I was. No one would rescue me this time. He was going to kill me.

He fired three more rounds, and monitors on the console shattered, raining down shattered glass on me.

"Your mother's dead, I see," Stone said. "They'll blame you, of course. Isn't that how this story goes?"

Get a grip. Think . . .

But the only thing I could think was to stall him and even that would do nothing.

"Racked with guilt from killing her own mother, a loving daughter takes her own life." Stone continued. "However the story really goes, I have to kill you, you understand." He paused and let the words settle on me. "How quickly and painlessly is up to you."

I felt myself starting to fade, as much from fear as with the loss of blood.

"Why are you doing this?" My voice sounded weak.

"It's quite simple. You took things that didn't belong to you, things that could cast my employer in an unfortunate light. I can't allow that."

He took a step, angling around the console. I heard the clink of a bullet casing spin across the floor as he kicked it.

I peered under the desk and saw his black shoes on the other side, close. A few more steps and he'd see me.

"Your friend, Pixel, died slowly," he said. "You, however, don't have to. Just stand up."

My eyes flicked toward the tank room and, driven by instinct more than logic, I lunged forward and scrambled through the doorway. I slammed the door shut behind me and jammed my thumb against the doorknob's button lock.

Panting hard, I leaned there against the door and squinted into the room's darkness. If only the Hacks could have allowed our bodies to travel through time and space and not just our consciousness, I would've gotten into the tank and escaped through another reality, because that was the only way out.

Eyes adjusting to my surroundings, I crawled toward the far side of the room. There had to be something I could use to defend myself. My hands bumped against the legs of the stainless steel table where Austin laid out his tools for calibrating the tanks. I stood and bumped the tray with my arm. Metal wrenches clanged and scattered across the floor.

I bent, reaching for the tool, and, glanced up as the man's wide shadow fell across the shade over the observation window. For a brief moment, he stood there, then moved toward the door.

My fingers groped at the scattered instruments until they grazed the handle of a long screwdriver. I snatched it up, gripping it like a knife in my left hand. I could barely hold it: pain raked my entire body and my hands were trembling.

I turned to face the door. My only chance was to blindside him and stab him when he came in. It was all pointless, but I didn't care. I wasn't going to just let him kill me.

My focus settled to the right of the door—a small space between the first tank and the window. I started to move but was cut short by a deafening boom that filled the room. The door splintered at the jamb, swung open and banged hard against the wall.

The man planted his foot back on the ground and stood in the doorway, gun by his side. He was dressed in what appeared to be the same clothes he'd worn at BlakBox—black suit, white shirt, black tie. His face was hard as flint and, even silhouetted by the light coming from the apartment, I could see the death in his eyes.

Completely relaxed and unconcerned, he watched me. He considered the screwdriver in my hand and tilted his head to the side until his neck cracked loudly. "Understand, this isn't personal," he said, setting his gun on the table, beside the mannequin heads. "It's only business."

With a scream I rushed forward, screwdriver raised.

In a blur of motion, his hands came forward. A sharp pain cracked through my wrist as the man skillfully knocked the tool from my grip then clamped his hand around my neck and squeezed.

I tried to gasp for breath, tried to scream, but no air went in and no sound came out. My pulse thumped in my head. My fingers clawed at his hands, trying desperately to peel them away. I stretched to reach his face, but my efforts were frustrated by his long arms.

He spun me around and wrapped his arm around my throat then carried me forward, as though I was nothing more than a rag doll. I thought he might take me into the apartment, force me to my knees, and put a gun to my head. I thought maybe he'd kill me next to Austin or my mom. That would've been better I suppose—quick and painless—but he had other intentions.

He held me for a moment, choking for breath, then dragged me to the second tank, the one full of water, arm still clamped tight on my throat. He was going to drown me.

The tank's rim hit my shins as he shoved forward. I fell and the water swallowed me. My arms flailed and I twisted around as I broke the surface, gasping for breath. Stone's hand grabbed my face and shoved it under. He held me down and I thought my lungs would explode.

This was it, I thought. I was going to die in the tank, like Austin.

His hand grabbed a fistful of my shirt and yanked me upright. I gulped a lungful of air, wheezing as he held me just above the water. I struggled to get my hands under me, to grab the lip of the tank, to brace myself on my knees—anything to keep my head above water.

"Tell me," he said in a flat tone. "Where is the information you sent your friend?"

"I don't know! I don't ha—"

He shoved me under again. I clawed and thrashed until my lungs burned and I thought I'd pass out. As dark stars crowded the edges of my sight he yanked me up again.

"Where?" he said again.

I shook my head and gasped. I couldn't find my breath to speak. Everything was tilting and fading. He plunged me under again. Water rushed into my nose and mouth. Staring up from beneath the water, I saw the blurred image of the man through the murky, blood-tinged water. It was my blood and it all seemed so surreal.

He jerked me upright again, this time pulling me closer to his face.

"I have to be sure, you understand."

"I don't know anything . . . I swear." My words were slurred by exhaustion and pain. "Nothing . . . I don't know . . ." My throat began to cinch tighter as the hot tears blurred the world.

"Think harder."

I shook my head. "No one . . . no one knows . . ."

He studied me with lifeless eyes. There was no hint of contempt or anger in them; they were simply dark and empty. I was simply an obstacle on his path to some objective or another, and he was here to remove me.

Gasping, I struggled to speak and he pulled me closer. I didn't know what Pixel had found. All I knew was that it had cost him his life, and it would cost me mine if I didn't find a way out of the situation.

And then something in me changed. *Why struggle?* I thought. *Why such a frantic desperation to keep breathing in this body? Why not just let go?*

My mother's words from beyond whispered through my mind. She'd found peace. This wasn't the end at all. So why was I so desperate to cling to my last heartbeat?

It's not that I suddenly *wanted* to die; I just no longer felt any need to resist what my mother had told me in my Hack. There was nothing to fear, she'd said.

Peace, like a warm blanket, settled over me for the first time. It's going to be okay, I thought, and I felt my face soften.

"You want to tell me something," I heard Stone say, leaning forward.

It's going to be okay.

I opened my mouth to speak, when the man's attention snapped to his left. In the doorway I saw movement and heard a voice that seemed far away. The world slowed to a crawl.

Stone released his grip on me and lunged to his left, blurring out of sight. I started to fall back into the water and heard the crack of gunfire. One, two, three muzzle flashes.

And then I slipped beneath the surface. I flailed, panicking, feeling myself fade and desperate to get back up. My face broke the surface and I gulped air.

A raspy gasp to my right. Stone was there, holding the lip of the tank, trying to pull himself up. His eyes were wide with shock and disbelief. Blood soaked through his once crisp white shirt.

Oddly none of this really seemed to concern me much.

Another shot rang out.

Stone's head snapped sideways, and he collapsed. My sight blurred. I was fading now. Slipping back into the water.

It's going to be okay . . . It's going to be okay, Mother . . .

I thought I heard a voice, but I was underwater again. I thought about opening my eyes, but they felt as heavy as iron. Either way it didn't matter. It was going to be okay.

A hand suddenly grabbed my shirt and pulled my head above water. This time I clearly heard someone say my name. Felt someone's arms under me, holding me. Then I felt his breath on my cheek and my ear.

"It's okay. I've got you," Austin said. "I've got you."

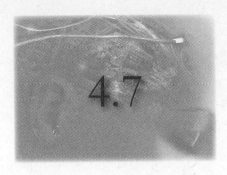

4.7

Two Days Later

BLAKBOX IMPLODED while the world watched. The story dominated the news cycle with the video clip of federal agents leading Walter Bell, handcuffed, into court.

Stone had been unaware that the cameras mounted in Austin's apartment were recording the whole time he was there; Austin had documented every Hack. Stone had unknowingly implicated Bell in Pixel's death and far more than that.

The FBI conducted raids on five of Bell's data centers and uncovered proof that he was the architect of an elaborate "dark net" used by terror organizations and rogue governments to traffic in state secrets. Bell had been the power broker behind it all, betraying his country for the sake of profit and power.

The talking heads on TV were already debating how fragile cyber security was even at the highest levels of government. Everything was for sale and no secret was ever truly secret. Privacy, they said, was dead. In cyberspace, anyone could hack into your life if they knew how.

But they only knew the half of it. Austin and I had seen far more.

I sat on the edge of my hospital bed and felt a deep sense of peace as I watched the TV, not because Bell was going to jail—although that certainly didn't hurt—but because it was all over.

Jill's life had been taken and so had Pixel's and Mom's. Yet, despite the sadness I felt, I was strangely at peace with their deaths. I would miss them all terribly, but in some way I was also happy for them. Death was no longer a monster to be feared because it wasn't the end. It was a new beginning and if it had taken Mom in such a kind way, with joy and comfort, then I believed it would've done the same for Pixel and Jill and for Dad and Tommy.

Death wasn't to be feared. It was simply the next step toward forever.

"Let me get that for you," Lettie said and tied my shoe. She hadn't left my bedside from the moment they'd admitted me.

"Thanks. I can't wait to get this thing off." I gently massaged my arm, which hung in a sling. Thankfully, the bullet had gone straight through, and the doctors were pleased enough with my recovery that they were discharging me.

"Well, don't rush it," Lettie said. "Things take time to heal."

I slid my feet to the floor and stood as a woman stepped into the room. Brenda Colson, the head of the FBI's cyber-crime division who'd stopped by my room the night I'd been admitted. Today she was dressed in a grey business suit and held a thick brown file folder under one arm.

"Ms. Parks . . ." The woman stepped up to me and extended her hand. "How are you feeling today?"

I shook her hand, glancing at Lettie. "Much better, thanks."

Brenda Colson had sat quietly in the corner that first night, merely observing while I was questioned about BlakBox, Austin, and Pixel. She had an easy smile and grey hair.

"I understand you've been cleared to go home," Agent Colson said.

"Yes ma'am," I said.

"Wonderful." Her attention snapped to Lettie then back to me. "Before you do, there are a few matters we need to resolve."

"Matters?" Lettie said. "What kind of matters?"

She flipped open the file folder and traced her finger down the page as she spoke. "Despite their CEO's personal woes, BlakBox's legal counsel is leveling a number of charges against you: trespassing, wire-tapping, extortion . . ." She paused and looked over the top of her glasses. "Then there's the matter of your mother's kidnapping, which is being taken under advisement by the Department of Justice, considering your mother's death."

I shifted my weight from one foot to the other.

"You're in a bit of a precarious position, Ms. Parks," she said. "Being seventeen, the law would normally see you as a minor and might mitigate the consequences you're facing. However, I understand that you're an emancipated minor, which changes your legal status to that of an adult. An adult fully accountable to answer for these charges."

The room was silent.

"However," she finally said, closing the file. "Intelligent, gifted young people like you don't belong in courtrooms or concrete cells, an opinion which my superiors share with me in your case."

"So that's good news," I said.

Agent Colson watched me, but showed no emotion. She was all business.

"Isn't it?" I asked.

"Well," she continued, "that depends on you."

"I don't understand."

"Through this particular investigation, it's come to our attention that, in the recent past, you've engaged in questionable activity online," Agent Colson said. "Activity of questionable legality and significant consequences if properly addressed."

"I, well . . ." My voice trembled.

"However," she continued, "We're prepared to drop the charges and make the inquiry go away. On one condition." She held up her index finger. "That you to come work for us."

"What?" Lettie said, stunned.

"Really?" I said.

The woman's stone-hard face eased. "It's rare to discover someone with your skills, especially at such a young age. Cyber security is the new battleground and, frankly, we can't afford to be outgunned. There's too much at stake. You and Austin are brilliant, two of the smartest hackers we've ever encountered, and we have a great need for individuals with your particular skill set. Brilliance like yours can't be wasted or, worse, used toward nefarious ends."

"Austin too?"

"I've already spoken to him." Colson looked at me. "I'm offering you a new life—the best ongoing training, access to the most cutting-edge technology, and a chance to do significant work that's challenging and vital. You'll be working under my direct supervision. I'm establishing a new West Coast division based here in the Bay Area. I'll push you harder than you think possible. But it'll be the best work you've ever done, that much I can promise."

"I'm not sure what to say," I said.

"Yes would be a good start." Colson said.

"Yes," I said. "Of course, yes."

"Good," Colson said. "My assistant will make contact with you to-morrow." She handed the folder to me. "A keepsake," she said with a grin.

I put it under my arm and gave a nod. "Yes, ma'am."

"Also," Agent Colson said, "I understand that you have some lingering medical expenses related to your mother. Those will be taken care of while we negotiate your compensation terms. I want your head in the game, not on scraping money together to pay bills."

I looked at Lettie. Tears were forming in her eyes. "Thank you," I said.

"You're welcome," she said. "See you next week."

I couldn't help but smile, watching her leave.

Lettie picked up my small overnight bag. "You ready?"

"I have just one stop to make first."

Lettie gave a knowing smile. "You go ahead. I'll meet you in the lobby."

"Thanks." I said and kissed her on the cheek before heading toward the elevator.

Austin was recovering in the room next to the one I'd taken Mom from a few days before. They said that everything I'd done to revive him, including injecting the adrenaline, may have been enough to resuscitate him, but they were having a difficult time believing it. He'd been dead too long.

Austin, propped up on pillows, watched me come into the room. He looked more at peace than I'd ever seen him despite the deep-blue puffs of skin under his eyes.

He'd survived death and was hardly worse for the wear.

"About time you dropped by," he said, smiling.

"I was . . . busy." I went to his side and took his hand. "How you feeling?"

"Alive." His eyes were bright. "I think you saved me. Thank you."

"I think it's the other way around." I leaned over and placed a kiss on his forehead. "Thank you. For everything."

Austin looked at me in a way no one ever had before. He didn't have to say that he cared about me, that he might even love me, because I knew it. I saw it in his smile and in his eyes.

"You have to tell me everything," I said, "What about your tumor?"

His eyebrow arched. "Gone."

"What!"

"They've run every kind of test that exists, but can't find a trace of it. Three different radiologists have examined me."

"You found Outlaw then?"

He tilted his head to the side, as if remembering something important. "I did, but not in the way I'd planned. You know the truth of it is that I didn't have to find him because *I'm* Outlaw. And so are you. We're not bound by the laws of this world. It just took these experiences for me to realize . . ." His voice trailed off.

"Realize what?"

"That death isn't death. It's not the end because we aren't just our minds or our bodies. We're far more than just physical beings having a spiritual experience. We're spiritual beings having a temporary physical experience." He paused. "All I know is the reality that's beyond all of this transcends words and comprehension. The only way to grasp it is to let go of our own limited understanding."

I smiled and squeezed his hand. "You look so . . . different. So alive. What did you see? What changed?"

"Everything changed," he said. "Everything. Turns out, some things can't be explained." He smiled.

"At least not yet," I said.

"Not yet, and maybe never. Either way it's okay. Some things are too big to comprehend. You have to leave space for mystery. A lot of space. And the only way to grasp it is to let go of everything else."

"That's what Mom told me."

"Deditio," he said. *Surrender.*

"Deditio," I repeated with a chuckle.

"Nothing will ever be the same. I feel like I'm seeing the world for the first time."

"Me too."

He nodded. "And it feels like just the beginning."

"I think you're right," I said. "Just the beginning."

And I leaned over and kissed him on the cheek.

Nothing would ever be the same.

ACKNOWLEDGMENTS

A massive shout-out to my friend and long-time partner in awakening, Kevin Kaiser. Together we take a journey through life, together we concoct wild scenarios that find their way into these stories, and together we imagine and commune with the tribe of Outlaws who gather in the world of story both on paper and in cyberspace. I can't adequately convey my gratitude for your partnership and bottomless creativity, so I'll just go with thank you. The Outlaw Chronicles would not be what they are without you. Neither would my life.

ABOUT THE AUTHOR

Ted Dekker is a *New York Times* best-selling author with more than six million books in print. His upbringing as the child of missionaries who lived among the headhunter tribes of Indonesia gives him a unique perspective outside the cultural bubble, enabling him to craft provocative insights, unforgettable characters, and adrenaline-laced plots in his fiction. Two of his forty-plus novels, *Thr3e* and *House,* have been made into feature films.

Dekker resides in Texas with his wife and children. Find him at TedDekker.com and Facebook.com/TedDekker.

NEW FROM TED DEKKER, MASTER OF SUSPENSE

THE OUTLAW CHRONICLES

A RAW ADRENALINE RUSH FROM FIRST PAGE TO LAST

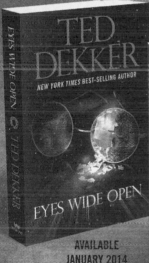

**AVAILABLE
JANUARY 2014**

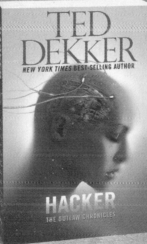

AVAILABLE JUNE 2014

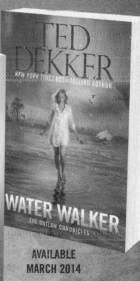

**AVAILABLE
MARCH 2014**

Head on over to TedDekker.com for more information

WORTHY
PUBLISHING

If you enjoyed this book, will you consider
sharing the message with others?

- Mention the book in a Facebook post, Twitter update, Pinterest pin, or blog post.

- Recommend this book to those in your small group, book club, workplace, and classes.

- Head over to www.facebook.com/TedDekker, "LIKE" the page, and post a comment as to what you enjoyed the most..

- Tweet "I recommend reading #HackerNovel by @TedDekker // @worthypub"

- Pick up a copy for someone you know who would be challenged and encouraged by this message.

- Write a book review online.

You can subscribe to Worthy Publishing's newsletter at worthypublishing.com

**WORTHY PUBLISHING
FACEBOOK PAGE**

**WORTHY PUBLISHING
WEBSITE**